OUTNUMBERED

D0547107

Smoke glared down at the man on the ground. "Did Murdock send you out to do us in?"

"I ain't sayin' nothin'," the man said.

Puma Buck stepped up to stand practically on top of the man. "If he's not gonna talk, Smoke, let me skin 'im," he said. "I ain't skinned nobody fer two, maybe three years now." He held out his big buffalo-skinning knife; it glinted in the firelight.

"No, no, please . . ." the man begged.

Smoke leaned over, his hands on his knees. "Then tell us what you know about Murdock's plans. How many men he has, when he plans to hit us . . ."

When he had his information, Smoke let the man go. When he was out of earshot, Smoke drained the last of his coffee. "I got an idea," he said. "What is the last thing a commander with an overwhelming superiority in numbers and firepower expects the opposing army to do?"

Puma grinned and nodded. "Attack? You can't mean we're gonna ride against Murdock and fifty men. That'd be suicide."

"A frontal assault's not exactly what I had in mind," Smoke said. "Sally brought some books back from her last trip out east. They were about some Japanese fighters called ninjas . . . individuals who swore allegiance to the warlords of feudal Japan, the shōgun. Ninjas were called "invisible killers" because they dressed all in black, attacked at night, and killed without being seen or heard."

Smoke paused, grinned. "We're about to become American ninjas."

BOOK YOUR PLACE ON OUR WEBSITE AND MAKE THE READING CONNECTION!

We've created a customized website just for our very special readers, where you can get the inside scoop on everything that's going on with Zebra, Pinnacle and Kensington books.

When you come online, you'll have the exciting opportunity to:

- View covers of upcoming books
- Read sample chapters
- Learn about our future publishing schedule (listed by publication month *and author*)
- Find out when your favorite authors will be visiting a city near you
- Search for and order backlist books from our online catalog
- Check out author bios and background information
- Send e-mail to your favorite authors
- Meet the Kensington staff online
- Join us in weekly chats with authors, readers and other guests
- Get writing guidelines
- AND MUCH MORE!

**Visit our website at
http://www.kensingtonbooks.com**

HONOR OF THE MOUNTAIN MAN

William W. Johnstone

PINNACLE BOOKS
Kensington Publishing Corp.
www.pinnaclebooks.com

PINNACLE BOOKS are published by

Kensington Publishing Corp.
850 Third Avenue
New York, NY 10022

Copyright © 1998 by William W. Johnstone

All rights reserved. No part of this book may be reproduced in any form or by any means without the prior written consent of the Publisher, excepting brief quotes used in reviews.

If you purchased this book without a cover you should be aware that this book is stolen property. It was reported as "unsold and destroyed" to the Publisher and neither the Author nor the Publisher has received any payment for this "stripped book."

All Kensington Titles, Imprints, and Distributed Lines are available at special quantity discounts for bulk purchases for sales promotion, premiums, fund-raising, and educational or institutional use. Special book excerpts or customized printings can also be created to fit specific needs. For details, write or phone the office of the Kensington special sales manager: Kensington Publishing Corp., 850 Third Avenue, New York, NY 10022, attn: Special Sales Department, Phone: 1-800-221-2647.

Pinnacle and the P logo Reg. U.S. Pat. & TM Off.

First Printing: January 1998
10 9 8 7 6 5

Printed in the United States of America

Prologue

Chihuahua, Mexico, sweltered under a brutal summer sun. The temperature was over 110 degrees; dogs, too exhausted by the heat to chase each other, lay panting in what scant shade there was.

Colonel Emilio Vasquez sat in a cantina called El Gato, enjoying its quiet coolness as he downed a mug of beer and chased it with a tumbler of tequila. He was second in command of the Rurales, local law enforcement officers made up primarily of uneducated men too lazy to work at honest labor and too cowardly to steal openly. Sergeant Juan Garcia, a huge bear of a man weighing almost three hundred pounds, was drinking with him. Garcia sleeved sweat off his forehead. *"Madre de Dios, es muy caliente,"* he said. Garcia was called *puerquito* by the other men, but never to his face. The Spanish word meant both little pig and a person who was filthy and disgusting. Vasquez glanced at Garcia, thinking his compadre fit the description, lacking both personal hygiene and any moral sense whatsoever.

Vasquez laughed. "Juanito, if you would not eat everything that did not eat you first, you wouldn't have to complain about the heat so much."

Garcia raised his eyebrows. "But, *mi corlonel*, the food, she tastes so good."

Vasquez sneered, about to reply, when his eyes caught a stain on the floor by the bar, covered with sawdust. "Geraldo," he called to the barman, "do we have to eat in a pigsty?"

Geraldo frowned in puzzlement. "What do you mean, Colonel Vasquez?"

Vasquez pointed at the bloodstain on the floor. "It has been almost a week since I taught those vaqueros how to respect my uniform, and their stinkin' blood still remains." He turned back to Garcia, waving a dismissive hand. "Have someone mop the floor pronto."

"Sí Señor Vasquez!"

As the bartender rushed to find a mop and a bucket, Vasquez thought back to the incident the previous week. . . .

Vasquez, Garcia, and two other Rurales entered the cantina. They were covered with a fine coat of trail dust from their ride in the desert. Three *bandidos* had raided a nearby ranch and Vasquez and his men chased them for two days. They caught them at noon and brought all three men back into town draped across their saddles, riddled with rifle bullets. Vasquez was in an irritable mood, because the men had been killed before he had a chance to work on them with his machete.

"Geraldo, tequila for me and my men," he called to the barman in a loud, obnoxious voice.

Vasquez and his three soldiers walked to their usual table, only to find it occupied by four cowboys. The men had large pitchers of beer on the table and were eating tamales and beans, sopping up the juice with folded-over tortillas.

Vasquez stood with his hands on his hips. "Excuse me, señors, but you are sitting at my table."

One of the men looked up, his weather-beaten, wrinkled face evidence of many years working outdoors under the brutal Mexican sun. He glanced around the cantina, seeing several unoccupied tables nearby. He grinned. "There are many places left to sit, señor." He waved a careless hand and went back to his eating. "Take any of them that pleases you."

Vasquez's face turned purple with rage. He whipped his sombrero from his head and swatted the man across the face with it. *"Bastardo!* You will address a colonel of the Rurales with more respect in the future."

The man jumped from his chair as one of his friends at the table tried to restrain him.

"Ernesto, it is nothing. We can move to another table."

Ernesto shook the man's hand off his arm, his eyes narrowed with hate. "We were here first, there is no need for us to move." He leaned his head to the side and spit on Vasquez's boots. "Find another table, you Rurale piece of dog shit!"

Vasquez's lips curled in a sneer. "No one talks to Emilio Vasquez like that," he growled.

Ernesto grinned mockingly. "Not to your face, perhaps, but you should hear what the villagers say about you behind your back."

"Oh? And what do they say, my brave friend?"

"That you Rurales are worse than the criminals you pretend to protect us from. You steal more than you're worth, and they laugh at you and your pompous ways when you're not around to hear them."

Vasquez drew the long-bladed machete from its scabbard on his belt in one lightning-quick move and slashed backhanded at Ernesto. The razor-sharp blade caught the cowboy in the upper right arm just below the shoulder.

Ernesto screamed in pain and grasped at his shoulder with his left hand. Another slash, and the machete nearly served his neck, killing him and ending his cries of terror.

When the men at the table with him kicked back their chairs and reached for their guns, Vasquez began to flail at them with the long knife as Garcia and his other soldiers drew their pistols and gunned down the men in a hail of bullets.

After the smoke cleared, four vaqueros lay in spreading pools of blood on the cantina floor. Vasquez kicked their bodies out of the way with his boot and sat at their table.

"Geraldo, clean up this mess and bring us our tequila, *muy pronto!*"

A small smile turned up the corners of Vasquez's mouth as he remembered the moment. He loved to kill with the machete, it was so much more . . . personal than using a pistol or a rifle. It was almost sexual in its intimacy, and usually caused Vasquez to become so excited that his first action after such a killing was to find a local prostitute and ease himself within her willing body.

"Garcia, if you are finished eating, it is time to go. General Sanchez has asked to see me." He puffed out his chest. "Probably wants to congratulate me on the swift apprehension of those *bandidos* last week."

He stood, leaving the cantina without bothering to pay for their drinks. He considered free alcohol his right for protecting the ignorant *campesinos* from local *bandidos* and Indians.

When they arrived at the Rurales command post, Vasquez was summoned into the office of General Arturo Sanchez, his commanding officer. Sanchez was looking out his window with hands clasped behind his back.

When he turned, his face was serious. "Emilio, I have received official complaints about your actions last week."

Vasquez's eyes narrowed. "Oh?"

Sanchez consulted a paper on his desk. "It seems that you killed several workers on Don Gonzalez's rancho." He tapped the paper with his index finger while staring at Vasquez. "Don Gonzalez says that you hacked three of his vaqueros to death with your machete for no reason."

"That is not true, your excellency. His men were drunk and insulted my honor while at the cantina in town. I did not know until later that they worked for Señor Gonzalez."

Sanchez nodded. "Well, *El Machete,*" he said, calling Vasquez by his nickname, "it seems Don Gonzalez has very important connections in Mexico City. He had complained to the governor of this province, and I have been instructed to arrest you on charge of murder."

"What? That is not possible!"

Sanchez shook his head. "Because of our long friendship, I will delay execution of my orders until tomorrow." He looked once again out of the window, turning his back on Vasquez. "If you happen to desert and leave Chihuahua before then, why, the matter will be solved to both our satisfaction."

Vasquez spit out the words *"Sí, mi comandante."* He turned on his heel and stalked angrily from the room. That *bastardo,* he thought, he has always known and approved of my methods. I will make him pay for abandoning me now.

Vasquez left the building in search of the men under his command he knew he could trust. Plans had to be made quickly.

That evening Vasquez and ten of his most trusted men, all as corrupt and vicious as he, broke into the command's stockade—over twenty-five murderers and rapists were housed in the jail, mixed breeds of Mestizo and Mescalero

Apache Indians and half-breeds and several notorious *bandidos* Vasquez and his men had captured.

Vasquez paced back and forth in front of their cells, offering them a chance to escape a firing squad and to ride free if they promised to obey his orders and ride for him.

With nothing to lose, the men all agreed, and Vasquez and Garcia unlocked their cells and provided them with guns and ammunition. While Garcia stole horses and tack from the command post stables, Vasquez slipped into Sanchez's bedroom. He tapped the sleeping man on the shoulder, wanting to look into his eyes while he killed him. Sanchez awakened, his eyes wide and bright in silvery moonlight.

"Adiós, cabrón," Vasquez snarled as he served Sanchez's neck with his machete.

Vasquez rejoined his group of desperadoes and led them off into the night, headed northwest toward the Rio Bravo and Del Rio, Texas.

Along the way they raided several haciendas for food and money, killing with cold abandon, meeting little resistance. After making a cold camp, they slept until dawn. The Rio Bravo, and freedom from pursuit, was less than ten miles away.

After a short ride, just as the sun was starting its ascent, the riders came upon a *ranchito* a few miles from the river crossing at Del Rio. The land was dry and its corn was withered and not worth stealing, but there were about twenty head of longhorn cattle milling near the adobe ranch house.

Vasquez signaled his men to a halt. "Hey, Juanito," he said to Sergeant Garcia, "I think we can get some money for those cattle across the border. What do you think?"

Garcia nodded. *"Sí.* There is a small town called Bracketville not too far away. I have an uncle who works for a ranch there. He say they always need more cattle."

Vasquez pulled his *pistola* from its holster and yelled, "Ride, vaqueros, ride!" He fired his pistol, and the group rode hard toward the little adobe hut, expecting an easy time of it.

As they approached at full gallop, two men ran from a small corral toward the house, trying to make it to safety. They were knocked off their feet in a fusillade of bullets, each shot several times.

Suddenly, a diminutive figure wearing a wide western hat and a brace of Colts strapped down low on his thighs stepped out of the doorway. Bullets began to pock the walls of the house, but he didn't flinch or move. He threw a Henry repeating rifle to his shoulder and began to cock and fire a steady stream of slugs into the *bandidos*. When two of the Apaches fell screaming to the ground, blood pouring from their chests, the other riders pulled their mounts around and began to ride in a circle near the house.

Vasquez screamed, "Kill him, kill the gringo!"

His men tried, firing over a hundred bullets at the little man, who remained where he stood, shooting calmly and accurately until his rifle was empty. When he threw the long gun down, the riders again tried to rush the hut, screaming and yelling at the top of their lungs.

Suddenly both the man's hands were filled with iron, and he proceeded to blow four more of Vasquez's men out of their saddles.

Vasquez pulled his men back out of pistol range and had several of the Rurales keep the man pinned down in the doorway while the Mescalero Apaches and half-breeds drove the cattle toward the Rio Grande.

A final shot from one of the riflemen caused a high-pitched scream to come from within the house, and the rancher holstered his pistols and ducked back out of sight. As they rode off, leaving their dead and wounded where they lay, Vasquez said to Garcia, "That hombre had the *cojones del toro!*"

Garcia shrugged. "Or maybe him just plenty *loco en la cabeza.*"

Joey Wells punched out his empties and reloaded both his Colts just in case the crazy marauders returned. Only then did he turn his attention to his wife and son, who lay in a spreading pool of blood on the dirt floor of his house. One quick look out the door to make sure the killers were gone, then he knelt by his wife's side.

She was unconscious, still clasping their three-year-old son in her arms. One of the bandit's bullets had torn through little Tom's right leg and into Betty's chest. The boy was moaning, barely conscious, and his leg hung at a funny angle. Joey whipped his bandanna off and tied it in a tight knot around the leg, slowing the bleeding to a trickle. He rolled Betty on her side, pulled a long, wicked-looking Arkansas Toothpick from a scabbard at the rear of his belt, and cut away her dress.

The bullet had entered her chest just below her left breast, hit a rib, and skidded around her rib cage just under the skin to exit out her back. There was no bloody froth on her lips, and her breathing was rapid but deep, without whistling. Joey knew from close association with gunshot wounds that hers was not immediately life-threatening.

He took a slab of fatback from the cupboard and placed it over her wound to slow the bleeding and tied it in place with what was left of her blouse.

He sat back on his heels, staring at his wife and son and their blood staining the dirt floor of their home, remembering what had happened to his first wife and son. . . .

* * *

It seemed almost to have happened to someone else instead of him, that day in 1858. Joey was young, but men married young in the mountains of Missouri in those days. He was a mountain man, as were his relatives who hailed from the blue ridges of Virginia, the peaks of Tennessee, and the broken crags of the Ozarks. The mountains and their ways of life were ingrained blood-deep in him: independence, self-reliance, and strength led to the peculiar code of the mountain man. To rectify a wrong, to seek vengeance for a hurt, was as all-important as returning a favor or keeping one's word once given. It was as strong as religion, and sometimes stronger, and the way of the Missouri Feud lived as long as the man did.

Joey Wells had come to Sutton County, Missouri, and brought forty acres, a quarter section, of bottom land with soil as black and rich as any in the state. His creek was full and his crops were growing as fast and tall as his new baby boy. If things continued to go his way, he'd buy the forty acres adjacent to the ones he now tilled.

That early spring day was cold, with wind swirling through wet pines and making a sound like a widow moaning at her man's funeral. The rain hit with the force of bullets, causing his lead mule to dance and stamp his feet, wanting the warm sanctuary of the half-finished barn.

Joey didn't mind the weather. His life was as full as he could hope, and he needed to get the crops in and well established before the spring rains began to fall and turned his fields into mud holes too wet to work. He hitched his mules to the turning plow while the sun was still minutes away from rising and the temperature only a few degrees above freezing. He cut a plug of tobacco and stuffed it in his mouth, chewing and waiting for the dawn so he could see to plow.

It was midmorning before Joey smelled smoke on the freshening breeze. He pulled back on the double reins and hollered, "Whoa there, mules, whoa there."

He followed his nose and saw the black clouds rising in giant puffs over the wooded ridge between him and his house. As he looked, he heard shots, and his blood turned cold with fear. His wife and son were in the cabin alone.

He left the mules where they stood, running wildly across the three miles to his house through briars and stinging nettle and brush, his face bloodied by branches unfelt in his hurry home. He splashed through his creek, staining the water with blood from his bare feet, clambering up the gully on the far side, pulling at roots and trees and grass to speed his progress.

He screamed in agony at the sight that befell him as he charged into the small clearing surrounding his house. He fell, exhausted and panting, to his knees, his voice a keening wail of sorrow. The timbers of his cabin were fallen in, flames eating what was left of Joey's dream of hearth and home. He scrambled to his feet and charged the fire until he was driven back, his face blistered and burned, his coveralls smoldering from the intense heat. He circled the cabin, screaming his wife's and boy's names over and over, until his voice was raspy and his soot-filled throat closed, as if that would somehow make them appear, alive and healthy.

It was almost nightfall before the flames subsided enough for him to search the ruins. He found them in what had been their bedroom. They were lying next to each other, the fire-blackened arms of his baby boy stretched out, his small fingers searching for his mother's, which would remain forever just out of reach. Sobbing and choking, Joey wrapped their bodies in burlap sacks and carried them to a large oak tree near the creek. He dug a single grave and placed them tenderly in the dirt. As the sun sank to the west and the stars broke through scattered clouds, he recited what he could remembered of a Christian burial ceremony. His final words were "An eye fer an eye, an' a tooth fer a tooth."

As tears made furrows in his soot-blackened cheeks, and sobs racked his lungs, Joey turned his face upward toward a slender moon and vowed revenge. It was the last time Joey Wells would cry.

Joey shook his head, snapping his mind back to the present. He had work to do if he wanted to save his wife's and his boy's lives. Walking quickly across sun-baked dirt, he went first to check on Carlos and Ricardo, his hired hands. They were both dead, killed instantly in the first rush of battle.

Joey turned, wearing a death grimace, pulled his Arkansas Toothpick from its scabbard, and walked slowly to check the six bodies lying in various locations around his house. Four were dead, two still breathing but unconscious.

He knelt next to the first one and, with a rapid back-and-forth motion slapped his face until the man opened pain-filled eyes. Joey leaned close to him, growling, "Who did this? Who is your leader?"

The Apache half-breed grinned, baring bloodstained teeth. "Fuck you, gringo, I tell you nothing!"

Joey didn't say anything, just grabbed the wounded man's collar and dragged him over to where the other man lay. This one, a Mexican, was conscious but unable to move. His spine was shattered where Joey's slug tore through it.

Joey asked him the same question. "Who is your leader, and why did you hit my place?"

The man gritted his teeth and shook his head. Evidently, he wasn't inclined to speak either.

Joey said, "Watch . . ." He pulled the Apache's head up by its hair and quickly sliced off both ears, causing the man to scream until his eyes bulged out. Joey grinned, a grin with no humor in it, at the other man. "Guess it's not true what they say about injuns not showin' any pain, huh?"

When the Mexican bandit again shook his head, Joey shrugged and with a lightning-quick motion moved his knife around the half-breed's head, then ripped his scalp off with a wet, sucking sound. One last scream, and the Apache died.

Joey turned again to the wounded man, who was wearing a dirty Mexican Rurale uniform. He slowly wiped his blade on the bandit's shirt. "Now, we kin do this one o' two ways . . . an easy way an' a hard way." He inclined his head and raised his eyebrows. "My wife an' kid're in that house, both shot by you bastards. I hope ya choose the hard way."

The Mexican licked his lips, his eyes flicking from the bloody knife blade to Joey's eyes, cold as stones. "It was Emilio Vasquez, *El Machete,* who bring us here. We just wanted your cattle, for money."

"Where they headin' next?"

"I do not know, señor."

Joey swung the knife down, penetrating the killer's hand and impaling it to the dirt. As he screamed and tried to pull it away, Joey said, "Wanna try thet question again?"

"Bracketville . . . they go to Bracketville to sell cattle. Aiyeee . . . my hand . . ."

"Hurts, does it?" Joey asked. When the man nodded, Joey watched his eyes as he jerked the knife free and swung it backhanded across the man's throat, slitting it from ear to ear.

He didn't turn to watch the bandit die, drowning in his own blood, but walked rapidly to the corral to attach his two horses to his buckboard. He needed to get his wife and son to Del Rio as soon as he could. The Mexican town of Jimenez was closer and on his side of the Rio Grande, but Joey knew there was no doctor there, at least none he would trust with his family.

It took him almost four hours to load his wife and son in the buckboard and make the trip to Del Rio. He was relived to hear that both would survive, though the doctor couldn't tell if the boy would ever be able to walk on his shattered leg. "It's in God's hands," the man said.

Joey nodded, his face grim. "I'll leave the healin' ta Him, long as He leaves the killin' ta me." He gave the doctor a handful of gold coins. "Take care o' my kin, doc, till I git back."

"But . . . where are you going. Your family needs you. . . ."

The look of naked hatred and fury in Joey's eyes stopped him in midsentence. "I gotta bury my hands and close up my house. Then I'm gonna kill every mother's son who had a hand in hurtin' me and mine. Tell Betty and little Tom I'll be back fer 'em when I'm done. She'll understand." He set his hat tight on his head. "She knows the way o' the Missouri Feud."

Chapter 1

Three days later Joey rode his big roan stallion, Red, into Brackettville. It was a small cattle town twenty five miles northwest of Del Rio, and a gathering place where ranchers from nearby spreads bought and sold stock of all kinds.

Joey was loaded for bear. He wore a brace of Colt .44s tied down low on his thighs, a shoulder holster with a Navy .36 under his left arm, his Arkansas Toothpick at his back, and he carried a Henry repeating rifle across his saddle horn and a Greener ten-gauge sawed-off shotgun in a saddle boot.

As he rode down the main street, his eyes flicked back and forth, covering his approach on both sides, including rooftops. It was a habit learned young, when after the Civil War he spent two years hunting and killing Kansas Redlegs until there were none left.

The war and its aftermath had turned young Joey Wells into a vicious killing machine, until he met Betty and tried to change his life. Now he was back on the trail, hunting nature's most deadly animals, other men.

He cut a corner off a slab of Bull Durham and stuck it in his mouth. He felt the familiar surge of adrenaline—a quickening of the heart, a dryness of the mouth, a quiver of muscles ready to act on a moment's notice. A minute later he leaned to the side and spit, thinking, "God help me, but I've missed this," as his mind drifted back to 1858. . . .

It didn't take Joey Wells long to discover who had burned his cabin and killed his wife and son, and why. There had been raids along the Missouri-Kansas border since 1854, but the burning of Wells's cabin had been the first incursion of the Kansas Redleg raids to hit Sutton County. The Redlegs were becoming infamous, leading raiders and killers and rapists into Missouri. Their leaders were infamous as well—Doc Jamison, Johnny Sutter, and a colonel named Waters. These men and the thugs they commanded hid behind a "cause," but they really cared only about killing and looting and burning.

After burying his family, Joey took to the bush, where he found others like himself—men who had been burned out, families either killed or driven off, men who had lost everything except the need for vengeance.

By the time the actual War Between the States began, these men, and Joey, were seasoned guerrilla fighters, men as at home on horseback or lying covered in leaves and bushes in thick timber as they were around a campfire. They could live for weeks on berries and squirrels and birds, and could sneak up to a man and steal his dinner from his plate without being seen. They were also mean and deadly as snakes, and just as quick to kill.

To these warriors there were no rules, no lines of battle, no command structure. It was simply kill or be killed, but be damned sure to take some with you when you shot your final load.

Finally, Union General Ewing made his biggest mistake of the war. He issued an order to arrest womenfolk, burn their homes, and kill everyone along the Missouri-Kansas border. This caused hundreds, even thousands, to join the guerrilla ranks of the Missouri Volunteers. Names began to be carved into history and legend, names written in the blood of hundreds of Union soldiers and sympathizers. Quantrill, Bloody Bill Anderson, Dave Johanson, George Tilden, Joey Wells; mere mention of these men could make grown men blanch and pale, and women grab their children and run for cover.

After Union raiders killed a mother and her young son in one of their many raids, her other two sons joined the ranks of the Missouri Volunteers, to ride with Bloody Bill Anderson. They were Frank and Jesse James.

These Volunteers perfected the art of guerrilla warfare. They used pistols mostly. Riding with reins in their teeth, guiding their mounts with their knees, a Colt pistol in each hand, they charged forces superior in numbers and weaponry time and again, to defeat them by sheer raw courage and fearlessness.

Joey reined Red in before a saloon with a sign over the front entrance lettered THE BULL AND COW. He flipped the reins around a hitching rail, slung his Henry over his shoulder, and stepped through the batwings. He stood just inside for a moment, letting his eyes adjust to the smoky gloom, checking right and left, evaluating whether there was any immediate danger. He saw no group of men who could be the ones he was trailing and relaxed slightly, ambling to the bar, putting his Henry in front of him, its hammer back.

"Whiskey," he growled, watching other patrons behind his back in a big mirror over the bar. None seemed to be taking any great notice of him.

The barman placed a bottle in front of him and a glass so dirty he couldn't see through it. Joey fixed him with a stare, eyes narrow. "You want me ta clean thet glass on yore shirt?"

The bartender blanched and hastily replaced the glass with a clean one. "An' gimme a bottle with a label on it, I don't want none o' this hoss piss here."

The man nodded rapidly. "Yessir, Old Kentucky okay?"

Joey didn't answer. He took the bottle and poured a tumblerful, drinking it down in one swallow. "Leave the jug."

"Yessir." The bartender took a rag and began wiping down the far end of the bar, as far away from Joey as he could get, head down, eyes averted, as if he could smell danger on him.

Joey took the bottle and walked to an empty table in a corner of the saloon, one where he had his back to a wall, and he sat facing the other tables, drinking slowly, watching and waiting.

At midnight a door slammed on the second story of the saloon and a very drunk, fat Mexican staggered down the stairs, an almost empty bottle of tequila in one hand and his sweat-stained sombrero in the other. He wore a Mexican Rurale uniform still covered with trail dust. At the bottom of the stairs he upended the bottle and drank the last of its contents, then let out a loud belch and stumbled toward the bar.

Joey called softly, "Amigo, over here, *por favor.*"

The drunk looked through bloodshot, bleary eyes toward Joey as he walked toward him. "What you want, mister?"

Joey inclined his head toward his bottle. "I got this here whiskey an' I don't like ta drink alone."

The man glared suspiciously at him. Evidently he wasn't used to Anglo strangers offering him free drinks. Joey whispered, "An' I'd like ta know 'bout the girls here. They worth a couple o' dollars?"

A grin spread across the Mexican's face, and he plopped down in a chair across from Joey. "*Sí, señor*. They not so young, but what you do in town this small?"

Joey signaled the barman for another glass and poured it full when it arrived. The fat man drank half of it down in one gulp, then hiccupped and laughed. "Not so much fire as tequila, but . . ." He shrugged.

Joey grinned. "Yeah, I know what you mean. Still, it'll git the job done, all right."

"My name is Tomás. Tomás Rodriguez." He nodded at Joey and drank the rest of the bourbon without pausing.

Joey sipped his, watching through slitted eyes. "I'm headin' on down Del Rio way. You ever been there?"

He nodded drunkenly. "*Sí*. Much better cantina in Del Rio. *Muchas señoritas, muchas tequila.*"

"I'm lookin' ta buy some longhorns. You know anybody down that way might have some ta sell?"

Rodriguez shook his head. "You want longhorns? Too bad. *Mi compadres* just sold ours two days before."

Joey smiled again. "You mean those cattle Vasquez sold here?"

The man looked up quickly, suspicion in his pig eyes. "You know Vasquez?"

Joey shrugged. "Sure, old friend of mine. Used ta call 'im El Machete back when I knowed him."

Rodriguez smiled broadly, showing several missing teeth. "Oh, you been to Chihuahua?"

"Yeah, once or twice."

Rodriguez leaned across the table and put his finger to his lips as if he were about to tell a secret. "Vasquez not in Chihuahua no more." He shook his head. "He goin' to Colorado, and I join him there."

"Colorado, huh? Why's ol' Machete goin' all the way ta Colorado?"

"Big *jefe* in Pueblo named Murdock going to hire us. Need vaqueros good with *pistolas.*" Rodriguez held up the empty bottle. "You got more whiskey?"

"Sure, it's across the street at the hotel, in my room. Come on and I'll get us another bottle."

Joey threw his arm around the drunk's shoulders and they stepped through the batwings, the Mexican singing some folksong in Spanish that Joey had never heard before. He walked him around a corner of the saloon and into the darkness of an alley. As the man realized something was wrong and straightened, pulling away, Joey pulled out his Arkansas Toothpick and held the point under Rodriguez's chin.

The fat man slowly raised his hands. "Why for you do this, gringo?"

"The only reason I ain't killin' ya right now, *bastardo,* is I don't want the U.S. law on my trail while I track down an' kill yore murderin' friends." The knife flashed and severed all four of the fingers on Rodriguez's right hand, then, with a backhanded swipe, Joey hit him dead in the middle of his forehead with the butt of the knife, knocking him instantly unconscious before he had time to scream. He dropped like a stone, blood pouring from his ruined hand.

After wiping his knife on the man's shirt, Joey walked around the corner to get on Red and head toward Pueblo, Colorado. As he stepped into the saddle, a voice came from the door of the saloon.

"I thought that was you the barman described, Wells."

Joey's hand was on his pistol butt before he saw who was talking to him. It was Louis Carbone, and standing next to him was his friend and constant companion, Al Martine.

Joey shook his head and grinned. "Looks like they'll let any ol' trash come up to Texas."

Carbone smiled. "You got time for to wet your whistle, killer?"

Joey looked to his left at the entrance to the alley. "Well, maybe just one, then I gotta be on my way."

Martine raised an eyebrow when he saw Joey's eyes flicker toward the alley. "Yore hurry wouldn't have nothin' to do with that hombre you escorted outta here, would it?"

Joey shook hands with the two men and they went back into the saloon. They showed him to their table, where there was a bottle of bourbon, half empty, and two mugs of beer. "Wanna beer?" Carbone asked.

"Naw, like I said, I gotta git goin' here 'fore too long. Whiskey'll do me just fine."

After they all downed a drink, Joey asked, "What're you two doin' all the way up here? Last I heared, you was stuck down there in Chihuahua, entertainin' all the señoritas."

"We came to buy some longhorns from Texas and run 'em back down to Mexico. Those Mexican crossbred cattle ain't worth spit."

"Say," Joey asked, "you boys know anything 'bout a galoot named Murdock ranchin' up Colorado way?"

The two looked at each other and grinned. "Yeah, and I hope the fact that you're askin' about him means he's gonna die real soon," Martine said.

"Oh?"

Carbone chuckled. "Yeah, Al's got a hard-on for the guy. 'Bout a year back, when we was last up here buying cattle, he got in a poker game with Murdock and lost half the money we had for cattle."

Martine scowled. "Later, I heard he ran a crooked game. He cleaned some ol' boy outta everything he had, includin' the deed to a ranch somewhere up in the mountain country. Coulda been Colorado, I guess."

"Last news we had was the Rangers tole him to git his butt outta Texas or they'd make 'im wished he had," Carbone added.

Joey's face turned hard. "Don't worry none 'bout gittin'

any revenge, Al. I'm headed up that way ta have a talk with Murdock and some men he's hired." Joey went on to tell the two about how the marauders had shot Betty and Tom.

Carbone put his hand on Joey's arm. "Don't worry none 'bout your family, compadre, Al and I will stay here and make sure they are well cared for while you take care of Vasquez and his men. But watch your ass. I hear Vasquez is crooked as a snake's trail, and twice as dangerous with that long knife of his."

"Thanks, Louis."

The men walked outside to stand next to their horses at the hitching rail.

Al narrowed his eyes. "If you happen to get up near Big Rock, Colorado, there's someone I'd like you to look up for us."

"Who'd that be?"

"Man name of Smoke Jensen. He did Louis and me a big favor a couple of years back, and I'd like you to take him a present from us."

"Smoke Jensen? Smoke Jensen the pistoleer?"

Martine said, "Come on over to my horse. I have something in my saddlebags for you to take with you."

Chapter 2

Smoke and Pearlie and Cal rode three abreast across the lush meadows of Sugarloaf, Smoke's ranch, keeping their horses at an easy canter. The fields were full of wildflowers, riotous colors not yet muted by the early frost, and the air was crisp and cold with a gunmetal smell of snow on the breezes. The sun was bright in a cloudless sky but brought little warmth.

They were riding the pastures and fields to make sure the spring calving hadn't left any cows down, their calves to starve. Spring rains had knocked some fences down, and Pearlie and Cal were checking to see which ones needed fixing first, so Pearlie could send the punchers out to repair the damage.

Out of the corner of his eye Smoke saw Cal flexing and swinging his left arm, a grimace of pain on his face. "How's the arm, Cal?"

The boy straightened in his saddle, wiping pain from his face. "Oh, it's fine, Smoke, no problem at all."

Pearlie gave Smoke a wink. "Yeah, it's fine, 'ceptin' I

reckon ol' Cal'll be able to tell us when a storm's comin', from the aching in that wound of his.''

Cal had only recently recovered from a bullet he took in his chest while helping Smoke in his fight against the man who called himself Sundance. Smoke sobered, his grin fading as he remembered how Cal and Pearlie had saved his life. . . .

Smoke planned to cover the north part of the trail himself and to slow down, or eliminate that bunch of paid assassins. He directed Cal and Pearlie farther down the mountain to harass and attack a second bunch headed up the mountain along a winding deer trail through tall timber.

By the time Cal and Pearlie made their way down the slopes to locate the gunmen's campfire, it was past ten o'clock at night. The snow had stopped falling, and the dark skies were beginning to clear.

Cal and Pearlie lay just outside the circle of light from the fire and listened to the outlaws as they prepared to turn in for the night.

One-Eye Jordan, his hand wrapped around a whiskey bottle and his speech slightly slurred, said, ''Black Jack, I'll lay a side wager that I'm the one puts lead in Smoke Jensen first.''

Black Jack Warner looked up from checking his Colt's loads, spun the cylinder, and answered, ''You're on, One-Eye. I've got two double-eagle gold pieces that say I'll not only drill Jensen first, but that I'll be the one who kills him.''

The Mexican and two Anglos who were watching from the other side of the fire chuckled and shook their heads. They apparently did not think much of their leader's wager, or were simply tired and wanted them to quit jawing so they could turn in and get some rest.

Finally, when One-Eye finished his bottle and tossed it in the flames, the men quit talking and rolled up in their blankets under a dusting of light snow.

Pearlie and Cal waited until the gunnies were snoring loudly, and then they stood, stretching muscles cramped from lying on the snow-covered ground. Being careful not to make too much noise, they circled the camp, noting the location and number of horses, the layout of surrounding terrain. They crept up on the group of sleeping gun hawks, moving slowly while counting bedrolls to make sure all of Sundance's men were accounted for.

Pearlie leaned over and cupped his hand around Cal's ear, whispering, "I count five bodies. That matches the number of horses."

Cal nodded, holding up five fingers to show he agreed. He took two sticks of dynamite from his pack and held them up so Pearlie could see, then he pointed to Pearlie and made a circular motion with his hand to indicate he wanted Pearlie to go around to the other side of camp and cover him.

Pearlie nodded and slipped a twelve-gauge shotgun off his shoulder. He broke it open and made sure both chambers were loaded, then snapped it shut gently so as not to make a sound. He gave Cal a wink as he slipped quietly into the darkness.

Cal waited five minutes to give Pearlie time to get into position. Taking a deep breath, he drew his Navy Colt with his right hand and held the dynamite in his left. He slowly made his way among the sleeping outlaws, being careful not to step on anything that might cause noise. When he was near the fire, he tossed both sticks of dynamite into the dying flames and quickly stepped out of camp. He ducked behind a thick ponderosa pine just as the dynamite exploded with an ear-splitting roar, blowing chunks of bark off the other side of the tree.

The screaming began before echoes from the explosion

stopped reverberating off the mountainside. Flaming pieces of wood spiraled through the darkness, hissing when they fell into drifts of snow.

Cal swung around his tree, both hands full of iron. One of the outlaws, his hair and shirt on fire, ran toward him, yelling and shooting his pistol wildly.

Cal fired both Colts, thumbing back hammers, pulling triggers so quickly the roaring gunshots seemed like a single blast. Pistols jumped and bucked in his hands, belching flame and smoke toward the running gunnie.

The bandit, shot in his chest and stomach, was thrown backward to land like a discarded rag doll on his back, smoke curling lazily from his flaming scalp.

One-Eye Jordan threw his smoldering blanket aside and stood, dazed and confused. His eye patch had been blown off, along with most of the left side of his face. He staggered a few steps, then pulled his pistol and aimed it at Cal, moving as if in slow motion.

Twin explosions erupted from Pearlie's scattergun, taking Jordan low in the back, splitting his torso with molten pieces of lead. His lifeless body flew across the clearing, where it landed atop another outlaw who had been killed in the dynamite blast.

One of the Mexican *bandidos*, shrieking curses in Spanish, crawled away from the fire on hands and knees. Scrabbling like a wounded crab toward the shelter of darkness, he looked over his shoulder to find Pearlie staring at him across the sights of a Colt .44.

"Aiyee . . . no . . ." he yelled, holding his hands in front of him as if they could stop the inevitable bullets. Pearlie shot him, the hot lead passing through his hand and entering the bandit's left eye, exploding his skull and sending brains and blood spurting into the air.

Black Jack Warner, who was thrown twenty feet in the air into a deep snowdrift, struggled to his feet. As he drew his pistol, he saw Pearlie shoot his compadre. Pearlie was turned away from Warner and did not see the stunned outlaw creep slowly toward him, drawing a bead on his back with a hogleg.

Cal glanced up, checking on bodies for signs of life. He saw Warner with his arm extended, about to shoot Pearlie in the back.

With no thought for his own safety, Cal yelled as he stood up, drawing his Navy Colt, triggering off a hasty shot.

Warner heard the shout and whirled, catching a bullet in his neck as he wheeled around. A death spasm curled his trigger finger, and his pistol fired as he fell.

Cal felt like a mule had kicked him in the chest as he was thrown backward. He lay in the snow, gasping for breath, staring at stars. In shock, he felt little pain—that would come much later. He knew he was hit hard and wondered briefly if he was going to die. His right arm was numb and wouldn't move, and his vision began to dim, as if snow clouds were again covering the stars.

Suddenly Pearlie's face appeared above him, tears streaming down his cheeks. "Hey, pardner, you saved my life," he said, worry pinching his forehead.

Cal gasped, trying to breathe. He felt as if the mule that had kicked him was now sitting on his chest. "Pearlie," he said in a hoarse whisper rasping through parched lips, "how're you doin'?"

Pearlie pulled Cal's shirt open and examined a blood-splattered hole in the right side of his ribs. He choked back a sob, then he muttered, "I'm fine, cowboy. How about you? You havin' much pain?"

Cal winced when, suddenly, his wound began to throb. "I feel like someone's tryin' to put a brand on my chest, an' it hurts like hell."

Pearlie rolled him to the side, looking for an exit wound. The bullet had struck his fourth rib, shattering it, and traveled around the chest just underneath the skin, causing a deep, bloody furrow, then exited from the side, just under Cal's right arm. The wound was oozing blood, but there was none of the spurting that would signify artery damage, and it looked as if the slug had not entered his chest cavity.

Cal groaned, coughed, and passed out. Pearlie tore his own shirt off and wrapped it around Cal, tying it as tightly as he could to stanch the flow of blood from the bullet hole. He sat back on his haunches, trying to think of something else he could do to help his friend. "Goddammit, kid," he whispered, sweat beading his forehead, "it shoulda been me lyin' there instead of you."

The sound of a twig snapping not far away caught Pearlie's attention, and he jerked his Colt, thumbing back the hammer.

"Hold on there, young'un," a voice called from the darkness, "it's jest me, ol' Puma, come to see what all this commotion's about."

Pearlie released the hammer and holstered his gun with a sigh of relief. "Puma! Boy, am I glad to see you!"

Puma sauntered into the light, then he saw Cal lying wounded at Pearlie's feet. He squatted down, laying his Sharps Big Fifty rifle near his feet, and bent over the kid. He lifted Pearlie's improvised dressing and examined Cal's wound. Pursing his lips, he whistled softly. "Whew . . . this child's got him some hurt."

He pulled a large Bowie knife from his scabbard and held it out to Pearlie. "Here. Put this in that fire and get me some fatback and lard out'n my saddlebag."

When Pearlie just stared at him, Puma's voice turned harsh. "Hurry, son, we don't have a surfeit of time if'n we want to save this'n."

Pearlie snatched the knife from Puma and hurried to carry out his request.

Puma took his bandanna and began wiping sweat from Cal's forehead, speaking to him in a low, soothing voice.

"You just rest easy, young beaver, ol' Puma's here now, an' yore gonna be jest fine."

When Pearlie returned carrying a sack of fatback and a small tin of lard, Puma asked him if he had any whiskey.

"Some, in my saddlebags, but . . ."

"Git it, and don't dawdle now, you hear?"

After Pearlie handed Puma the whiskey, the old mountain man cradled Cal's head in his arms and slowly poured half the bottle down his throat, stopped to let him cough and gag, then gave him the rest of the liquor.

Without looking up, he said, "Git my blade outta the fire, it oughta be 'bout ready by now."

Pearlie fished the knife out of the coals, its blade glowing red hot and steaming in the chilly air. He carried it to Puma and gave it to him, dreading what was to come next.

"Pearlie, you sit on the young'un's legs and try an' keep him from moving too much. I'll sit on his left arm and hold down his right."

When they were in position, Puma pulled a two-inch cartridge from his pocket and placed it between Cal's teeth. "Bite down on this, boy, an' don't worry none if'n you have to yell every now'n then. There ain't nobody left alive to hear you."

Cal nodded, fear in his eyes, jaws clenched around the bullet.

Puma laid the glowing knife blade sideways on Cal's wound and dragged it along his skin, cauterizing the flesh. It hissed and steamed, and the smell of burning meat caused Pearlie to turn his head and empty his stomach in the snow.

Cal's face turned blotchy red and every muscle in his body tensed, but he made no sound while the knife did its work.

When he was through, Puma stuck his blade in the snow to cool it, sleeving sweat off his forehead. He looked down at Cal, who was breathing hard through his nose, bullet sticking out of his lips like an unlit cigarette. "Smoke was right, Cal," Puma whispered. "You're one hairy little son of bitch. You were born with the bark on, all right."

Cal spit the bullet out and mumbled, "Do you think you could move, Pearlie? Yore about to break my legs."

Pearlie laughed. "Shore, Cal. I wouldn't want to cause you no extra amount of pain."

Cal chuckled, then he winced and moaned. "Oh. It hurts so bad when I laugh."

While they were talking, Puma gently washed the wound with snow, then packed the furrow with crushed chewing tobacco.

"What's that for?" Pearlie asked.

"Tabaccy will heal just about anything," Puma answered as he dipped his fingers in the lard and spread a thin layer over the tobacco-covered wound.

Cal looked down at his chest, then up at Pearlie. "Would you build me a cigarette, Pearlie? I think I'd rather burn a twist of tobacco than wear it."

Puma sliced a hunk of fatback off a larger piece, laid it over Cal's chest, and tied it down with Pearlie's shirt. "There, that oughta keep you from bleedin' to death till you git down to Big Rock an' the doctor."

Pearlie handed Cal a cigarette and lit it for him. "How are we gonna git him down to town, Puma? I don't think he can sit a horse."

Puma stood up and walked off into the darkness, fetching two geldings back, leading them into the light. He tied a dally rope from one to the other and then turned to the two younger men. "We'll sit Cal in the saddle, and you'll ride double behind him, with yore arms around him holdin' the reins. That way, if'n he faints or passes out, you can hold him in the saddle. 'Bout halfway down, change horses when this'n gits tired." He glanced up at the stars. "I figure you'll make it to town about daylight."

Pearlie said, "But what about Smoke? How'll he know

what happened to us? He's expectin' us back at camp in the morning."

Puma smiled. "Don't you worry none about that. I'll tell him what you done and where you're gone to. Now, git goin' if'n you want to make it in time fer breakfast."

The two men lifted Cal into the saddle, and Pearlie climbed on behind, his arms around the younger man. "Just a minute," Cal said, feeling his empty holster. "Where's my Navy?"

"Don't worry about it," Pearlie said, "I'll get you another one."

Cal shook his head. "No. That was Smoke's gun when he came up here with Preacher. It means somethin' special to me, an' I won't leave without it."

Puma dug in the snow where Cal had fallen until he found the pistol. He brushed it off and handed it to the teenager. "Here ya go, beaver. You might want to check yore loads 'fore you put it in yore holster." He glanced back, surveying the outlaws' bodies lying around camp. "Looks like you mighta used a few cartridges in the fracas earlier."

Pearlie grinned as they rode off. "That we did, Puma, that we did."

Cal had been as close to death as a man could come and still survive. His wound left him bedridden for three months, with Smoke and Pearlie taking turns sitting by his bedside, feeding him beef stew and later steaks to build up his strength and help replace the blood he had lost. For his part, Cal never complained about the excruciating pain, gritting his teeth and forcing food down when he wasn't hungry so he could heal faster.*

* *Vengeance of the Mountain Man*

*   *   *

Pearlie chuckled. "He's so proud of that wound, he's even taken to working with his shirt off so's the other punchers kin see that ugly ol' scar. Guess he wants 'em to know he's a genuine pistoleer."

Cal, blushing furiously, said, "Shut yore mouth, Pearlie! I don't neither!"

Smoke grinned to himself. From the way the two cowpokes jawed at each other, you'd never guess they were best friends. Such was the way of the West and of the boys who grew to be men too fast.

"Why," Pearlie continued, unwilling to let the teenager off so easy. "I reckon at the next Fourth of July picnic in Big Rock he'll be parading around bare-chested, askin' all the young ladies if'n they wanna touch his famous scar."

"Pearlie, I swear to God, I'm gonna whup you if'n you don't shut yore trap!"

Smoke's grin faded as he cut his eyes to the side, peering from under his hat brim. He slowed his big Palouse stallion, Horse, to a walk and without saying anything reached down and slipped rawhide thongs off the hammers of his Colt .44s, then leaned forward to loosen his Henry repeating rifle in its saddle boot.

Pearlie noticed Smoke's actions and sat straighter in his saddle, pulling his Stetson down tight. "Trouble, Smoke?"

"Maybe." He glanced right and left, eyes searching the tree line on either side of the meadow they were riding across. "I saw a reflection off a glass in those trees to the right, and something flushed a covey of quail out of that copse of trees to our left. I hope you boys are loaded up six and six."

Cal and Pearlie both began to survey the nearby forest as they loosened pistols in their holsters.

"We need to get to cover. When I give the word, spur your mounts toward that tank up ahead." He inclined his head at a small pond used to water cattle that lay a hundred yards distant. It had been dug by hand and was surrounded by an embankment of earth several feet high on all sides. It wasn't much, but it was all they had.

After a moment Smoke leaned forward and shouted, "Now! Shag your mounts, boys!"

The three men lay over their saddle horns and rode hell bent for leather just as a group of riders broke cover on either side of them, puffs of smoke and distant pops of gunfire ringing out to break the stillness of the morning air.

As their horses strained and grunted, sweat flying from their bulging muscles, hooves throwing clods of dirt into the air, a rifle bullet whined overhead, slapping Pearlie's hat off. "Goddamn son of a bitch," he growled through gritted teeth, blinking his eyes against sweat running off his forehead.

They didn't slow as their broncs jumped the embankment, splashing into the shallow waterhole. They shucked rifles from saddle boots and dove out of their saddles to sprawl against the covering wall of dirt, Smoke on one side, Cal and Pearlie on the other. Small geysers of soil exploded as bullets slammed into the ground around them, stinging eyes and faces.

Smoke flipped his Henry over the edge of the mound, cocking and firing so fast, the booming of the big gun sounded as one roar. As Cal and Pearlie returned fire, the air filled with billowing clouds of cordite and their ears rang from cracking explosions of their rifles.

Six men rode hard toward Smoke's side, firing rifles and pistols over their horses' heads. Smoke's first shot took the lead rider full in the chest, punching through, blowing out his spine, and catapulting him backward off his mount. Smoke's second shot missed, but his third caught another rider in the face, exploding his head into a fine red mist, killing him instantly. As the other three bushwhackers turned their broncs to the side to escape his withering fire, Smoke blasted two of them out of their saddles to lie writhing among the wildflowers, staining them with blood and guts.

The other two riders finally got their horses turned and were hightailing it for the cover of the trees, leaning almost flat over their saddle horns, trying to get to safety.

Smoke, oblivious to the lead peppering the ground around him from behind, scrambled to the top of the dirt ridge and took careful aim, elevating the barrel of his long gun until its bead was a foot above one of the fleeing gunmen. Taking his time, he gently caressed the trigger and squeezed off a final shot, grunting as the big Henry slammed back into his shoulder. Three seconds later, the ambusher straightened in his saddle, flinging his arms wide before toppling to the side to lie unmoving in the dirt. The other rider glanced over his shoulder to watch his comrade hit the ground, but didn't slow his mount as it disappeared into the tree line.

Two more explosions rang out behind Smoke before he heard Pearlie growl, "Got ya, ya son of a bitch. That hat cost me two dollars."

Cal said, "That's it for this side, Smoke. We dusted 'em all."

Smoke turned, eyes narrowed against the morning sun. "You boys all right?"

"Well, goddamn!" said Pearlie, looking at Cal, who had a red stain on his left shoulder where a bullet took a chunk out of his left arm. "Cal, I swear, boy, you a regular magnet fer lead."

"It's okay, it's jest a scratch," Cal replied as he reloaded his Colt Navy pistol.

Pearlie stepped to his side and began to tie his bandanna around the wound. "Shit, Smoke, now we'll never git this boy to wear a shirt!"

Smoke punched cartridges into his Henry until it was full. He looked around at the bloody corpses surrounding them. "Pearlie, you and Cal go check those galoots and make sure they're all dead. I'll take this side."

"And if they're not?"

Smoke shrugged. "See if you can find out why they jumped us and who sent them." He eared back the hammer on the Henry and climbed out of the waterhole, walking slowly toward the five men lying nearby. His eyes searched the trees, but there was no sign of the one who got away.

Only one of the gunmen Smoke shot was still alive. He had a bubbly red froth on his lips and a gaping wound on the right side of his chest, indicating a shot lung. Smoke crouched next to him, slapping his face gently until he opened his eyes.

"Goddamn you, Smoke Jensen," he croaked through wet lips. "You done kilt me."

"Not yet, cowboy, but you're close. Why'd you draw down on me and my men?"

"Fer the money." He moaned and touched his wound, then raised his hand to see the blood covering it. Turning fear-widened eyes to Smoke, he whispered, "It's funny, Jensen. I'm hit hard, but it don't hurt much."

Smoke frowned. "It will if you last long enough. What money are you talking about?"

The gunny coughed once, grimacing as the pain began. "Jesse found a paper on you in New Mexico. Said you was worth ten thousand alive er dead." He coughed again, said, "Oh, Jesus . . ." and died, empty eyes staring at eternity.

Smoke reached down and fingered his eyes shut, sighed, and walked over to the first man he shot. He lay on his back, arms flung wide, dead face looking somehow surprised. Smoke pulled a folded paper from the ambusher's shirt pocket. He wiped bloodstains off on the man's shirt and spread it open. It was a wanted poster dated several years before. There was a drawn picture of a younger Smoke Jensen on it and the offer of a reward of ten thousand dollars for his capture, dead or alive.

Smoke shook his head. The fools, he thought, this poster was recalled years ago. It was just after Lee Slater and his gang shot up Big Rock, the town Smoke founded, and wounded Smoke's wife, Sally. Smoke chased them up into the piny San Juan Mountains. A judge back east, related to Slater, issued a phony warrant on Smoke, causing a passel of bounty hunters to go up into the mountains after him. Smoke came down out of those peaks alone—the bounty hunters stayed up there, where they had died. U.S. marshal Mills Walsdorf got the warrant declared null and void, and the papers were supposed to have been re-called.*

Smoke snorted. "I guess they missed of few of those posters. I wonder how many more are out there, drawing bountiers to me like flies to molasses." He walked slowly across the meadow toward the waterhole, detouring slightly to make sure the other three gun hawks were dead. Cal and Pearlie had rounded up the men's horses and were waiting for him when he got there.

"Any survivors?" Smoke asked.

"Naw," Pearlie answered, "they's all dead as yesterday's news."

"You want us to bury 'em, Mr. Smoke?" Cal asked.

Smoke shook his head. "No, winter storm's coming soon. Wolves and coyotes got to eat, same as worms. Leave 'em where they lie." He removed his hat and ran his hands through his sand-colored hair. "Far as I can see, they don't deserve the sweat of honest men."

He slipped his Henry into its saddle boot. "Put dally ropes on those broncs and we'll take them back to the

* *Code of the Mountain Man*

ranch house." He looked at the horses as he swung into his saddle. "They're a sorry lot, but they'll do as spares in the remuda." He pointed at the bodies. "Cal, while Pearlie's getting the horses ready, why don't you round up those outlaws' pistols and rifles and ammunition. No need letting them lay out here to rust."

It was almost dusk when they arrived at Smoke's cabin. Cal and Pearlie saw to the horses and guns and Smoke went into the house. His wife, Sally, wiped her hands on her apron and threw her arms around Smoke's neck, hugging him tightly. She stiffened, stepped back, and wrinkled her nose. "You stink of gunpowder. Did you have some trouble?"

He unbuckled his gun belt and hung it on a peg next to the door. "A little." He handed her the wanted poster with his picture on it. "A few bounty hunters thought they'd get rich the easy way." He grinned at her when she looked up from reading the paper. "They found out it wasn't so easy after all."

Sally's eyes turned toward the bunkhouse. "Are Cal and Pearlie all right?"

"Cal got a minor wound in his shoulder. Pearlie says it'll give him another scar to brag about."

She frowned. "Smoke Jensen, you go get that boy right now and bring him back over here. I'll boil some water and dress his wound so it doesn't get infected." She turned, saying to herself, "If I know you men, you just wrapped a dirty old bandanna around it."

Smoke turned quickly to hide his smile. "Yes, ma'am." He walked out the door to fetch Cal. Over the years, Sally had patched up more bullet wounds than most doctors, a good many of which had been on Smoke himself.

*   *   *

That night, as they got ready for bed, Sally asked, "What are you going to do about those men who died?"

"I'll ride into Big Rock in the morning and report it to Monte Carson. I need to have him wire New Mexico and see if any more of those posters are still out there."

Chapter 3

It was a typical fall Saturday in Big Rock, Colorado. The town was full of cowboys from nearby ranches come to spend their wages and raise hell. Louis Longmont sat at his usual table in the saloon he owned, playing solitaire and drinking coffee. A piano player with garters on his sleeves was plinking in a corner, and two tables had stud poker games going, with stakes too small to interest Louis. Several hung-over cowpokes were trying to force down steak and eggs without much enthusiasm, faces haggard and eyes bloodshot from too much whiskey the night before. Cigar and cigarette smoke hung in the air like morning fog, giving the room a gloomy atmosphere in spite of the bright sunshine outside.

Louis was a lean, hawk-faced man with strong, slender hands and long fingers. His nails were carefully manicured, and his hands clean. His hair was jet black, and he sported a pencil-thin mustache. He was dressed as usual in a black suit, with a white shirt and dark ascot—the ascot something he'd picked up on a trip to England a few years back. He wore low-heeled boots, shined until they glistened, and carried a pistol hung low in a tied-down holster on his right thigh; it was not for show alone, for Louis was snake quick with a short gun. A feared, deadly gunman when pushed, he preferred to make his living teaching would-be gamblers how to lose their money at poker when they failed to correctly figure the odds.

He reached an impasse in his game and threw his cards down in disgust, looking up as the batwings were flung wide. A man entered slowly, stepping to the side when he got inside, so his back was to a wall. He stood there, letting his eyes adjust to the darkened interior of the saloon. Louis recognized the actions of an experienced pistoleer: how the man's eyes scanned the room, flicking back and forth before he proceeded to the bar. The cowboy was short, about five feet nine inches, Louis figured, and was covered with a fine coat of trail dust. He had a nasty-looking scar on his right cheek, running from the corner of his eye to disappear in the edge of his handlebar mustache. The scar had contracted as it healed, shortening and drawing his lip up in a perpetual sneer. His small gray eyes were as cold and deadly as a snake's, and he wore a brace of Colt .44s on his hips, tied down low, and carried a Colt Navy .36 in a shoulder holster. Louis, an experienced gunfighter himself, speculated he had never seen a more dangerous hombre in all his years. He looks as tough as a just-woke grizzly, he thought.

As hair on the back of his neck prickled and stirred, Louis shifted slightly in his seat, straightening his right leg and reaching down to loosen the rawhide thong on his Colt, just in case.

The stranger flipped a gold double eagle on the bar, took possession of a bottle of whiskey, and spoke a few words in a low tone to the bartender. After a moment the barman inclined his head toward Louis, then busied himself wiping the counter with a rag, casting worried glances at Louis out of the corner of his eye.

The newcomer turned, leaning his back against the bar, and stared at Louis. His eyes flicked up and down, noting the way Louis had shifted his position and how his right hand was resting on his thigh near the handle of his Colt. His expression softened and his lips moved slightly, turning up in what might have been a smile in any other face. He evidently recognized Louis as a man of his own kind, a brother predator in a world of prey.

Louis watched the gunman's eyes, thinking to himself, this man has stared death in the face on many occasions and has never known fear. With a slow, deliberate motion, his gaze never straying, Louis picked up his china coffee cup with his left hand and drained it to moisten his suddenly dry mouth, wondering just what the stranger had in mind, and whether he had finally met the man who was going to beat him to the draw and put him in the ground.

The pistoleer grabbed his whiskey with his left hand and began to saunter toward Louis, his right hand hanging at his side. As he passed one of the poker tables, a puncher threw his playing cards down and jumped up from the table with a snort of anger. "Goddamned cards just won't fall for me today," he said as he turned abruptly toward the bar, colliding with the stranger.

The cowboy, too much into his whiskey to recognize his danger, peered at the newcomer through bleary, red-rimmed eyes, spoiling for a fight. "Why don't you watch where yer goin', shorty?" he growled.

The gunman's expression never changed, though Louis thought he detected a kind of weary acceptance in his eyes, as if he had been there many times before. In a voice smooth with soft consonants of the South in it, he replied, "I believe ya need a lesson in manners, sir."

The drunken cowboy sneered. "And you think yore man enough to give me that lesson?"

In less time than it took Louis to blink, the pistoleer's Colt was drawn, cocked, and the barrel was pressed under the puncher's chin, pushing his head back. "Unless ya want yore brains decoratin' the ceiling, I'd suggest ya apologize to the people here fer yore poor upbringin' and fer yore mama not never teachin' ya any better than to jaw at yore betters."

The room became deathly quiet. One of the other men at the table moved slightly, and the stranger said without looking at him, "Friend, 'less ya want that arm blown plumb off, I'd haul in yore horns till I'm through with this'n."

Fear-sweat poured off the cowboy's face, and his eyes rolled, trying to see the gun stuck in his throat. "I'm . . . I'm right sorry, sir. It was my fault and I—I apologize fer my remarks."

The gunman stepped back, holstered his Colt, and glanced at a wet spot on the front of the drunk's trousers. "Apology accepted, sir." His eyes cut to the man at the table, who had frozen in position, afraid to move a muscle. "Ya made a wise choice not ta buy chips in this game, friend. It's a hard life ta go through with only one hand." Without another word he ambled over to stand next to Louis's table, his back to the wall, where he could observe the room as he talked.

"Ya be Mr. Longmont?"

Louis nodded, eyebrows raised. "Yes, sir, I am. And to whom do I have the pleasure of speaking?"

"I be Joseph Wells, 'though most calls me Joey."

At the mention of his name, the men at the poker table got hastily to their feet and grabbed their friend by his arm and hustled him out the door, looking back over their shoulders at the living legend who almost curled him up.

Louis didn't offer his hand, but smiled at Wells. "Pleased to make your acquaintance, Mr. Wells." He nodded at an empty chair across the table from him. "Would you care to take a seat and have some food?"

Wells scanned the room again with his snake eyes before he pulled a chair around and sat, his back still to a wall. "Don't mind if'n I do, thank ye kindly."

Louis waved a hand, and a young black waiter came to his table. "Jeremiah, Mr. Wells would like to order."

"Yes, sir," the boy replied as he looked inquiringly at Wells.

"I'll have a beefsteak cooked jest long enough ta keep it from crawling off'n my plate, four hen's eggs scrambled, an' some tomaters if'n ya have any."

The boy nodded rapidly and turned to leave.

"An' some *cafecito,* hot, black, and strong enough to float a horseshoe," Wells added.

Louis grinned. "I like to see a man with a healthy appetite." He glanced at a thick layer of trail dust on Wells's buckskin coat. "You have the look of a man a long time on the trail."

"That's a fact. All the way from Mexico, pretty near a month now."

The waiter appeared and placed a coffee mug on the table, filled it with steaming black coffee from a silver server, and added some to Louis's cup before setting the pot on the table. Wells pulled a cork from his whiskey bottle and poured a dollop of he amber liquid into his coffee. He offered the bottle to Louis, who shook his head.

Wells shrugged, blew on his coffee to cool it, and drank the entire cup down in one long draft. He leaned back, took his fixings out, and built himself a cigarette. Striking a lucifer on his boot, he lit the cigarette. He left it in his mouth while he spoke, squinting one eye against the smoke. "That's might good coffee." He refilled his cup and again topped it off with a touch of whiskey. "Shore beats that mesquite bean coffee I been drinking fer the last month."

Louis nodded, reviewing in his mind what he had heard about the famous Joey Wells. Wells had been born in the foothills of Missouri. He was barely in his teens when he fought in the Civil War for the Confederate Army. Riding with a group called the Missouri Volunteers, he became a fearless, vicious killer, eagerly absorbing every trick of guerrilla warfare known from the mountain men and hill-billies he fought with. After Lee's surrender at Appomattox, Wells's group attempted to turn themselves in. They reported to a Union Army outpost and handed over their weapons, expecting to be sent home like other Confederate soldiers had been. Instead, the entire group was assassinated. All except Wells and a few others, who were late getting to the surrender site. From a hill nearby they watched their unarmed comrades being gunned down. Under the code of the Missouri Feud, they vowed to fight the Union to the death.

After Joey and his men perpetrated several raids upon unsuspecting Union soldiers and camps, killing viciously to fulfill their vow of vengeance, a group of hired killers and thugs known as the Kansas Redlegs was assigned to hunt down the remaining Missouri Volunteers. After several years of raids and counterraids, Joey was the last surviving member of his renegade group. It took him another year and a half, using every trick he had learned, to track down and kill all of the remaining Redlegs, over a hundred and fifty men. Along the way he became a legend, a figure mothers would use to scare their children into doing their chores, a figure men would whisper about around campfires at night. With each telling, his legend grew, magnified by penny dreadfuls and shilling shockers, until there was no place left in America for him to run to.

After the last Redleg lay dead at his feet, Joey was said to have gone to Mexico and set up a ranch there. Rumor had it the Texas Rangers had struck a bargain with him, vowing to leave him in peace if he stayed south of the border.

Louis fired up another cigar, sipped his coffee, and wondered what had happened to cause Wells to break his truce and head north to Colorado. Of course, he didn't ask. In the West, sticking your nose in another's business was an invitation to have someone shoot it off.

After his food was served, Wells leaned forward and ate with a single-minded concentration, not speaking again until his plate was bare. He filled his empty coffee cup with whiskey, built another cigarette, and leaned back with a contented sigh. Smoke floated from the butt in his mouth and caused him to squint as he stared at Louis from under his hat brim. "A while back, I met some fellahs down Chihuahua way tole me 'bout a couple o' friends of theirs in Colorado. One was named Longmont."

Louis motioned to the waiter to bring him some brandy, then nodded, waiting for Wells to continue. "Yep. Said this Longmont dressed like a dandy and talked real fancy, but not to let that fool me. This Longmont was a real bad pistoleer and knew his way around a Colt, and was maybe the second-fastest man with a short gun they'd ever seen."

Louis dipped the butt of his stogie in his brandy, then stuck it in his mouth and puffed, sending a cloud of blue smoke toward the ceiling. "These men say anything else?" he asked, eyebrows raised.

"Uh-huh. Said this Longmont would do ta ride the river with, and if'n he was yore friend, he'd stand toe ta toe with ya against the devil hisself if need be."

Louis threw back his head and laughed. "Well, excusing your friends for engaging in a small amount of hyperbole, I suppose their assessment of my character is basically correct."

Wells's lips curled in a small smile. "Like they said, ya talk real purty."

"And who was the other man your friends mentioned?"

"Hombre named Smoke Jensen. They said Jensen was so fast, he could snatch a double eagle off'n a rattler's head and leave change 'fore the snake could strike."

Louis drowned his quiet smile in coffee. "Your friends have quite a way with words themselves. Might I ask what their names are?"

" 'Couple o' Mexes named Louis Carbone and Al Martine. Got 'em a little *ranchito* down near Chihuahua." Wells dropped his cigarette on the floor and ground it out with his boot. "They be pretty fair with short guns theyselves, fer Mexes."

Louis nodded, remembering the last time he had seen Carbone and Martine. The pair had hired out their guns to a rotten, no-good back-shooter named Lee Slater. Slater bit off more than he could chew when he and his men rode through Big Rock, shooting up the town and raising hell. Problem was, they also wounded and almost killed Sally Jensen, Smoke's wife. Smoke went after them, and in the end faced down the gang in the very streets of Big Rock, where it all started. . . .

Lee Slater stepped out of the shadows, his hands wrapped around the butts of Colts, as were Smoke's. "I'm gonna kill you, Jensen!" he screamed.

A rifle barked, the slug striking Lee in the middle of his back and exiting out the front. The outlaw gang leader lay dead on the hot, dusty street.

Sally Jensen stepped back into Louis's gambling hall and jacked another round into her carbine.

Smoke smiled at her and walked down the boardwalk.

"Looking for me, amigo?" Al Martine spoke from the shadows of a doorway. His guns were in leather.

"Not really. Ride on, Al."

"Why would you make such an offer to me? I am an outlaw, a killer. I hunted you in the mountains."

"You have a family, Al?"

"*Sí*. A father and mother, brothers and sister, all down in Mexico."

"Why don't you go pay them a visit? Hang up your guns for a time?"

The Mexican smiled and finished rolling a cigarette. He lit it and held it to Smoke's lips.

"Thanks, Al."

"Thank you, Smoke. I shall be in Chihuahua. If you ever need me, send word, everybody knows where to find me. I will come very quickly."

"I might do that."

"Adios, compadre." Al stepped off the boardwalk and was gone. A few moments later, Sheriff Silva and a posse rode up in a cloud of dust.

"That's it, Smoke," the sheriff announced. "It's all over. You're a free man, and all these other yahoos are gonna be behind bars."

"Suits me," Smoke said, and holstered his guns.

"No, it ain't over!" The scream came from up the street. Everybody looked. Pecos stood there, his hands over the butts of his fancy engraved .45s.

"Oh, crap!" Smoke said.

"Don't do it, kid!" Louis Carbone called from the board-walk. "It's over. He'll kill you, boy."

"Hell with you, you greasy son of a bitch!" Pecos yelled.

Carbone stiffened, cut his eyes to Smoke.

"Man sure shouldn't have to take a cut like that, Carbone," Smoke told him.

Carbone stepped out into the street, his big silver spurs jingling. "Kid, you can insult me all day. But you cannot insult my mother."

Pecos laughed and told him what he thought about Carbone's sister too.

Carbone shot him before the Kid could even clear

leather. The Pecos Kid died in the dusty street of a town that would be gone in ten years. He was buried in an unmarked grave.

"If you hurry, Carbone," Smoke called, "I think you can catch up with Martine. Me and him smoked a cigarette together a few minutes ago, and he told me he was going back to Chihuahua to visit his folks."

Carbone grinned and saluted Smoke. A minute later he was riding out of town, heading south.*

Louis grinned at the memory. Carbone and Martine had been given a second chance at life through the generosity of Smoke Jensen. He hoped they took advantage of it. "How are Carbone and Martine doing?"

Wells shrugged. "Pretty fair. Ain't much fer ranchin' though. Spend most of their time drinkin' tequila and shaggin' every señorita within a hundred miles, most of the señoras too, I 'spect."

Louis laughed again. "That would certainly be like Al and Louis all right."

"They said they owed you and Jensen a debt of honor fer how you all helped them out a while back." Wells reached into a leather pouch slung over his shoulder on a rawhide thong.

Louis tensed, his hand moving toward his Colt. Wells noticed the motion and shook his head slightly. "Don't you worry none, Mr. Longmont. I ain't here to do you or your'n any harm. I'm jest deliverin' somethin' fer Carbone and Martine. A token o' their 'preciation, they called it."

He opened his pouch and took out a set of silver spurs with large, pointed-star rowels and hand-tooled leather straps, and a large shiny Bowie knife with a handle inlaid with silver and turquoise. "The knife's fer Jensen, the spurs are fer you."

Louis was about to tell Wells thanks, when the batwings opened and two men cradling Greener ten-gauge shotguns stepped through the door.

Chapter 4

Wells straightened and half rose from his chair, his hands hovering over his Colts until Louis put a hand on his shoulder. "That's all right, Joey, they're friends of mine. You're in no danger in my establishment."

As Wells sat back down, Sheriff Monte Carson and his deputy, Jim, approached their table. "Everything all right here, Louis?" Monte asked, his thumb on the hammer of his Greener.

"Certainly, Monte. Why do you ask?"

"A couple of punchers came over to the jail and said Joey Wells was in town and drew down on 'em. They said it looked to them like he was loaded for bear and had some business with you."

Louis smiled reassuringly at Monte. "Unhand those scatterguns and you and Jim join us for some coffee. Mr. Wells here and I were just having a pleasant conversation about Louis Carbone and Al Martine."

"Carbone and Martine? Last I heard, those two reprobates were down in Mexico, tryin' to raise longhorns." He chuckled. "You got to be smart as a rock to try and herd longhorns."

"About all they seem to be raising at the present time is hell, according to Mr. Wells," Louis said.

Monte fixed his gaze on Wells. "Mr. Wells, I'm Monte Carson, sheriff of Big Rock, and this is my deputy, Jim Morris." He gave a half smile. "I hope we're gonna be friends, and that you're not planning any . . . excitement here in my town."

Wells stared back at Monte, his gaze unflinching. "Sheriff, I been on horseback fer over a month now, an' the only excitement I plan is ta find a bed fer me an' a rubdown an' some grain fer my hoss."

"I hope you won't take offense at my nosiness, but just what brings you to Big Rock?"

Wells hesitated. A private man, he wasn't used to discussing his affairs with strangers. After a moment he glanced at Louis and shrugged. "No offense taken, sir," he said to Monte. "I reckon it's yore job and ya got a right ta ask." He took a small drink of his whiskey and began to make a cigarette as he talked, his eyes on his hands as he folded the paper and sprinkled tobacco on it from a small cloth sack. " 'Bout six weeks back a group of Mexican Rurales and half-breed Mescalero Apaches raided my ranch down in Mexico, jest 'cross the border from Del Rio." He screwed the butt in the corner of his mouth and lit it, then raised his eyes to Monte's. "They killed two of my hands an' wounded my wife and son an' stole twenty of my beeves."

Jim blurted out, eyes wide, "They shot yore wife and kid?" His surprise came from the fact that in the West, women were treated with respect and deference by most cowboys. Men had been known to be shot or hanged for merely treating a woman with disrespect, and the thought of involving wives and children in feuds between menfolk was unthinkable to most citizens.

"Yeah. Soon's the raiders was gone, I took Betty and little Tom 'crost the Rio Bravo into Del Rio and had the doc there patch 'em up." Wells looked down at his hands, clenched white-knuckled on the table before him. "Still don't know if'n my boy's gonna be able to walk. They shattered his leg bone with a rifle bullet."

"How many were there that attacked you?" asked Louis.

"Thirty, maybe thirty-five." Wells gave a tight smile. "I was a mite too busy to count 'em at the time. They left six fer the buzzards ta eat at my place."

When Wells paused, Monte asked, "That why you're up this way?"

"Yep. After I got my kin taken care of, I tracked the murderin' bastards ta a town called Bracketville, where they sold my cattle. One of 'em stayed behind to sample the nightlife, an' he tole me he an' the others had been hired by a man name of Murdock ta work at a ranch over ta Pueblo, Colorado. Seems this Murdock won the ranch in a crooked poker game just 'fore he was run outta Texas by some Rangers who didn't like his back-shootin' ways."

Monte frowned. "I've heard of Jacob Murdock. The ex-sheriff of Pueblo is a friend of mine. He says Murdock is crooked as a snake's trail. According to my friend, Murdock's men threatened to kill the townspeople if they didn't vote for his kid brother, Sam Murdock, for sheriff." Monte waved at the waiter, held up two fingers, and pointed at the coffeepot.

Jim said, "That's be Ben Tolson?"

"Yeah. Ben tole me that ever since Murdock took over the ranch, the Lazy M he calls it, there's been complaints of cattle and calves missing and turning up on Murdock's spread."

Wells paid close attention as Monte spoke. One of the lessons he'd learned in his years as a hunted outlaw was to gather as much information about his opponents as he could. He had a term for it. He called it "having an edge."

He knew he had beaten men as fast as, and maybe faster with a gun than he was. He did it by always making sure he had an edge; the sun at his back and in the other's eyes, an element of surprise, or just the simple fact he always made sure to have grain to feed his big roan stallion instead of hay. He had outrun and outlasted many a pursuer, because grain gives a horse more "bottom," the ability to run longer, while hay-fed mounts give out.

"Didn't Tolson investigate the complaints?" Louis asked.

"Sure," Monte answered. "But witnesses against Murdock had a nasty habit of gettin' themselves killed before they could testify against him, and 'fore long Ben was out of a job." Monte cut his eyes to Wells. "You got a tough row to hoe if you're plannin' to go up against Murdock, especially if he's got thirty new gun hawks on his payroll and his brother as sheriff."

Wells shrugged, patting his Colt Navy in his shoulder holster. "Don't matter none ta me. Better men than this Murdock been tryin' ta plant me fer years." His eyes grew hard and seemed to change color, causing the hair on the back of Monte's neck to stir. "I'm still forked end down an' all of them are food fer worms."

Wells looked up, eyes narrowed as the batwings opened and a man entered. Dressed in buckskin shirt and trousers, wearing a brace of Colt .44s tied down low, the left-hand gun butt forward, he stopped just inside the door and paused to let his eyes adjust to the semidarkness, just as Wells had before. He was a few inches over six feet tall, with massive shoulders and arms straining his buckskin shirt. His eyes were blue as spring skies and cold as winter ice, and his hair was blond. Wells knew without asking he was looking at Smoke Jensen, a man as famous, and as deadly, as he was.

As Smoke approached their table, Louis smiled and gestured. "Howdy, Smoke. Come join us."

Smoke stood there, his eyes appraising Wells, while he waited to be introduced. He nodded greetings to Monte and Jim as Louis said, "Smoke Jensen, meet Mr. Joey Wells."

Wells stood, his head reaching only to the middle of Smoke's chest. He stuck out his hand. "Pleased ta meet cha, Mr. Jensen."

Smoke's big hand swallowed Wells's. "Likewise, Mr. Wells." He hesitated, then said with a serious expression, "If only half of what I've heard about you is true, I hope your visit to Big Rock is a social one."

Wells nodded. "I've heard a mite about ya too." He picked up the Bowie knife from the table and handed it to Smoke. "Louis Carbone and Al Martine send their regards."

Smoke took the knife, turning it over in his hands, admiring its workmanship. "Carbone and Martine, huh?"

"Yeah. Said this was ta remind ya they still owe ya a debt, an' ta let 'em know if'n ya ever need 'em."

Smoke hooked another chair from a nearby table with his boot and pulled it over. The waiter appeared with a fresh pot of coffee and a handful of mugs. While they drank their coffee, Smoke and Wells talked cattle talk, discussing the difficulties of raising longhorns in Mexico and shorthorns in Colorado. From their conversation, one would never know they were two of the most feared gunfighters in the territory.

Wells managed a laugh or two when Smoke and Louis recounted some tales of Carbone's and Martine's exploits during the Lee Slater fracas of a few years back. Smoke got the feeling Wells hadn't had much to laugh about for some time. He also found, to his surprise, he liked the man. Wells was straightforward, with none of the arrogance or swagger seen in most shootists Smoke had met.

After a while, saying they had rounds to make, Monte

and Jim left. While Smoke ate his breakfast, Louis gave him a short version of why Wells came to Colorado.

Smoke glanced up from his bacon and eggs. "You figuring on going up against Murdock and his gang alone?"

Wells nodded. "Don't know no other way. One thing I learnt in the war, sometimes a lone man kin do more damage than an entire brigade."

Smoke considered what Wells said. "You're probably right. If this Murdock is as crooked as Monte says, he's most likely got his ranch set up like a fort. A frontal assault wouldn't stand a chance of succeeding. And his brother, the sheriff, would be sure to warn him if a group of strangers showed up."

"One man, though, slippin' in under cover o' darkness, could be in an' out 'fore they knew what hit 'em."

Louis tipped smoke from his nostrils and contemplated the plume as it rose toward the ceiling. "Getting in won't be the problem. Getting out is another matter."

Wells's face grew hard. "I figger ta take some lead all right, but if'n word gits around in Mexico that you kin shoot up Joey Wells and not pay the price, then I'm good as dead anyhow."

"There is that to consider," Smoke said as he finished his coffee and stood. "However, if you're not in too big a hurry to kill those *bandidos,* I'd be proud to have you spend a day or two out at Sugarloaf."

Wells hesitated. "Well . . ."

Smoke shrugged. "It's a long ride to Pueblo, and you don't want to take on that bunch until you're well rested."

"And you won't find a better cook or hostess in Colorado than Sally Jensen," Louis added.

"You gents talked me into it. I'll just feed and water my hoss and we kin be on our way."

"While you do that, I've got to go see Monte about some wanted posters on me that are still floating around New

Mexico. It shouldn't take me more than a half hour or so."

Wells reached into his pocket, but Louis held up his hand. "There's no charge for the food. Consider yourself my guest as long as you're in town, Mr. Wells."

Wells stuck out his hand. "Like I said, my friends call me Joey."

He and Smoke walked through the batwings and Smoke pointed out the livery stable before he turned to walk toward Monte's office.

Wells stepped into his saddle and began to walk his big roan stallion down the street, eyes searching rooftops and alleys out of lifelong habit. As he passed the general store, he saw a figure step out of shadows, a rifle to his shoulder pointing at Smoke's back. Wells drew and fired in one motion, his .44-caliber slug entering the ambusher's left eye, blowing out the back of his head.

When the Colt boomed, Smoke crouched, wheeling, his hands full of iron. He saw Wells's pistol leaking smoke, still aimed at the bushwhacker as he toppled backward. The streets filled with people, Monte and Jim coming on the run with Greeners leveled at Wells.

"Hold on, Monte!" Smoke yelled. "Joey saved my life!"

A crowd gathered around the body as Smoke bent to check him for life. He was dead as a stone. "This is one of the gang of bounty hunters that attacked me this morning."

"Bounty hunters? There's no bounty on you," Monte said.

Smoke pulled the folded poster from his shirt pocket and handed it to the sheriff. "It's a long story. Come on over to your office and I'll fill you in."

Before leaving, he stuck out his hand, staring into Wells's eyes. "Joey, I owe you."

In the West, this was more than a statement—it was a

pledge. A promise that whenever or wherever Wells needed help, Smoke would be there for him.

Wells took Smoke's hand, shrugging. "I never could abide back shooters." He leaned over and spit in the corpse's face before leading his horse toward the livery.

Monte said in a low voice, "I guess this means you're gonna help him go up against Murdock."

Smoke grinned without answering, his face alive with savage anticipation.

Chapter 5

Sally and Joey hit it off immediately. Perhaps she saw in the small, proud man the same qualities that had attracted her to Smoke Jensen—his independence, his refusal to allow anyone to hurt his family or friends without paying the price, and his complete lack of pretension and arrogance. For his part, Sally reminded Joey of his wife, Betty. Fiercely loyal to her man, she accepted without question any friend of Smoke's as a friend of hers, and nothing was too good for the gentleman who had saved her lover's life.

Sally outdid herself with supper, stuffing the two men with beefsteak, homemade biscuits, and fresh vegetables from her garden until they couldn't eat another bite. After the meal she shooed them out to the porch with mugs of rich, dark coffee and cigars while she cleaned the kitchen.

Smoke called Cal and Pearlie from the bunkhouse to meet his guest, and the two young cowboys were thrilled to make the acquaintance of such a living legend. Cal even brought over a couple of dime novels written by Ned

Buntline that had Joey's picture on the cover, blowing away a group of Kansas Redlegs.

Smoke laughed when Joey blushed, embarrassed by the teenager's obvious hero worship. The pistoleer finally got serious, looking directly into Cal's eyes as he said, "Cal boy, killin' a man ain't hardly never nothin' ta be proud of, no more'n killin' a rattler is. Truth is, ever one o' those Redlegs forfeited their right ta live by what they done in the war." He hesitated while he puffed on his cigar, watching smoke drift on the cool night breeze. "Killin' in a war, face-ta-face in battle, is one thing, an' I don't have no hard feelin's again any soldiers, blue or gray, who fought with honor. But the Redlegs turned their backs on honor an' gunned down unarmed men an' boys who'd given up their weapons an' surrendered."

Cal said, "Tell us what happened, Mr. Wells. How did you let them git the drop on you?"

Joey smiled sadly, his eyes far away. "It'd been a long, cold war, boy. My men and I had been livin' in our saddles for what seemed like months, with no word of back home or kinfolk nor nothin'. We'd been livin' like animals, hunted, runnin' when we had to, only ta stop and turn occasionally and attack back at 'em when they was least expectin' it."

Joey paused to build a cigarette, stick it in the corner of his mouth, and take a drink of coffee before he continued. "The Redlegs raided and burned Dayton, Missouri, an' we retaliated by doin' the same thing ta Aubry, Kansas. They dogged our tails all the way back ta the mountains on that little fracas."

He leaned back against a porch post and stared at the stars as he spoke. "We slept in our saddles, or in the timber under bushes an' leaves an' grass, shivering, never darin' ta unsaddle our hosses." He glanced at Cal. "Slept with the reins in our hands most o' the time. Covered our hosses' hooves with burlap or cloth to muffle the noise they made and tried to slip through the Indian Nations back to Texas. Had to take some time to heal our wounded and replace our grub an' ammunition.''

"When you got safely back to Texas, why didn't you just stay there?" asked Cal, his eyes wide in the starlight.

Joey shook his head. "T'weren't the way of it, Cal boy. The Missouri Feud don't say you fight till yore tired an' hungry an' then quit. Nope, the way o' the feud is ta fight till ya win or ya die."

Joey reached up a finger to flick the ask off his cigarette, then continued. "As the 'Federates began to lose more an' more o' their battles, an' the blue-bellies began to git thick as fleas on a hound dog along the border, we started to lose some o' the best we had. Bloody Bill died with his hands filled with iron, Bill Quantrill was kilt in a runnin' gunfight, and lots more whose names I cain't recollect just now was lost to the feud.

"When Lee surrendered at Appomattox, word started circulatin' that we'd git amnesty pardons if'n we surrendered." He nodded, looking down at his hands clasped around his mug of coffee. "Lots of the boys were gittin' homesick, wantin' ta see their mamas and papas and wives again.

"We sat 'round the campfire, talkin' it up an' down and all around. One of the fellahs said he'd been ta town and saw a poster that said if'n we'd raise our hands and promise not ta cause no more grief and be loyal ta the Union, an' turn in our guns, we'd be set free ta go on back home."

He looked at Smoke. "You fought in the war, Smoke. You must know how good that sounded ta boys who'd been in the bush fightin' fer nigh on three year or more."

Smoke nodded, staring at his cigar tip, watching the smoke curl and twist on the evening breeze. "Yes. After a while it seems you only dreamed about home, and many young men began to feel it wasn't real, only the fighting and dying were real."

Joey grinned, his scar making the smile into a sneer.

"That's the way it was, all right. I sat there 'round that fire, my hat pulled down low, holdin' the reins of my hoss as I always did, and thought it over. By then I was might near the oldest and toughest of the bunch, an' I knew they was waitin' ta see which way I'd tilt.

"I didn't want no more friends ta die in my arms or 'cause o' me and my feud. I didn't say nothin' when ol' George Tilden tole 'em he was ridin' in. He got up and stepped into his saddle, and they all to a man follered him."

He grinned again. "Damn if they wasn't a ferocious-lookin' bunch o' men. Most of us carried three or four pistols, a shotgun or two, and maybe a rifle in a saddle boot. Lot of knives too, but we didn't git ta use them overly much, most of our fightin' bein' from horseback.

"They stopped when they saw I was still squattin' by the fire. Davey Williams asked me if'n I was goin' in, an' I tole him I reckoned not.

"Tilden tipped his hat an' wished me luck, as did the others. They rode off toward the Union camp five miles to the south, ready to make their peace an' git on home."

Pearlie asked softly, "Why didn't you go, Joey?"

Joey flipped his cigarette out into the night, took a cigar when Smoke offered it, and thought silently for a moment. "It's a hard thing to explain, Pearlie. I guess I just didn't have no place to go home to. My cabin was burnt ta the ground an' my family all kilt." He shook his head, his eyes glittering in the light as he struck a lucifer and held the burning flame to his stogie. "An' the mountain code I'd always been raised ta believe in said ya didn't quit a feud till yore enemies was all dead." He cut his eyes to Pearlie, and the fierce look in them made Pearlie sit back, as if he were afraid he might be attacked.

"My loyalty was ta my dead wife and baby, and my obligation was ta the feud." He shrugged. "It was as simple an' as complicated as that, I guess.

"One boy stayed with me, Collin Burrows. He'd been ridin' with me more'n two years an' he said he didn't have no place ta go neither."

Cal said, "What happened when the others tried to turn themselves in?"

Joey's eyes took on a haunted look, as if the ghosts of his past were not far from his thoughts.

"Tilden led our boys right up to the Union camp, hands held high, white 'kerchiefs tied to rifle barrels."

Joey took the cigar out of his mouth, spit on the ground, then replaced it between his lips. "Colonel Waters an' his second in command, Johnny Sutter, welcomed 'em in with big grins on their faces, tellin' 'em they was doin' the smart thing."

He sighed. "Collin an' me watched from a ridge overlookin' the camp. We stood there in mistin' rain with our hands over our mounts' noses so they wouldn't smell the other hosses and nicker. After Colonel Waters got all our boys guns an' such, he walked back to his tent and closed the flap."

Joey's eyes narrowed. "Guess he didn't have the stomach to watch what was gonna happen next. Sutter lined the boys up and tole 'em ta raise they right hands an' swear allegiance to the Union. While they was swearin', Sutter gave a signal an' some blue-bellies pulled up a tarp on a wagon containin' a Gatlin' gun."

Joey paused and Cal sucked in his breath, knowing what was coming.

"Their soldiers cranked the handle on that gun and mowed my boys down like they was cuttin' wheat in a harvest."

Pearlie said, "Oh, no! What'd you do?"

Joey pursed his lips. "Collin an' me swung into our saddles an' charged right into that camp, both our hands filled with iron. I put a ball into Sutter's arm, spinnin' him around, and then took out five or six others with my Colts.

Collin did the same, an' we jest kept right on ridin' on through the camp, screamin' an' givin' our rebel yells."

Cal's eyes were big in the moonlight. "And you both got away?"

Joey shook his head. "We got away, but Collin took a rifle bullet in his chest. Took 'im four days ta die, four days o' pain an' agony as we hid from the blue-bellies in swamps and creek bottoms while they searched fer us."

"Did you kill Sutter?" Smoke asked.

Joey's lips curled. "Not then. He survived that wound. Took me another year and a half 'fore I finally stood face-ta-face with him and blew him to hell for what he done that day."

He glanced at Smoke, his eyes cold and hard. "When those soldiers shot my friends down like that, they became no better'n animals an' deserved what they got."

Smoke nodded. "Kind of like those *bandidos* of Murdock's."

"Yep," Joey said, staring at the end of his cigar, glowing in the darkness.

"Bandidos?" asked Pearlie.

When Joey didn't answer, Smoke told Cal and Pearlie about how the Rurales and Apaches raided Joey's ranch and wounded his wife and son, and how Joey planned to make them pay for what they had done.

"But," Cal protested, "you can't go up against an entire gang of thirty or forty men by yourself."

Smoke spoke up before Joey had a chance to reply. "He isn't going to be alone—I intend to be there with him."

Joey looked up quickly. "That ain't my plan, Smoke!"

"I know, but seeing as how I'd be lying in Big Rock with my brains decorating the dirt if you hadn't taken a hand, I'm obligated to return the favor."

"But . . ."

"No buts, Joey. It's a matter of honor, and two men stand a better chance of coming out of this alive than only one."

Cal and Pearlie glanced at each other, smiled, and nodded. Pearlie said, "An' four men stand a better chance than two. Cal and I'd be proud to ride with you and Smoke, Joey."

Joey looked from one to the other of his new friends gathered around him on the porch, his eyes soft. "Thank you, boys, but a man's got to kill his own snakes and saddle his own horse."

Cal snorted, smiling. " 'Cept when a snake needs killin', it don't much matter who kills it, long as it gits kilt! Now"— he hitched up his belt and expanded his chest—"when do we ride?"

Joey laughed and looked at Smoke. "This boy's plumb full o' piss an' vinegar!" Joey hesitated a moment, then said, "Tell ya what. I'll mosey on over ta Pueblo, an' if I see I can't get the job done alone, I'll send for you boys first thing."

Smoke shook his head, his eyes sad. "If that's your last word, we have to accept your wishes, but I still think you're making a mistake."

Joey shrugged. "Won't be the first I made."

Smoke nodded at Cal and Pearlie. "Now, you two rough-and-tumble pistoleers get on over to the bunkhouse and get some sleep. Daylight's going to come mighty early, and you still got some fences to mend before first snowfall."

The two young men took off toward the bunkhouse with disappointed glances back over their shoulders.

Joey shook his head, smiling. "You got a couple o' good boys there, Smoke. They kin o' your'n?"

"No. I just got lucky in the hiring, I guess," Smoke said, thinking of the different ways the two youngsters had come to work for him. Calvin Woods, going on seventeen now, had been just fourteen when Smoke and Sally had taken him in as a hired hand. It was during the spring branding, and Sally was on her way back from Big Rock to Sugarloaf. The buckboard was piled high with supplies, because branding hundreds of calves makes for hungry punchers. . . .

As Sally slowed the team to make a bend in the trail, a rail-thin young man stepped from the bushes at the side of the road with a pistol in his hand.

"Hold it right there, miss."

Applying the brake with her right foot, Sally slipped her hand under a pile of gingham cloth on the seat. She grasped the handle of her short-barreled Colt .44 and eared back the hammer, letting the sound of the horses' hooves and the squealing of the brake pad on the wheel mask the sound. "What can I do for you, young man?" she asked, her voice firm and without fear. She knew she could draw and drill the young highwayman before he could raise his pistol to fire.

"Well, uh, you can throw some of those beans and a cut of that fatback over here, and maybe a portion of that Arbuckle's coffee too."

Sally's eyebrows rose. "Don't you want my money?"

The boy frowned and shook his head. "Why, no, ma'am. I ain't no thief, I'm jest hungry."

"And if I don't give you my food, are you going to shoot me with that big Colt Navy?"

He hesitated a moment, then grinned ruefully. "No, ma'am, I guess not." He twirled the pistol around his finger and slipped it into his belt, turned, and began to walk down the road toward Big Rock.

Sally watched the youngster amble off, noting his tat-

tered shirt, dirty pants with holes in the knees and torn
pockets, and boots that looked as if they had been salvaged
from a garbage dump. "Young man," she called, "come
back here, please."

He turned, a smirk on his face, spreading his hands.
"Look, lady, you don't have to worry. I don't even have
any bullets." With a lightning-fast move he drew the gun
from his pants, aimed away from Sally, and pulled the
trigger. There was a click but no explosion as the hammer
fell on an empty cylinder.

Sally smiled. "Oh, I'm not worried." In a movement
every bit as fast as his, she whipped out her short-barreled
.44 and fired, clipping a pine cone from a branch, causing
it to fall and bounce off his head.

The boy's knees buckled and he ducked, saying, "Jiminy
Christmas!"

Mimicking him, Sally twirled her Colt and stuck it in
the waistband of her britches. "What's your name, boy?"

The boy blushed and looked down at his feet. "Calvin,
ma'am, Calvin Woods."

She leaned forward, elbows on knees, and stared into
the young man's eyes. "Calvin, no one has to go hungry
in this country, not if they're willing to work."

He looked up at her through narrowed eyes, as if he
found life a little different than she described it.

"If you're willing to put in an honest day's work, I'll see
that you get an honest day's pay, and all the food you can
eat."

Calvin stood a little straighter, shoulders back and head
held high. "Ma'am, I've got to be straight with you. I ain't
no experienced cowhand. I come from a hardscrabble
farm and we only had us one milk cow and a couple of
goats and chickens, and lots of dirt that weren't worth
nothing for growin' things. My ma and pa and me never

had nothin', but we never begged and we never stooped to takin' handouts.''

Sally thought, *I like this boy. Proud, and not willing to take charity if he can help it.* ''Calvin, if you're willing to work, and don't mind getting your hands dirty and your muscles sore, I've got some hands that'll have you punching beeves like you were born to it in no time at all.''

A smile lit up his face, making him seem even younger than his years. ''Even if I don't have no saddle, nor a horse to put it on?''

She laughed out loud. ''Yes. We've got plenty of ponies and saddles.'' She glanced down at his raggedy boots. ''We can probably even round up some boots and spurs that'll fit you.''

He walked over and jumped in the back of the buckboard. ''Ma'am, I don't know who you are, but you just hired you the hardest-workin' hand you've ever seen.''

Back at Sugarloaf, she sent him in to Cookie and told him to eat his fill. When Smoke and the other punchers rode into the cabin yard at the end of the day, she introduced Calvin around. As Cal was shaking hands with the men, Smoke looked over at her and winked. He knew she could never resist a stray dog or cat, and her heart was as large as the Big Lonesome itself.

Smoke walked up to Cal and cleared his throat. ''Son, I hear you drew down on my wife.''

Cal gulped. ''Yessir, Mr. Jensen. I did.'' He squared his shoulders and looked Smoke in the eye, not flinching though he was obviously frightened of the tall man with the incredibly wide shoulders standing before him.

Smoke smiled and clapped the boy on the back. ''Just wanted you to know you stared death in the eye, boy. Not many galoots are still walking upright who ever pulled a gun on Sally. She's a better shot than any man I've ever seen except me, and sometimes I wonder about me.''

The boy laughed with relief as Smoke turned and called out, "Pearlie, get your lazy butt over here."

A tall, lanky cowboy ambled over to Smoke and Cal, munching on a biscuit stuffed with roast beef. His face was lined with wrinkles and tanned a dark brown from hours under the sun, but his eyes were sky blue and twinkled with good-natured humor.

"Yessir, boss," he mumbled around a mouthful of food.

Smoke put his hand on Pearlie's shoulder. "Cal, this here chowhound is Pearlie. He eats more than any two hands, and he's never been known to do a lick of work he could get out of, but he knows beeves and horses as well as any puncher I have. I want you to follow him around and let him teach you what you need to know."

Cal nodded, "Yessir, Mr. Smoke."

"Now, let me see that iron you have in your pants."

Cal pulled out the ancient Colt Navy and handed it to Smoke. When Smoke opened the loading gate, the rusted cylinder fell to the ground, causing Pearlie and Smoke to laugh and Cal's face to flame red. "This is the piece you pulled on Sally?"

The boy nodded, looking at the ground.

Pearlie shook his head. "Cal, you're one lucky pup. Hell, if'n you'd tried to fire that thing, it'd of blown your hand clean off."

Smoke inclined his head toward the bunkhouse. "Pearlie, take Cal over to the tack house and get him fixed up with what he needs, including a gun belt and a Colt that won't fall apart the first time he pulls it. You might also help pick him out a shavetail to ride. I'll expect him to start earning his keep tomorrow."

"Yessir, Smoke." Pearlie put his arm around Cal's shoulders and led him off toward the bunkhouse. "Now, the first thing you gotta learn, Cal, is how to get on Cookie's good side. A puncher rides on his belly, and it 'pears to me that you need some fattin' up 'fore you can begin to punch cows."*

Pearlie had come to work for Smoke in as roundabout a way as Cal had. He was hiring his gun out to Tilden Franklin in Fontana when Franklin went crazy and tried to take over Sugarloaf, Smoke and Sally's spread. After Franklin's men raped and killed a young girl in the fracas, Pearlie sided with Smoke, and the aging gunfighters he had called in to help put an end to Franklin's reign of terror.**

Pearlie was now honorary foreman of Smoke's ranch, though he was only a shade over twenty years old himself.

Joey pitched his cigar out into the night air, watching sparks fly as it tumbled to the ground. "Awfully lucky, I'd say."

Later that night, as Smoke and Sally undressed for bed, she turned to him. "Smoke, I know you feel honor bound to offer to help Joey out against this Murdock gang. . . ."

He walked to her and wrapped his arms around her, pulling her head against his chest. "Darling, it's something I have to do. That man doesn't stand a chance if he goes it alone."

She tilted her head back and kissed him lightly on his chin. "I know, sweetheart, and I'm not going to ask you not to go." She pushed him back and held him at arm's length, staring into his eyes. "I just want you to promise me that you'll be careful if he asks you to help. If you go and get yourself killed, I'll be really angry with you!"

He stuck out an index finger and made an X over his

* *Vengeance of the Mountain Man*
** *Trail of the Mountain Man*

chest. "Cross my heart, I'll be careful. I just hope he comes to his senses before it's too late." Then he smiled and leaned over to blow out the lantern. "Now I think it's about time I thanked you for that wonderful supper you cooked."

She laughed low in her throat as she pulled her night-dress over her head. "Why, sir, whatever do you mean?"

Chapter 6

Joey had Red and his packhorse loaded and ready for travel before dawn the next day. Sally fixed a breakfast of scrambled eggs and bacon and biscuits with mounds of grape jelly for their farewell meal. Cal and Pearlie were invited and pestered Joey for tales of his exploits chasing Redlegs, until Smoke finally said, "Boys, let the man eat and enjoy his food. He's got a long way to travel and, if he's like most cowboys, his camp meals aren't going to be near this good."

Joey nodded as he stuffed more eggs and bacon into his mouth. "That's right. My Betty is a fine woman, but I swear she could learn something about cookin' biscuits from Mrs. Jensen."

Sally handed him a sack. "I fixed you a batch of bear sign. I never met a man yet who didn't appreciate pastries."

Pearlie raised his eyebrows. "I hope you have some left over for the hands, Miss Sally. My stomach's been sorely missing your bear sign lately."

"Oh, there might be one or two still in the oven."

Cal snorted. "One or two? Heck, Pearlie's not happy 'less he's got seven or eight to himself."

Joey stood and wiped jelly from his lips with a napkin. "Smoke, boys, Mrs. Jensen, I 'preciate yore hospitality, but I got to git goin'." He patted his stomach. "That is if I ain't gained so much weight with all this good cookin' that Red won't be able to carry me."

He mounted up, waved once more, and walked Red off down the trail toward Big Rock without looking back.

Smoke stood with his arm around Sally, watching him ride off. "That man was born with the bark on, as Preacher would say."

Joey was at the last turn of the trail, where Smoke's property ended and the road turned toward Big Rock, when Red perked up his ears and shook his head, snorting.

Joey eased back on the reins, having learned to trust the big roan's instincts. "Somethin' up there, big fellow?" he whispered to the stallion. He peered through an early morning ground fog, but all he could see was a narrow path as it bent around a stand of pines about twenty yards ahead. He cocked his head, listening. There was something wrong; the bird sounds that had accompanied him all the way from Smoke's cabin were silent.

He eased his Greener short-barreled scattergun out of his saddle boot, released hammer thongs on his Colts, and stepped quietly from his saddle. He untied his dally rope to the packhorse and slapped it on its rump, sending it trotting down the path.

Watching where he stepped to avoid making any noise, he slipped off the trail into dense undergrowth of pines and scrub trees to his right and tiptoed through timber toward the bend ahead.

As he approached the spot, he smelled smoke. Someone was smoking a cigarette up ahead, someone who shouldn't be there. He eased up to an Indian hawthorn bush and peeked through the branches.

There were two Mexicans, and what appeared to be two Mescalero Apaches squatted behind trees, all with guns drawn, all watching the trail. Joey waited until his pack-horse came into sight, and the men pointed their pistols at the animal, then he stepped from cover, earring back the hammers on his Greener.

At the harsh metallic click of the hammers being cocked, the men glanced back over their shoulders. "Mornin', gents. Lookin' fer me?" Joey growled.

As the men whirled, bringing up their guns, Joey let loose with both barrels of the express gun. The shotgun exploded and kicked back, shooting fire and heavy loads of buckshot into the two Apaches, almost blowing them in half, sending their bodies jerking and twisting to sprawl dead on the ground.

In the same motion, Joey dropped the Greener and slapped leather, drawing his Colts in a movement so fast, the Mexican bandits barely had time to cock and aim their pistols before he was spraying lead at them.

The first one took bullets in the chest and face, dying where he stood. The second got off one shot, which hit Joey in the side of his rib cage, tearing a chunk of meat out of his back as the bullet exited. The force of the bullet spun him around, saving his life as the ambusher's next slug went high and wide, pocking bark off a pine tree, where Joey had been standing.

Just before he hit the ground, Joey snap-fired another round, hitting the gunman in the forehead, exploding his head in a red mist and dropping him like a stone.

Joey lay there on a soft carpet of pine needles, fire burning in his chest, clutching his left arm tight against his body, trying to stop the bleeding. The small clearing was choked with gun smoke, and the heavy smell of cordite made Joey cough, groaning at the pain it caused him. He lay back against the pine tree, thinking of the time he had nursed Collin Burrows after his chest wound, wondering if he was going to end up the same way. . . .

Joey helped Collin from his horse, his arms around the boy's shoulders. He was so weak from loss of blood, he couldn't stand without help. Joey lowered him to the ground under thick branches of an oak tree, hoping it would keep some of the driving rain off him. He covered Collin with a saddle blanket and went to search for the roots, mosses, and bark his grandmother had used to make poultices to heal injuries when he was a boy.

He built a small fire and mashed the moss and leaves together in a tin cup, pouring in water. When the liquid boiled, he would add pieces of the bark to make a tea that might get Collin through the night. From the way the blood was dripping from his mouth, and the bright red bubbly nature of it, he was lung shot, hit hard and dying.

Joey watched the rain, cursing the war and all the men in it. He had seen too many young men, boys really, die for a cause they knew little about. As he sat in the rain, he whittled on the bark, stripping off small splinters to boil into tea.

After a moment, Collin groaned and began to talk to himself, delirious with fever and pain and infection. "Dad, where are ye? Mom's lookin' fer sis, an' ya gotta help me find her. . . ." His voice trailed off as he drifted into a fitful sleep. Joey smoothed the hair back out of his eyes, laying his hand for a moment against his cheek, as if it might soothe his pain a bit.

After dark fell, a group of Redlegs rode close by, and Joey lay over Collin, covering his mouth with his hand to keep him from crying out and giving away their position. When they had gone, Joey removed his hand, and noticed there was no breathing. He sighed, climbed stiffly to his feet, and walked to his horse to get his shovel. He would bury Collin in the mud of Missouri, dirt he had fought honorably to defend for reasons he probably never understood.

Joey felt lightheaded, but shook the feeling off, knowing he would die there if he passed out. Pushing thoughts of Collin from his mind and ignoring his discomfort, he crawled on hands and knees twenty yards to the middle of the trail and whistled for Red. The big horse trotted up moments later, bending its head to sniff and lick at Joey, nervously stamping its feet as it smelled blood and gun smoke in the air.

Joey pulled himself to his feet using his horse's reins and clung to the saddle. He opened his saddlebag and took out an extra shirt he carried there, stuffing it as hard as he could against his wound. Too weak to climb into the saddle, he lay across it and pulled Red's head back toward the Jensens' ranch house. "Come on, big fellah, git me back there," he groaned. Red began to walk back up the trail, turning his head to see why his master didn't get in the saddle as usual.

Joey had traveled less than a hundred yards before Smoke and Cal and Pearlie came galloping down the path to meet him, guns drawn, expressions grim.

Without pausing to ask questions, Smoke leaned sideways in his saddle and swung his big arm around Joey's waist and lifted him effortlessly onto his lap. "Cal, shag your mount into Big Rock and get Doc Spalding back here pronto! Pearlie, you scout around here and make sure there isn't anyone left alive, and bring Joey's horses back to Sugarloaf when you're done."

He jerked Horse's head around and took off back up the trail as fast as his Palouse could ride.

* * *

Dr. Cotton Spalding took a final stitch in a gaping hole in Joey's back and tied the silk in a surgeon's knot, bringing the edges of the wound neatly together. As he cut the strands, he looked over at Sally. "You did a good job stopping his bleeding, Sally. You probably saved this young man's life."

Sally gave a lopsided grin, glancing at Smoke. "I've had plenty of practice on my husband, doctor."

Joey sleeved sweat off his forehead and tried to look over his shoulder at his back. "How soon 'fore I can ride, doc?"

Cotton shook his head. "If the wound doesn't suppurate, and you get plenty of rest and nutritious food, about two weeks, I'd say. I'll take the stitches out in ten days, another couple of days to get the kinks and stiffness out, and you'll be good as new. Luckily, the bullet missed your lung and stayed in the meat of the latissimus dorsi muscle on your side. You'll be plenty sore, but from the looks of all these other scars on your body, you're used to being shot."

Joey nodded, a rueful grin on his pale face. "Yes, I've taken a little lead in my days."

Cotton snorted. "More than a little, I'd say." He washed blood off his hands in a basin next to the bed and stood up.

"Sally, make sure he eats lots of beef and stew and soup with meat in it. That'll help him replace the blood he's lost. Change his dressings twice a day, and call me if he starts to chill or have a fever."

"Thank you, Cotton," Smoke said.

"Yeah, thanks, doc," Joey added. "I owe you one."

The doctor looked down at Joey, "Pay me back by staying out of the path of any bullets in the near future."

"You kin bet on it," Joey replied.

After the doctor left, Smoke pulled up a chair and sat next to Joey's bed. "You know who those men were who ambushed you, Joey?"

He nodded. "Most likely part of the band of raiders that stole my cattle and shot up my ranch."

Smoke looked puzzled. "Any idea how they knew you were after them, or where you would be?"

Joey shrugged. "Only thing I can figger is that Mex I questioned in Bracketville. I cold-cocked him right before Carbone and Martine stopped me in front of the saloon. He must've come to and heard them tellin' me ta stop by Big Rock an' look you up. I guess he sent Murdock a telegraph and Murdock sent those men to keep me from comin' after him and messin' up his plans."

Smoke nodded. "That makes sense. Maybe when we get to Pueblo, we can ask Murdock about it."

Joey's eyes narrowed. "Whatta ya mean, we, Smoke? I thought we settled all that."

Smoke shook his head. "That was before someone tried to kill a guest on my spread. Remember when you said if word got around that they could shoot up your ranch, you might as well pack it in?"

Joey nodded.

"Same thing goes here in Colorado. I am not without my enemies, and I cannot afford to let anyone think they can ride in here and try to kill someone on my place and get away with it." He spread his arms. "So I'm going to Pueblo to speak with Mr. Jacob Murdock, with or without you. You have a choice, to ride with me, or both of us can go our separate ways."

Joey smiled. "Well, when you put it that way, I can see that your honor demands you answer this assault." He arched an eyebrow. "You sure you wasn't born in Missouri, Smoke?"

* * *

Pueblo was like a town under siege. People walked around, heads down, avoiding Sam Murdock and his deputies whenever possible. It was as if criminals were running the city. He and his men walked the streets and boardwalks arrogantly, and the slightest sign of disrespect or questioning of their authority was liable to be met with a blow from the butt of a rifle, or worse.

Several businessmen who questioned the results of the recent sheriff's election had their businesses broken into and their stocks ruined. One of the town councilmen was found with his throat cut after publicly calling for a wire to be sent to the governor's office asking for help. That effectively ended any active resistance to Sam Murdock's reign of terror in Pueblo.

Ben Tolson moved out of town to a small cabin and bided his time. He knew sooner or later Murdock would make a mistake, and he planned to be there to help the town pick up the pieces.

Colonel Emilio Vasquez stood quietly just inside the tree line, staring at the pasture before him. A small herd of cattle moved slowly in moonlight, munching grass while their calves bleated loudly, demanding milk. Vasquez earned his nickname, El Machete, by his habit of hacking *peóns* and *campesinos* to death with a long, razor-sharp, broad-bladed knife. Jacob Murdock's offer of triple wages for men who weren't afraid to do a little killing was tailor made for him and his group of twenty-five of some of the worst killers in Mexico.

When Vasquez and his men had reined up in front of Murdock's ranch house, he hired them on the spot. While in Texas, Murdock often heard tales of El Machete and knew he was just the kind of cold-blooded killer he needed to build his empire in Colorado.

Over tequila and cigars in his study, Murdock told Vasquez he would make him rich so long as he obeyed the rancher without question.

Vasquez's lips curled in an evil grin. "I love this country. Where else can *un hombre* get *mucho dinero* for doing what he love—killing gringos!"

Now Vasquez was about to earn his money. Jonah Williams, the rancher who owned the cattle Vasquez was observing, had complained to Sheriff Ben Tolson before he lost the election that a number of his calves were missing, and he thought they were on Murdock's spread. When Jacob Murdock's brother was installed as sheriff, Williams let it be known he was going to ask for U.S. marshals to investigate his charges.

Murdock gave Vasquez the job of changing Williams's mind any way he could.

Vasquez squinted, seeing a lone rider approaching the herd from the direction of Williams's ranch house, barely visible in the distance. He knew Williams had a habit of checking his cattle every night before he went to bed. He walked back into the trees and grabbed his horse's reins from his second-in-command, Sergeant Juan Garcia. The sergeant was every bit as vicious and cruel as Vasquez, though not nearly as intelligent.

As he stepped into his saddle, Vasquez grunted, *"Listo?"*

"Sí mi capitan," Garcia replied with a grin. "The gringo will sleep well tonight, eh?"

Vasquez tilted his head back to gaze at the moon and stars shining brilliantly in a cold, clear sky. *"Sí* Juanito. It is *un grande noche* for dying, is it not?"

The two *bandidos* laughed as they walked their horses out of the trees and toward the beeves in the valley. When they were about fifty yards from the cattle, Vasquez and Garcia dismounted. Vasquez reached up and adjusted the scabbard he had slung across his shoulder with a rawhide strap. The scabbard was positioned so the handle of the machete it held was sticking up behind his neck, within easy reach.

Jonah Williams saw the two riders and veered his mount toward them, pulling his Winchester from its saddle boot and earing back its hammer. When he rode up, Garcia was bent over with his horse's leg pulled up, peering at its hoof.

"What're you two men doin' on my spread?" he called, leveling the rifle at them.

Vasquez grinned, his yellow-stained teeth gleaming in the moonlight as he spread his hands wide and shrugged. *"Buenos noches, señor.* My compadre's horse, she pulled up lame."

Williams walked his bronc closer until he was in front of Vasquez. "That don't answer my question, does it? Now, you gents keep them hands where I can see 'em and tell me what you're doin' out here in the middle of the night."

Vasquez raised his hands until they were next to his head. He continued to grin, watching Williams's eyes as Garcia straightened and began to turn. When Williams's eyes flicked to the side to watch Garcia and his rifle barrel turned toward him, Vasquez grabbed the handle of his machete and drew it in one lightning-quick movement. The three-foot-long blade sparkled and reflected the moon as it whistled down, severing Williams's right arm just below his elbow.

Williams screamed and dropped his rifle, grabbing at his bloody stump with his left hand. Vasquez swung backhanded, catching Williams on the side of his head with the blunt edge of the machete, knocking him sideways off his mount.

While Williams lay on the ground, semiconscious, blood pumping out of his ruined arm, Vasquez and Garcia jumped into their saddles and rode in a circle to a far side of the herd. Once there, they drew their pistols and began firing into the air and yelling, sending frightened animals stampeding over the dying rancher, trampling him to death.

The killers wheeled their horses and trotted off toward Murdock's ranch. Vasquez laughed. "Like I said, compadre, it's a good night for dying."

Murdock was in his study, smoking a cigar and sipping bourbon while going over his books, when the door opened and Vasquez swaggered in.

Murdock frowned as he looked up, his hand wrapped around the butt of a Colt in his desk drawer. "Don't you know to knock before entering a man's home, Vasquez?"

Vasquez grinned insolently and spread his hands wide as he gave a small bow. "Pardon, señor, I meant no offense."

Murdock's nose wrinkled. The man smelled as if he had drunk an entire bottle of tequila. "Well, what do you have to report?"

Vasquez plucked a cigar out of the humidor on Murdock's desk, bit an end off, and spit it on the floor before lighting it with a lucifer he struck on his front tooth. "Señor Williams will not be here to look for his calves. The poor hombre fell off his horse in front of his cattle and they ran over him. I think he be plenty dead."

Murdock nodded, a slow smile creasing his face. "Oh, I'm sorry to hear that." He puffed his cigar and watched smoke spiral toward the ceiling as he leaned back in his chair and put his boots on his desk. "I hope our new sheriff doesn't try to arrest you for this killing," Murdock said with a wide grin.

Vasquez chuckled. "Maybe you could put in word for me?"

"Oh, I think Sam has more important things on his mind than investigating the accidental death of a small rancher." He stroked his chin. "I wonder if the widow Williams will want to sell the ranch now that her husband's deceased?"

Vasquez's eyes narrowed. "You want to *buy* his cattle?"

Murdock shrugged. "At the right price, of course." He pointed his stogie at Vasquez. "I want you to ride into town and have Sam and his men spread the word that it would be . . . unhealthy for anyone else to make a bid on Williams's place."

Vasquez grinned as he picked up Murdock's bottle of bourbon and drank from it. "*Sí*, I tell Sam to make the other gringos understand."

Chapter 7

Joey recuperated at Smoke's ranch for thirteen days. Dr. Spalding removed his stitches on the eleventh day, stating he had never seen a man heal so quickly.

Joey told him, "Doc, this ol' body's had plenty practice healin' itself from bullet holes. It ought ta know how by now."

The last two days, Smoke and Joey had been hunting turkey and pheasant and relaxing before taking off for Pueblo and Jacob Murdock. As they walked a field, carrying twenty-gauge American Arms shotguns loaded with bird shot over their shoulders, Smoke asked, "Tell me about how you finally got to Sutter, Joey. After almost two years of you killing every other Redleg in the country, he must have known you were coming after him."

Joey smiled. "Oh, that he did, Smoke. The coward never went anywhere without his squad of guards with him. He always rode with seven men, seasoned killers every one, when he was out huntin' me."

"Where did the final showdown take place?"

"Just south of San Antonio, Texas. I'd gone to Texas to let the heat die down, and to heal up some minor wounds I'd suffered in my last fracas. I spent a week in San Antone"—he cut his eyes at Smoke and smiled—"some mighty pretty señoritas, 'specially to a man who's been on the run fer almost two year."

Just then they flushed a covey of pheasant and both men leveled their shotguns and fired in the blink of an eye. Three birds fell to the ground, while one flew off in a circle, one leg hanging down.

"You got yours, I missed one of mine," Smoke said.

Joey shrugged. "It's a might easier when they don't shoot back, ain't it?"

As Smoke chuckled and nodded, Joey continued with his story. "I guess I must've pissed off someone in town, or they heard about the money on my head. Anyway, some lowlife wired Sutter an' his men I was in San Antonio and they came bustin' on down to do me in." He bent to pick up his birds and put them in the burlap sack he had tied to his belt. "I was sleepin' in the hotel when I heard boots on the stairs." He smiled at Smoke. "Them guards was mean, but they wasn't too bright. Didn't bother to take his shoes off to try an' sneak up on me. If'n he had, I'd be forked end up now."

He pulled a plug of Bull Durham out and sliced off a chunk, biting it off his knife as he cut it. After he chewed for a moment, he continued. "One thing ya learn on the owl hoot trail when yore bein' hunted is ta always sleep ready fer action. I had my boots an' guns on in about two seconds an' was halfway out the window when he kicked in my door. He wasted two bullets shootin' the señorita, who was screamin' an' hollerin' to beat the band, and I put a .44 slug in his left eye. I guess the sight o' blood an' brains blowing out the back of his head discouraged the two with him, fer they hightailed it back down the stairs."

He spit and sleeved a dribble off his chin with the back

of his arm. "Sutter an' the others was waitin' fer me on the street below, an' there didn't appear to be a surplus o' options fer me at that point."

"What did you do?"

"I went right back in the window, lit a lantern, and set the hotel on fire, then I went out in the hall and started screamin' and hollerin' *fire* as loud as I could." He grinned as he spit again. "Hell, ya shoulda seen it, Smoke. Naked women an' gents dressed only in their boots an' hats all scramblin' down those stairs and climbin' out o' windows and such, it was a sight ta see. When the smoke got heavy enough, I just joined in the crowd o' people and slid out right under Sutter an' his men's noses, keepin' my head down an' my hands filled with iron just in case."

"Then what?"

"I got Red an' shagged on out of town fer a mile or two an' made a cold camp."

"Weren't you afraid they would try and follow you?"

He shook his head. "Naw. They'd had ta ride day an' night ta catch me in town, an' I knowed they was dead tired. 'Sides, they didn't have no idea which way I went when I left town."

"I see, so you knew you had some time before they would get on your trail."

"Yep, but the next thing is the best. What's the first thing a man's gonna do after weeks o' ridin' the trail when he gets to a decent-sized town?"

"Only three things I know of. Get some good food, get some whiskey or a woman, and take a bath."

Joey nodded. "An' if'n ya been ridin' hard fer three or four days, ya gonna want ta git the bath first, so ya can enjoy the other two later."

Smoke smiled. "You didn't . . ."

"Yeah, I did. I caught 'em in a bathhouse, with more than their pants down. I killed the first three with my Arkansas Toothpick so there wouldn't be any noise ta alert the others. Slit their throats an' just let 'em sink down in the water.'' He grinned. ''Probably set that bathhouse man's business back when word got around what had happened. Anyway, the other four guards was in the next room, all soakin' an' smokin' an' braggin' about how they was gonna git the prettiest woman. Sutter, being the leader, had gone first and was up in his room shaving by then.

''I stepped into the room, hands hangin' down, fingers flexin' like they do when ya know yore gonna have ta draw, an' them fellows' eyes just about popped outta their heads.'' He cut his eyes at Smoke again. ''If'n they'd been anybody else 'sides Redlegs, I'd of given 'em a chance. As it was, while they was scramblin' to git outta the tubs and grab they guns, I just filled my hands and began to blast away. They was all dead, all seven of 'em without gittin' off a single shot.

''I punched out my empties, reloaded my Colts, an' went out in the street below Sutter's window. I knew he'd heard the shots and knew I was back, so I yelled up at him and told him ta come on out if'n he wasn't no coward.''

''The sheriff or his deputies give you any problems?''

Joey's teeth gleamed in the Colorado sunshine. ''Not when I tole 'em who I was and who I was fixin' ta kill. Them Texicans are good ol' boys, an' they had a soft spot in they hearts fer us gray-bellies.''

''Did Sutter come out?''

''Not at first, but finally when he saw there wasn't no other way, he came on out in the street. We faced each other and I asked him where Colonel Waters was, him bein' the only other Redleg I hadn't already kilt. He said the dirty yellow coward had run off back east, said he was tired of war and fightin' an' such. I looked him in the eye an' tole him his commanding officer was a back-shootin' coward, just like Sutter and all his men were.

''Well, that did it. There were too many people standin' around watchin' fer him to take that and not respond.

When his hand twitched toward his holster, I drew and shot him in the stomach, doubling him over and curlin' him up."

Smoke and Joey walked another twenty yards before Joey added, "I was sure sorry it took him only two days to die." He looked at Smoke. "I wanted him to last at least four, like Collin did."

They flushed another two coveys of pheasant, and Smoke brought down a large tom turkey. Figuring they had plenty for dinner, they took their burlap sacks back to the ranch house. Joey and Smoke were out behind the bunkhouse, cleaning their birds, when Monte Carson rode up, his horse lathered as if he had galloped the entire way.

Smoke waved a bloody hand covered with feathers at the sheriff. "Hey, Monte. Park your horse and stay for dinner. Sally's going to fix fried turkey and pheasant."

Monte jumped to the ground, breathing hard. "I got some news you two might want to hear."

"Oh?" Smoke asked. "Does it concern Jacob Murdock?"

"Yeah." Monte sleeved sweat off his forehead. "You think Sally might have some coffee made?" He reached back and rubbed his butt with both hands. "Either I been too long at a desk job, or they're making saddles harder than they used to!"

Smoke and Joey grinned as they washed their hands in a rain barrel. "Or maybe you're just getting old, Monte," Smoke said as he clapped the sheriff on the back and led the men toward his porch.

Sally came out and gave Monte a brief hug. "Good morning, Monte. We don't get to see you out here often enough. Would you like some breakfast or coffee?"

"Just coffee, please, Sally." He patted his ample paunch. "I've got to cut back on the vittles or get a bigger horse."

Sally smiled as she took the birds Smoke and Joey had cleaned and went into the cabin. A few minutes later she reappeared with three mugs and a steaming pot of coffee.

After the men were settled in their chairs with mugs in their hands, she placed a platter covered with fresh biscuits next to them, along with jars of butter and jam. "I'll leave you men to your talk while I cook those birds for lunch." She looked inquiringly at Monte. "Will you be able to stay, Monte?"

He licked his lips. "For a taste of your fried pheasant and turkey? Of course!"

After she left, Smoke spoke around a mouthful of biscuit. "What have you heard about Murdock, Monte?"

Joey looked up from smearing butter on his bread, interested in what was coming.

"Well, I wired Ben Tolson a couple of days ago and asked him to keep me informed of any goings-on at the Lazy M."

"Ya tell him why ya wanted to know?" drawled Joey.

Monte grinned. "My mama raised only one fool, an' that was my brother Billy."

After Smoke and Joey chuckled, he continued. "I got a wire back from Tolson this morning, bright and early."

"What's the news, sheriff?" Smoke asked.

"Seems a week or so after the sheriff's election, a rancher named Williams said he was going to ask U.S. marshals to investigate Murdock's operation. He claimed Murdock was rustling his calves."

Joey nodded, eyes squinted in concentration as he listened. "That don't surprise me none. Any man who'd hire the likes o' Vasquez an' his gang wouldn't be above stealin' another man's beeves."

"Uh-huh," Smoke said. "And that's probably not all he's got in mind, or he wouldn't need that many gunnies on his payroll."

Monte added, "Williams's wife brought his body into town two days ago in a buckboard. Said he got killed the night before in a stampede out at his ranch."

Smoke frowned. "Well, that happens. Is there anything to tie Murdock or his men to the killing?"

"Yeah, his wife couldn't explain how her husband managed to get his right arm chopped off clean at the elbow."

Joey's face hardened as he whispered, "El Machete."

Smoke and Monte stared at him. "El Machete?" Monte asked. "What's that?"

Joey explained to them that the leader of the Rurales who rode against him, Vasquez, was known to use a machete, and that he was a vicious killer who enjoyed hacking men to death, especially gringos.

"What's the new sheriff going to do about it?" Smoke asked.

Monte shrugged. "What do you think? There weren't any witnesses, and Murdock has twenty men who'll swear he never left his ranch that night."

"That figgers," Joey said. "Murdock don't sound like a man who'd do his own dirty work."

"That's not all. Tolson says Williams's wife has put her spread up for sale. She's going to go back east as soon as the funeral's over."

"Oh?"

"Yeah. Tolson says it's a prime piece of land, lots of water and grass and a sizable herd of shorthorns." He began to build a cigarette as he talked. "Williams's place abuts the Lazy M, and the river that runs through it supplies all of Murdock's water. Tolson says whoever buys it will have control over the water Murdock needs to feed his stock."

Joey rubbed his chin. "That's right interestin'."

Monte lit his cigarette and took a deep puff. "Even more interesting is the fact that no one seems eager to buy the place. Two local ranchers who put in early bids on the place withdrew their money after having the shit kicked out of 'em by persons unknown."

Joey said, "Those persons unknown were probably wearin' badges when they did the kickin'."

Smoke nodded, a slow grin curling his lips. He looked at Joey. "Joey, I've got an idea. How about you and I investing in a ranch in Pueblo? Might be a way to cause Murdock a passel of trouble."

Joey shrugged. "I ain't exactly flush with cash right now, Smoke. 'Bout all my savin's are tied up down in Mexico."

Smoke smiled. "Oh, money's no problem. I think I can convince the bank in Big Rock that investing in prime ranch property in Pueblo is a good idea . . . especially since Sally is president of the bank board and owns the building it's in."

"But, Smoke, I don't know nothin' 'bout ranchin' in Colorado."

"I'm not saying we have to run the ranch forever. But from what Monte's told us, Murdock is getting rich and powerful off the backs of poor people." He pulled a cigar out and lit it. "It's been my experience that the best way to hurt rich men is to take away all their money and power. That's a lesson Murdock won't soon forget!"

"When you put it that way, the idee does have some appeal to it."

Monte shook his head. "I hope you boys don't think Murdock is gonna just lie down and let you ruin him. He's sure to send his men against you, and with the sheriff being his kin, you don't stand much of a chance of a fair fight."

Joey looked at him, his eyes cold as glacier ice. "That's the part o' the plan I like best. When the law's crooked, an' people in town know it, it gives us an edge later if marshals are called in. If'n the Murdock brothers and their phony lawmen come after us, the real law cain't hardly take their part after this fracas is over."

Smoke smiled and spread his hands. "That's right. We'd just be innocent ranchers defending our property."

Monte snorted, still shaking his head. "You two are about

as innocent as a fox in a henhouse with feathers all over his snout!''

Pueblo, Colorado, though not a large town when compared to Denver or Silver City, was considerably bigger than Big Rock and had both stagecoach and train service. Smoke and Joey took a Wells, Fargo and Company stage to get there as soon as possible. Cal and Pearlie followed by train so they could bring Smoke's Palouse stallion, Horse, and Joey's big roan stallion, Red, along with them.

Smoke decided not to bring any of his hands along, not wanting to tip their hand to Sam Murdock too early, and he figured they would be able to recruit plenty of help from ranchers who had been driven out of business by Murdock.

Their stage arrived at dusk, and ex-sheriff Ben Tolson was on hand to meet it, having been wired by Monte Carson to expect them. When they climbed down, Tolson walked up and stuck out his hand to Smoke. ''Mr. Jensen, I'm honored to make your acquaintance. Any friend of Monte's is a friend of mine.''

Smoke took his hand. ''Howdy, Ben. Monte speaks very highly of you.''

Tolson rubbed his chin, grinning. ''Well, Monte and I go back a ways. We rode together a couple o' times when we were young pups, hiring out our guns in the range wars of a few years back.''

Tolson was a large man with broad shoulders and thick, muscled arms, hands gnarled with early arthritis. He had a handlebar mustache and small goatee, neatly trimmed, under dark, bushy eyebrows. Smoke thought he didn't look like a man to trifle with.

''Like Monte, when I got married I figgered it was time to plant myself and quit galavantin' all over the country.''

He looked down at his hands, flexing them. "Plus, this rheumatiz makes using a short gun kind o' tricky."

"Ben, this is Mr. Joey Wells," Smoke said, inclining his head toward Joey.

Tolson's eyes narrowed for just a moment before he gave a lopsided grin and stuck out his hand. "I've heard a mite about you, Mr. Wells. You cast a long shadow fer such a young man."

Joey's lips curled up in what might have been a smile if his eyes hadn't remained as hard as stones. "In spite of what you've probably heard, Ben, I ain't never drawed on a man who didn't pull iron on me first, an' I ain't never kilt nobody that didn't deserve it."

"What do you plan to do now that Murdock's hijacked your town, Ben?" Smoke said to break the tension between the two men.

Tolson frowned. "Hell, I don't rightly know." He looked over his shoulder to see if anyone was listening. "Jacob Murdock and his worthless brother, Sam, have been ridin' roughshod over the smaller ranchers hereabouts and the businessmen in town who supported me during the election." He shook his head. "Most of those folks have been friends of mine for years . . . I don't want to let 'em down."

Smoke's expression grew serious. "Isn't there something you can do about it?"

"Not without proof that the election was rigged." Tolson patted his chest where his tin star used to lie. "When I put that badge on, I took an oath to uphold the law, and the law says the people have a right to elect whoever they want for sheriff, unless I can *prove* they stole the votes." He shook his head as he pulled a plug of tobacco out of his pocket and sliced a chunk off. He chewed a couple of times, then leaned to the side and spit a stream of brown juice into the dirt. "I can't prove anything against Murdock without havin' some witnesses who'll testify in court, and since the election, the only ones who tried to speak out have ended up deader than a stick. Now people who are willin' to talk are few and far between."

He spit again, showing Smoke and Joey what he thought of people too afraid to speak out against the Murdock brothers. "Things were simpler in the old days. Then, I would've had a . . . private talk with Murdock and tole him how much healthier it'd be if he and his no-good kin moved on down the line."

"Still sounds like a good idee to me," Joey drawled in his soft Southern accent.

Tolson cut his eyes to Joey. "Yeah, well, you don't have a governor who's tryin' to make Colorado Territory a state. One complaint from Murdock, who is still the duty-elected sheriff of Pueblo, and I'd have a passel of U.S. marshals down here chewin' on me like buzzards on a deer carcass." He shook his head and spit again. "No, much as I like Monte, and much as I respect your reputation, Smoke, I can't be a part of any vigilante justice here in Pueblo." He shook his head. "If I did that, I'd be no better than Murdock and his crew."

Smoke smiled and spread his hands, an innocent look on his face. "You don't have to worry about us, Ben. Mr. Wells and I are just honest ranchers come down here to inquire about buying a spread we hear is coming up for sale."

Ben chuckled. "Yeah, I bet. Anyway, I just wanted you gents to know where I stand. If we can get proof, or someone willing to testify, I'll stand with you against the Murdocks. Otherwise, I got to keep my head down until that time comes." Tolson glanced at the Colts hung low on their hips and Henry rifles slung over their shoulders. "I can see you men don't travel light."

Joey stuck a cigarette in the corner of his mouth and struck a lucifer on the hammer of his Colt. As the match flared, making his eyes glow with a feral glint, he growled,

"Like you said, Ben, it's a dangerous country, an' the law cain't always protect a fellah."

Monte nodded, his own eyes hard in the flickering light. "You know, I almost hope Murdock does come after you boys, and I hope I'm there to see it. If anybody can take that man down a notch or two, you two can!"

He pointed over his shoulder. "Take your bags on over to Mrs. Pike's hotel. The food ain't great, but it's cheap and it's plentiful."

Joey wiped his mouth with his sleeve. "They serve whiskey there? After twenty-four hours on that stage, my mouth's so dry, I could plant cotton in it."

Tolson chuckled. "After you fill your bellies, come on over to the Silver Dollar Saloon. Murdock's usually there playin' poker till about midnight in a high-stakes game." He grinned and winked. "I figure it's about time he sees what he's up against."

Chapter 8

It was going on ten o'clock before Smoke and Joey had eaten their fill, washed the trail dust off, and changed into fresh clothes. On their way to the saloon, Smoke put his hand on Joey's shoulder. "Joey, we're liable to run into the men who attacked your ranch and shot up your family in the saloon. Do you think they'll recognize you?"

Joey gave a sardonic grin. "No. The onliest ones got close enough ta see my face didn't survive the sight. The ones that got away stayed well outta range."

Smoke's expression was solemn. "Do you think you can hold your temper and stick to our plan?"

Joey nodded. "Only by knowin' that's the only way we kin git *all* the bastards an' not jest one er two."

As they stepped up to the batwings, Smoke loosened the rawhide hammer thongs on his Colts and whispered, "Be sharp, Joey."

"Only way ta be, Smoke, an' live ta see my wife an' boy again."

The saloon was like hundreds of others in the gold rush

and ranching towns of the West. A long wooden bar across one wall, a piano in a corner being tortured by a player with more enthusiasm than talent, and gaming tables scattered throughout the room. In spite of numerous kerosene lanterns, the room was gloomy and dark, the air suffused with a suffocating cloud of cigar and cigarette smoke combined with the pungent aroma of unwashed bodies and stale beer and whiskey.

Ben Tolson was at a table to one side of the room, sitting by himself with a mug of beer in front of him. He had his Greener across his lap.

As they entered, Tolson gave a small nod toward a table in the far corner of the room. A large, blustery man with carrot-red hair and muttonchop sideburns sat there, laughing too loudly and acting as if he owned the place. He wore a black coat and vest over a white shirt with a ruffled front and sported a large gold-nugget ring on the little finger of his left hand. Three other men, also wearing suits, were seated at the table. Two Anglos and two Mexicans were standing behind Murdock, eyes searching the room for any sign of danger to their boss, their hands resting on their pistol butts.

There was no sign of anyone who might be Sheriff Sam Murdock or any of his deputies in the saloon.

Joey stiffened, then spoke low out of the side of his mouth on the way to the bar. "El Machete."

He looked toward the tall, lean Mexican standing next to Murdock.

Smoke and Joey walked across the room and leaned on the counter, facing one another so they could each cover the other's back.

Joey flipped a gold double eagle toward the barman. "Bottle o' whiskey, an' I want one with a label on it."

"Yes, sir!" the bartender said as he pulled a bottle from beneath the bar and placed it and two glasses in front of them.

Joey poured drinks while Smoke observed El Machete out of the corner of his eye. The killer was staring at Joey, eyes squinted, a puzzled expression on his face as if he was trying to remember where he had seen him before.

Smoke lit a stogie while Joey made a cigarette and stuck it in the corner of his mouth. As smoke curled up around his face, Joey asked the barman in a loud voice, "I hear tell there's a ranch up fer sale hereabouts?"

The bartender stopped wiping the counter and cut his eyes toward Murdock before replying, "Oh? Where'd you hear that?"

"Around," answered Joey. He drained his glass without removing the cigarette from his mouth and poured another.

Smoke, peering over Joey's shoulder, noticed they had Murdock's full attention. He had stopped talking and was staring in their direction, as if trying to hear what Joey was saying over the noise of the cowboys in the saloon.

"I also hear it's a prime piece o' land with good water an' stock."

The barman began to sweat as he inched away from them. "I wouldn't know nothin' about that, mister. I just tend bar here." He busied himself with his rag, keeping his head down and his gaze averted as if he was afraid of being seen talking to them.

Murdock nodded over his shoulder at El Machete, who whispered something in Sergeant Garcia's ear, causing the big man to grin widely. He hitched up his belt and walked toward the bar.

Smoke leaned over and spoke low. "Uh-oh, trouble coming."

The fat Mexican stood behind Joey and placed a ham-sized hand on his shoulder. "Señor, I think you make a beeg mistake."

Joey winked at Smoke, then stared at Garcia. He looked

like a child next to the huge man, his head barely reaching Garcia's chest. "You talkin' to me, mister?"

"*Sí*. The *ranchito* you askin' about, she is spoken for already."

Joey leaned his head back to glare up into Garcia's eyes, blowing smoke in his face. "Oh? That ain't what I heard."

The saloon became deathly quiet. The cowboys stopped their jawing, and sensing a confrontation watched to see what would happen. Even the piano player stopped beating the keys and spun on his stool to see what was going on. Smoke noticed out of the corner of his eye that Ben Tolson had put his beer down and placed his hand on the butt of his scattergun, ready for trouble. The ex-gunman had a slight smirk on his face, enjoying the action.

Garcia stuck out an index finger as big as a sausage and poked Joey's shoulder with it as he spoke. "Señor, I tole you, there is nothing in this place for you."

Joey stepped away from the bar and squared his shoulders, his eyes changing color as he stared at Garcia. "The last man touched me like that is eatin' with his left hand now." He glanced down at Garcia's ample paunch. "From the looks o' yore belly, ya need both hands to shovel in yore tortillas an' frijoles, so why don't ya back off an' I'll not hurt ya?"

Garcia threw back his head and laughed, then swung a fist at Joey's head. Quick as a snake, Joey reached up and grabbed the hand in midair with his left hand, squeezing. Knuckle bones cracked with a sound like dry twigs snapping.

Garcia screamed, "Aiyeee," and dropped to his knees. As the Mexican fumbled at his belt for his pistol with his left hand, Joey drew in one fluid motion and slammed the barrel of his Colt across the man's face, flaying his forehead open with the raised front sight and snapping his head back. Garcia's eyes crossed and glazed over. After a few seconds the outlaw fell facedown on the floor, his boots beating a tattoo on the boards as he flopped like a fish out of water, blood pumping from his wound to cover his face and chest and pool on the wooden floor.

El Machete took a step forward and Joey glared at him. Joey extended his arm, hammer back on his pistol, pointing it between Vasquez's eyes. "Hey, Mex, this trash a friend of your'n?"

Vasquez stopped, his hands out from his sides, his face burning red at the insult. He nodded slowly, hate filling his eyes. "Sí."

"Then why don't ya take his fat ass outta here 'fore I kill him?" Joey snorted in disgust, holstered his gun, and turned his back on the infuriated man as if he posed no threat.

Joey poured himself another drink and said in a loud voice so all could hear, "It's gittin' so a man cain't have a peaceable drink anymore without some greaser son of a bitch gittin' in his face!"

Vasquez slapped leather, but stopped when Smoke's pistol appeared in his hand as if by magic. The mountain man eared back the hammer on his Colt with a loud click and put the barrel against the side of Vasquez's head. "Your fat friend started it, Vasquez. Now, why don't you and your compadres take him out of here 'fore my friend puts a window in your skull?"

Murdock glared at Smoke and Joey, a speculative gleam in his eye. He growled from the corner, "Vasquez, take him back to the ranch, I'll handle this."

It took Vasquez and three other men to lift Garcia and carry him from the saloon, sweating and grunting under the load. Smoke and Joey glanced at Murdock, their lips curled in derisive smiles, then holstered their pistols. They took their whiskey and glasses and sat at a table to the far side of the saloon, where they had an unobstructed view of the room and a wall at their backs.

Murdock got up from his table and walked over to where

Tolson sat, observing the action with a slight smile on his face. After talking with Tolson for a few minutes, beady pig-eyes watching Joey and Smoke, Murdock returned to his poker game. A half hour later the game broke up. Murdock pocketed his winnings and motioned for the bartender to bring him a bottle of whiskey. He spoke quietly to one of his two remaining bodyguards, who stared at Smoke and Joey as Murdock talked.

The cowboy, an Anglo with his pistol tied down low on his right hip in a fancy rig, sauntered toward Smoke and Joey's table, scowling and trying to look mean. He stopped in front of them, legs spread and hands on hips. "Mr. Murdock wants to talk with you," he snarled.

Smoke took the stogie out of his mouth and tapped an inch of ash on the man's boots. "Okay."

When Smoke and Joey remained seated, the gunny got a puzzled look on his face. "I tole you, Mr. Murdock wants to talk to you!" he repeated.

Joey shrugged, not looking up as he made another cigarette. "Yore boss has somethin' ta say, send him over. We'll listen."

Murdock's man stood there, chewing his lips, trying to decide what to do next. "You want Mr. Murdock to come to you?" he asked, not believing his ears.

Smoke shrugged as though he didn't particularly care one way or the other.

"He ain't gonna like that much."

Smoke looked at Joey. "You care what Mr. Murdock likes or don't like?"

Joey's lips curled in a half smile as he stuck the cigarette in the corner of his mouth and lit it. "Not enough so's ya can tell it."

The gun hawk's face blushed red, and his right hand dropped near the handle of his pistol, fingers flexing.

Joey's smile faded and his eyes narrowed, cold and intent as a rattler's about to strike. "Cowboy, ya wanna live ta see tomorrow, you trot over there like a good little dog an' tell yore boss what we said." His shoulders moved in a small shrug. "Otherwise, make yore play an' I'll kill ya where ya stand. Makes no difference ta me either way."

The man saw death in Joey's eyes, and sweat began to bead on his forehead. With a mumbled curse he spun on his heel abruptly and stalked back across the room toward Murdock. They talked for a moment before Murdock smiled, shaking his head. He picked up his whiskey and walked to their table, followed by his two guards.

"Mr. Jensen, Mr. Wells, I'm Jacob Murdock. I'd like to have a word with you."

Smoke nodded. "We know who you are, Murdock. You're welcome to sit and chat, but send your trained dogs there back to your table. We don't want them stinking up our end of the room."

One of the men stepped forward, but Murdock stopped him with an outstretched arm. "Well, I can see you are as tough as your reputation makes you out to be, Mr. Jensen."

Joey smiled insolently. "Yeah, he was born with the bark on, all right."

Murdock inclined his head at his men, sending them back to his table to wait for him. He took a seat and poured himself a glass of whiskey. "Mr. Wells, Mr. Jensen, I'd like to propose a toast. To   the possibility of a mutually profitable business venture." He held up his glass.

Smoke and Joey glanced at each other, then back at Murdock. Neither man picked up his glass. "Before we go to drinkin' together, Murdock, why don't ya git ta the meat of the thing? Say what ya came here to say, plain an' simple," Joey said.

Murdock looked unsure of himself, his eyes darting back and forth between Smoke and Joey, his fat fingers nervously twisting the hair of his sideburns.

He raised his glass to drink, and Smoke noticed his hand was trembling slightly. An expert at reading men, Smoke knew this to be a sure sign of a coward, nervous without his gun hands to back his play. Smoke glanced at Joey, knowing he realized it too.

"When Ben Tolson over there told me who you were, I got to wondering why two famous pistoleers had come to Pueblo, and why you are interested in buying a ranch out here in the middle of nowhere."

Smoke and Joey remained silent, leaning back in their chairs, sipping their whiskey and smoking, neither bothering to reply.

Murdock, confronted by silence, cleared his throat, dropping his eyes to stare at his drink. "If it's work you're looking for, I'm paying triple wages to men who know how to handle a gun." He raised his gaze, a hopeful expression on his face. "I'm planning on building the biggest spread in these parts, and I can make you rich." He hesitated, then added, "And if you're not partial to ranching, my brother is sheriff of Pueblo now, and I feel sure he can always use a couple of men who are good with their guns."

Joey snorted. "Smoke's already rich, Murdock. He could buy and sell ya ten times over without breakin' a sweat." He shrugged. "As fer me workin' fer ya or yore worthless little shit of a brother, if I saw either one of ya on fire, I wouldn't piss on ya to put ya out!"

Murdock looked stunned. It was obvious few men had the courage to talk to him in this fashion. He scowled, glancing at Smoke. "Them your feelings too, Jensen?"

Smoke dropped his cigar into Murdock's whiskey glass and leaned forward, speaking loud enough for everyone in the room to hear. "Let me be frank with you, Murdock. Joey and I don't have any use for men like you. To us, you're lower than pond scum. Not only do you rob and steal what other men have spent their entire lives building, but you're too cowardly to do it yourself. You hire stupid men who are as worthless as you to do your dirty work." He stuck a finger in Murdock's face. "Joey and I intend to put you out of business, Murdock. We're going to take everything you've got and give it back to the people you stole it from.''

Murdock's face reddened and his head snapped back as if he had been slapped. As he opened his mouth to reply, Joey interrupted to say in a loud voice, "An' ya kin tell those bastards that ride fer your brand that if'n they git in our way, we'll kill every mother's son of 'em."

Murdock's eyes narrowed. "You talk awfully big for just two men," he snarled.

Smoke smiled. "Oh, two men?" He stood and glanced around the saloon at the cowboys, who were silent, listening to what was being said. "People of Pueblo," he called in a loud voice, "I'm Smoke Jensen, and my partner here is Joey Wells." He smiled at the reaction on the punchers' faces when they recognized his and Joey's names. "We intend to buy the Williams spread when it comes up for auction and we're going to be hiring hands in the morning." He started to sit, then stood back up. "Oh, and incidentally, we also intend to shut Mr. Murdock's operation down and send his ass back where he came from, him and that sorry bastard of a brother of his. If you boys know anyone that kind of work would appeal to, send 'em over to the hotel at nine in the morning."

Before Smoke could sit down, Murdock's two bodyguards jumped up from their table and grabbed iron. Murdock dove out of his chair onto the floor as Smoke and Joey drew their Colts in the blink of an eye and fired.

Though spectators would argue for weeks over who fired first, the big .44s exploded as one, the slugs taking the two gunmen in their chests and blowing them backward to land spread-eagle on the table, their pistols still in holsters. The action was over so fast, Ben Tolson didn't have time to raise his shotgun before the echoing blasts died away.

Smoke looked down at Murdock sprawled cowering on the floor, his hands covering his head. Smoke nudged him none too gently with his boot. "I think it's time you went on home, Murdock, and tell your boys we'll be seeing them."

Murdock scrambled to his feet and took one look at the ruined bodies of his gunnies. "That was cold-blooded murder! I'll see that the sheriff hangs the both of you."

Smoke looked around at the crowded saloon. "Anybody here see us murder anyone, or was it self-defense?"

Several of the cowboys, evidently no friends of Murdock's, spoke up. "They drawed on you first, mister. We all seen it."

Another man, awe in his voice, said, "At least, they *tried* to draw first."

Murdock muttered a curse and stomped out of the saloon, his eyes glaring hate at the men in the room.

Smoke and Joey sauntered over to the two dead men. Smoke's bullet had taken his man square in the heart, while Joey's was a couple of inches to the center, having entered the man's breastbone and blown out his spine.

Smoke grinned as he punched out his brass and reloaded. "Looks like your aim was off a tad, Joey."

Joey made a disgusted face. "Yeah, 'course, I did git off the first shot."

Smoke laughed. "Oh, is that so?"

Tolson walked up, shaking his head. "Mary Mother of Christ, I never seen nothin' so fast in all my born days. You men are quick as greased lightnin'! Them boys didn't even clear leather 'fore they was dead."

Jacob Murdock was as mad as he could ever remember being. He was pacing his study, cursing under his breath, while Vasquez and one of his men who had some medical training were trying to put stitches in Garcia's face so he wouldn't bleed to death.

As Murdock reached for his decanter of bourbon, he

heard the fat Mexican scream, *"Madre de Dios . . ."* Serves the fat bastard right, thought Murdock, letting a little sawed-off runt like that Joey Wells beat the shit out of him.

After a moment Vasquez sauntered into the room. "I think he will live, but it will be some time before he ride and shoot again."

Murdock whirled and pointed his finger at Vasquez. "Tell the stupid son of a bitch that he'll get no pay until he's fit to work again!"

Vasquez's eyes narrowed, but all he said was "As you wish, señor." After a moment he lowered his eyes, walked to Murdock's desk, took a fat cigar out of his humidor, and rolled it as he slid it under his nose. "Ah, *es muy bueno.*" He struck a lucifer on his pistol butt and lit the cigar, then poured some of Murdock's whiskey into a crystal goblet.

He dropped onto a couch, put his feet up on a small table in front of the sofa, and sat there, smoking and drinking and watching Murdock pace.

Murdock took a deep drink of his bourbon and said, "I thought you told me these men you hired are all tough hombres."

Vasquez shrugged. "They are plenty tough, señor. But that does not mean that there are not men who are tougher, or most fast with pistols." He narrowed his eyes. "I do not think I seen anyone faster than those two gringos tonight." He shrugged again and upended his glass, drinking it dry. "Of course, fast is no good against many guns at one time, or against guns one cannot see. I will take care of these mens, do not worry."

Murdock stubbed out his cigar in an ashtray on his desk. "Don't worry? How can I not worry? The auction of the Williams ranch is tomorrow morning. What if this crazy man does what he says and buys the ranch?"

Vasquez stood and stretched and yawned. "I said, do not worry, señor. Your brother and his men will be there, and I and my men will be there. This Smoke Jensen and

Joey Wells may be fast with *las pistolas,* but they are not loco enough to go up against all of us tomorrow. You will see.''

Murdock finished his bourbon and turned red, fearful eyes on Vasquez. "You better be right, Emilio, you better be right.''

Chapter 9

By the time Joey and Smoke finished breakfast the next morning, there were over thirty cowboys lined up outside the hotel, looking for work. They hadn't seen anything of Sheriff Sam Murdock yet, and figured he and his men were waiting until they could make their play in a nonpublic place. There were just too many witnesses to the gunplay the night before for Sam Murdock to try and arrest them.

Smoke left Joey to do the hiring while he walked to the train depot to meet Cal and Pearlie. He hated to admit it, but only two days into their scheme to dethrone Murdock he was already sick of being in a city. Smoke had been a mountain man for about as long as he could remember, and more than two or three days without being on horseback up in his beloved high lonesome and he became homesick. He grunted, thinking to himself he also missed lying next to Sally at night in their own bed at Sugarloaf.

The train pulled into the station with squealing brakes and great hissing clouds of steam, its whistle echoing a mournful scream. Smoke walked back along the tracks until he came to the livestock car. It had two-by-four boards with spaces between and mounds of hay on the floor. Just as he got there, the big door was slid back and Cal and Pearlie jumped down, shouting, "Hey, boss, we made it!"

Sprigs of hay stuck out of their hair and they were dusty and covered with soot, their shirts showing many small holes where hot cinders from the engine had burned through, but they seemed very happy to have arrived. "Whoo-eee, Smoke," Cal shouted, "you should have seen us move! That engine was flying as fast as the wind on the down slopes." He shook his head and sleeved sweat and dust off his forehead. "I never traveled so fast in all my born days."

Smoke grinned and shook the boys' hands. "Glad you made it okay. How are the horses . . . any trouble?"

"Naw," Pearlie drawled, "not too much. Horse did okay, but that Red of Joey's is a snake-eyed bronc, all right."

"Oh?"

Cal snickered. "Seems as how Pearlie's got hisself a scar or two now."

Pearlie shoved Cal. "Listen, pup, I'm still ramrod of Sugarloaf, an' don't you forgit it an' let yore mouth overload yore butt."

"What happened?" asked Smoke, smiling at the young men's play.

Pearlie shrugged. "Nuthin'. I bought me a sack o' apples at the stop at Junction City an' gave one to each of our horses and kept a couple for me and Cal." He looked over his shoulder at the big red roan's nose, which was sticking through the spaces in the side of the boxcar, sniffing him. "Ol' Red there, he musta figgered since he was the biggest, he deserved more than just one apple."

Cal couldn't wait. "You should've seen it, Smoke. One minute Pearlie was liftin' that apple toward his mouth an' the next the apple and Pearlie's arm up to the elbow was in Red's mouth. If'n Pearlie'd been any slower, we'd be callin' him lefty now.''

Smoke bit his lip to keep from laughing at the mental image of the young man trying to get the big red horse to let his arm go. ''He hurt you any?''

Pearlie's face flamed as he gave Cal a look that would peel varnish off a table. ''Naw, he wasn't tryin' to hurt me, he was jest hungry.''

Smoke whistled and Horse came to the open door of the car, snuffling and nickering at the sound of his master's call. ''Get that ramp set up and let's get these mounts out and let them walk off their stiffness.''

Soon the three men were leading their horses toward the livery stable, while Cal and Pearlie stared around at the town with wide, wondering eyes. ''Smoke, I ain't never seen so many people in one place at one time,'' whispered Cal.

''Me neither,'' said Pearlie. ''They's packed together like beeves in a corral at brandin' time. Seems to me they'd git on each other's nerves, livin' so close together all the time.''

Smoke nodded. ''Quite often they do, Pearlie. There aren't many days go by that several of them aren't killed by their neighbors.'' He glanced around at the teeming crowds of people, horses, wagons, and buckboards jostling along the streets and boardwalks. ''That's why I like the high lonesome so much. If God wanted man to live like ants, all swarming over one another, He wouldn't have made so much space and so few people.''

They arrived at the livery and made arrangements for their horses to be boarded, specifying a daily rubdown and grain to be available for them at all times.

On the way to the hotel, Pearlie asked Smoke if he thought the dining room might still be open. ''I swear, Smoke, I must've lost four or five pounds on that train. I ain't eaten a decent meal since I left Sugarloaf.''

116   *William W. Johnstone*

"We'll see if the cook there can't scare you up a dozen eggs and some bacon and biscuits," Smoke answered.

Pearlie held up his hand with his thumb and index finger two inches apart. "And maybe a small steak, an' some taters, fried like Louis Longmont's cook André does 'em?"

Smoke laughed. "Yeah, but remember, we're here to buy a ranch, and I can't have you eating up all our money before it goes up for sale."

In the hotel dining room, while Cal and Pearlie shoveled in groceries like they hadn't eaten in a week, Smoke filled them in on the events of the night before at the saloon.

"Jiminy," exclaimed Cal, eyes wide, "I'd give a month's wages to have seen that!"

Joey squinted at the young puncher through smoke trailing from the cigarette in his mouth. "If'n it's gunplay yore wantin' ta see, Cal boy, you'll git yore fill of it 'fore this fracas is over. Jacob Murdock and his brother don't strike me as men ta take kindly ta our messin' up their plans."

Smoke nodded, his expression serious. "Joey's right. Murdock's a back-shooter if I've ever seen one." He glanced around the table at his friends. "From now on, we better all ride with our guns loose, loaded up six and six. I want us to travel in pairs, with one watching the other's back. I figure either Murdock's men or the sheriff and his deputies will make another play at us before the auction tomorrow, and I want us to be ready for it."

Joey motioned for the waiter to bring another round of coffee. "When do ya think it'll happen, Smoke?"

"My guess is he'll wait until it's dark, then send some men to call on us while we're asleep. He won't dare do anything in the open, not till his back's up against a wall." He leaned forward, speaking low. "Now, here's what we're going to do . . ."

* * *

At two o'clock in the morning, with heavy storm clouds scudding across the sky and obscuring the moon, the hotel was quiet. Two men walked their horses into the alley between the hotel and a dry goods store. Silent as ghosts, they climbed up to stand on their saddles and pulled themselves onto the balcony that circled the second story of the building. Tiptoeing quietly, they unlimbered shotguns from rawhide straps on their backs and eared back the hammers.

At the end of the balcony they peered into the open window of the room supposed to be occupied by Smoke and Joey. In the darkness they could just make out two forms lying covered on the beds in the room and could see gun belts and hats hung on bedposts and boots standing next to the beds.

Jesse Salazar looked at his friend and grinned widely, his gold tooth gleaming in the sparse moonlight reflected off the clouds. The other man nodded, and they aimed their scatterguns at the forms under the covers and fired four barrels of buckshot into the rooms, shredding sheets and mattresses and blowing bed frames into kindling wood.

Surrounded by billowing clouds of cordite gun smoke, they laughed and began to run back down the balcony to where they left their mounts.

The two assassins stopped abruptly when they saw four men standing side by side, watching them.

"Evenin', gents. You lookin' fer us?" drawled Joey Wells.

Salazar screamed, *"Madre de Dios"* as he dropped his shotgun and grabbed for his pistol.

Four Colts boomed, spitting flame and smoke and shattering the stillness of the night. Salazar took two bullets in the chest from Smoke and one in the throat from Cal. His accomplice was hit twice in the belly by Pearlie, and twice in the face by Joey, once between the eyes, and one bullet entered his open mouth and exited out the back of his head, taking most of his brains with it. Both Salazar and his partner were blown off the balcony to fall spinning to the ground, dead before they hit the dirt.

As hotel lights began to wink on and a crowd gathered, Joey took a cigarette out of his mouth and flipped it over the balcony rail to land smoldering on Salazar's shirt. He yawned. "Well, that takes care o' that. Me fer some shut-eye, boys. It's been a long day."

Smoke punched out his empties and reloaded his Colt. "I'll explain what happened to the sheriff when he gets here. Hell"—he looked around at the gathering crowd—"he was probably watching it anyway."

"You think you'll need any help, Smoke?" Pearlie asked.

Smoke shook his head. "No. Too many people around to see what he does. Sam Murdock is a coward just like his brother. He won't do anything tonight. You boys better get some sleep . . . but keep your windows locked and the curtains drawn."

While Smoke talked to Sheriff Sam Murdock, who at first tried to arrest him, until the crowd shouted him down, Cal and Pearlie prepared their room for their night's sleep.

Pearlie took the mattresses off their two beds and propped one over the windows and the other over the door. He sat on the wooden bottom of the bed and began to take his boots off.

Cal stood with hands on hips, looking at what his partner had done. "Just how are we supposed to sleep, Pearlie? You done took all the mattresses and put 'em where we cain't git to 'em."

Pearlie shook his head. "Better that than to wake up dead, Cal boy. Now, git yore butt in bed and git some shut-eye."

Cal stooped to remove his boots. "That's easy for you to say, Pearlie, you could sleep in a buckboard goin' down Rocky Road back home. I'm tired of sleepin' in places not fit fer man nor beast, like that cattle car on the way down here.''

"Hell, what're you complainin' about? We had plenty of food and water and hay to lie down on. What more could a man want?''

Cal peered at him as he leaned over to blow out the lantern. "Well, I don't call having to use horse apples as pillows livin' in the lap of luxury!"

It seemed as if everyone in town was gathered at the courthouse the next morning. Judge Cornelius Wyatt banged his gavel for silence and glared out at the crowd over wire-rimmed spectacles perched on the end of his nose. "Order in the court!" he shouted. After the towns-people got quiet, he continued in a normal tone of voice. "We're here this morning to settle a matter before this court concerning the sale of Mrs. Williams's ranch. Ora Mae Williams and some of her friends"—he looked directly at Ben Tolson, who was sitting in the back row—"have asked me to preside to make sure there are no . . . irregularities in the proceedings.''

He glanced to his side, where Sheriff Sam Murdock and one of his deputies were standing with shotguns cradled in their arms, eyes scanning the crowd for trouble. Murdock's eyes lingered for a moment on Smoke and Jocy, sitting in the rear, narrowing as if daring the two to bid on the property.

Judge Wyatt picked up a sheet of paper and began to read aloud from it. "The property consists of two sections, about thirteen hundred acres, ranch house, bunkhouse and outbuildings, three corrals, and two wells. There are roughly five hundred head of cattle that go with the ranch. The boundaries are, on the north a line from—" He hesi-tated, took his glasses off, and glared around the room.

"Oh, hell, everyone here knows where the ranch is. I'll forgo reading the boundary lines and start the bids."

Jacob Murdock, sitting in the front row with five of his hired guns, raised his hand and called out, "I bid three thousand dollars."

"I have three thousand bid. Any other offers?"

A voice from the rear of the room spoke up. "Judge, I have in my hand a letter of credit drawn on the Bank of Big Rock, Colorado. I ask that you determine how much cash Mr. Murdock has on hand before we proceed any further."

The judge squinted his eyes, peering nearsightedly toward the speaker. "With what purpose, Mr.—uh—just who am I speaking to?"

"Smoke Jensen, your honor. I plan to bid one thousand dollars more than whatever amount Murdock can come up with." Smoke smiled and spread his arms. "No need to prolong these proceedings any more than is necessary."

Murdock and Vasquez jumped to their feet, El Machete's hand close to his pistol. There was a loud murmur from the crowd of citizens, and Cal and Pearlie and several cowboys Joey had hired stood, staring at the Mexican, their hands near their guns. There was a loud double-click as Sam Murdock and his deputy cared back the hammers on their shotguns.

Jacob Murdock put his hand on Vasquez's arm and shook his head at his brother. He said to the judge, "Your honor, I must protest this most unusual statement by Mr. Jensen."

Wyatt peered down at Murdock, his lips pursed. "Well, Mr. Murdock, it is a bit unusual, but . . . in no way is it illegal." He smiled. "In fact, it seems very straightforward to me. Do you have a letter of credit from a bank indicating the amount of cash you have available for the purchase of this property?"

"Why, uh, no, your honor." Murdock frowned and

glanced around at the people in the room. "But everyone here knows I'm good for whatever I bid."

The judge scowled. "That's not the question, Mr. Murdock." He waved the papers in his hand in the air. "Mrs. Williams has stipulated in her bill of sale that the purchase is to be cash only, no promissory notes." He looked out over the room. "Is anyone here from the bank?"

A short, fat man in a black suit stood, nodding nervously as he cut his eyes toward Murdock and his gunmen, then toward the sheriff in front of the room. "Yes, your honor. I'm Thaddeus Gump, president of the board of directors of the bank here in Pueblo."

Judge Wyatt leaned back, crossing his arms. "Well, you heard what Mr. Jensen said. Just how much money does Mr. Murdock have on deposit with your bank?"

Gump licked his lips, his eyes flicking back and forth like a cornered rat. He took a handkerchief out of his pocket and blotted sweat from his forehead. "Uh, if I could have a moment to confer with Mr. Murdock, your honor?"

Wyatt banged his gavel. "I'll recess for five minutes for you and Mr. Murdock to come up with a bid, then I'm going to sell this parcel to the highest bidder."

Murdock and Gump walked to a corner of the room and talked for a moment, Murdock gesturing angrily and shaking his finger in Gump's face. Finally, a red-faced, sweating Gump approached the judge. "Your honor, with cash on hand and by virtue of a mortgage on the Lazy M ranch, the bank is prepared to offer up to nineteen thousand dollars for the Williams ranch."

Murdock smirked at Smoke, evidently thinking he had won. He knew the ranch wasn't worth more than eight or nine thousand dollars and seemed to feel sure an ex-gunfighter like Smoke Jensen wouldn't be able to cover that amount.

The judge raised his eyebrows. He, too, knew that was an unheard-of amount of money for the property in question. He shook his head and looked at Smoke. "Mr. Jensen?"

Smoke walked to the front of the room. He wanted to see the look in Murdock's eyes when he answered. "Your honor, I bid twenty thousand dollars for the Williams ranch." He handed Wyatt his letter of credit and stood there as the judge read it.

Wyatt's eyes widened and his mouth dropped open. He looked up. "This guarantee is for any amount up to one hundred thousand dollars!"

As everyone in the courtroom began to talk at one time, Murdock jumped to his feet, his face red with anger. "Your honor, I must again protest this proceeding! How are we to know this letter of credit, no doubt from some small-town bank, is genuine?"

Judge Wyatt smiled and held out the paper for Murdock to read. "Oh, I'd say it's good. It's signed by Henry Wells, president of Wells, Fargo and Company." He banged his gavel. "Mr. Jensen, you've bought yourself a ranch!"

The people in the room, no friends of Murdock's and his men, crowded around Smoke and Joey, clapping them on the back and congratulating them.

Murdock threw the letter at the judge and stormed from the room, followed by El Machete and his other gunmen. Vasquez paused as he passed Smoke to growl, "You'll never live to work that ranch, gringo." He fingered the handle of his machete as he glared at Smoke.

Joey squeezed between them, looking up with his face just inches from the Mexican's. "I'm gonna enjoy makin' you eat that blade, *cabrón*."

At the word *cabrón*, the worst insult a Mexican could get, Vasquez's face blanched, his lips pulled back in a snarl, and his hand fell to his pistol.

Before the gunny's gun was half out of its holster, Joey's Colt was drawn, cocked, and stuck against his stomach.

"Go ahead, pepper-belly, an' I'll blow yore guts all over the floor!"

Sheriff Sam Murdock stepped up and put the barrel of his shotgun between the two men. "What's goin' on here? Wells threatenin' you, Vasquez?"

Tolson, accompanied by at least ten local businessmen and cowboys, said, "Hold on there, Sam." His voice dripped with scorn. "Everyone here saw what happened. Vasquez made his play first." He gave a snort of disgust. "Your boss is waiting for you outside." He inclined his head toward the door. "I'd suggest you get on out there 'fore someone has to carry you out on a board."

The sheriff's face blazed red and his eyes narrowed with hate. The Mexican let his pistol slide back down into its holster and said to Joey, "*Cuidado, buscadero.* I see you later." He stalked out of the room, followed by Sam Murdock and his deputy.

As Smoke, Joey, Cal, and Pearlie walked to the hotel, Cal asked, "What did those Mexican words he said to you mean, Joey?"

Joey smirked. "Roughly translated, it meant watch yore ass, tough guy."

Chapter 10

Smoke, Joey, Cal, and Pearlie were having lunch at the hotel, celebrating their victory over the Murdock brothers, when Ben Tolson walked up, a worried look on his face.

Smoke waved a hand. "Pull up a chair and join us, Ben."

Joey paused, his fork halfway to his mouth. "Hey, compadre, you look like someone shot yore hoss. Anything the matter?"

Tolson signaled their waiter for coffee and leaned forward, speaking low. "Yeah. Sam Murdock's over at the Silver Dollar, getting alkalied. He's shooting his mouth off about how he's gonna make sure none of you live to set foot on the Williams ranch."

Joey snorted. "That's just whiskey talk. He's too smart ta try somethin' like that."

Tolson shook his head. "No, you got it wrong, Joey. Jacob Murdock's the smart one, Sam's an idiot. He's just liable to try and make good on his threats."

Smoke shrugged. "Well, Ben, what do you suggest we do about it? I'm not about to give the ranch back."

Ben took his coffee from the waiter, added sugar, and blew on it to cool it. He sipped for a moment in silence, then looked at Smoke. "How about you and your men coming out to my cabin? You could stay out there until the papers for the ranch are ready. It'd at least get you out of town and out of Sam's sight."

Joey shook his head. "That wouldn't exactly be a good idee, Ben. Think on it a minute. Long as we're here in town, anything Sam an' his brother do will be seen by a lot of people."

Smoke interrupted. "Joey's right, Ben. If we go out to your place, either of the Murdocks could hit us and later claim it was done by someone else, or even that we started the trouble." He shook his head. "No, I think the best thing for us to do is stay right here in Pueblo."

Joey said, "I'll tell ya what, pardner, you could help us by spreadin' the word around ta your friends ta kinda hang around town the next day or so and observe what goes on. That way, if Murdock is dumb enough to call us out or try an' ambush us, there'll be plenty of your friends that kin vouch fer us."

Tolson nodded. "You're right, I just hadn't thought it through." He drained his coffee cup and stood. "I'll tell everyone I can count on to be honest to keep a sharp eye out, and I'll be around too, just in case you need an extra gun or two."

Smoke looked up. "We don't intend to get you involved in our troubles, Ben."

"I told you before, Smoke. I won't stand for vigilante justice, or for innocent people getting gunned down in my town." He grinned widely. "Even if they're not quite as innocent as they claim."

As the group finished lunch, Smoke said, "Cal, Pearlie, I want you to be extra careful. Keep your guns loose and loaded up six and six, and watch each other's back. Don't let Murdock or his men goad you into making the first move."

He spoke to Joey. "What about the men you hired for the ranch? Can we count on them if worse comes to worst?"

Joey shook his head. "I don't think so, Smoke. They're ready to do whatever I ask 'em, but they're punchers, not shootists. I wouldn't want any of 'em ta git hurt on my account."

"Okay," Smoke said, "then that means it's just the four of us, five if we count Ben. I hear Murdock has at least ten deputies, though I don't know how many will follow his lead in this."

"Have you seen 'em, Smoke?" Cal piped up. "They look like he hired 'em outta a jail. They ain't one of 'em I'd trust to walk my dog."

Pearlie looked at him, eyebrows raised. "You ain't got a dog, Cal."

Joey chuckled. "He's right, Smoke. We gotta figger they all gonna be agin us if push comes ta shove."

Pearlie grinned, fearless as always. "If we git in a gunfight, I don't want to stand next to Cal, the bullets just seem to seek him out!"

Smoke smiled. "You and Cal go up to our rooms and bring down Joey's Greener and my American Arms express guns and some shells. If we have to shoot into a crowd, there's less chance of some innocent bystander getting killed if we use the scatterguns."

After the two younger men left to fetch the shotguns, Smoke looked at Joey. "I hate it that I've gotten those two mixed up in this. It isn't their fight."

Joey smiled and put his hand on Smoke's arm. "Yes, it is, Smoke. They ride for you, and you're ridin' agin Murdock, so they's agin Murdock too. It's a matter of their honor, just as it is ours. When you ride for a brand, you also ride for the man behind the brand."

Smoke shook his head. "It's more than that with Cal

and Pearlie. Since my children have been in Europe with Sally's family, those two have become like my own kin."

"I know," said Joey. "An' I know they look on you as they would their own paw. But when it comes time to stand up and be a man, you cain't hold 'em back."

Cal and Pearlie returned then, carrying the shotguns. Both were short-barreled, enabling them to be held and fired almost like pistols. Smoke and Joey took the guns, and each put a handful of shells in their pockets.

Smoke stood, looking at his partners. "Time we quit hiding in this hotel and step outside and see what Murdock has planned."

As he finished talking, Ben Tolson entered the room, carrying his own Greener. "Looks like bad news, boys. Sam Murdock and his men are all on the street, hanging around the boardwalk, waiting for you to come out."

"Oh?"

"Yeah, and he's told the townspeople to get off the streets, that he's gonna arrest you for murdering those two men in the saloon the other night."

"That'll never stand up in court," Smoke said.

Tolson shook his head. "Murdock don't plan to ever let it come to trial. If you let him take you to jail, you'll be dead before dawn."

Smoke flipped his American Arms shotgun open and checked the loads, then snapped it shut. "Okay, if that's the way he wants it, that's the way it'll be." He looked at the others. "Ready?"

All nodded, and the five men walked through the hotel door and out into the Colorado sunshine, side by side, pistols loose and shotguns cradled in their left arms so their right hands were free.

Smoke saw Murdock step out into the street to his left, three of his men with him. He glanced to the right, where another seven men were standing on the boardwalk, watching with hands near pistols.

Smoke spoke low, out of the side of his mouth. "Joey and I'll take Murdock and the men with him, you three take the gents to the right if they join in."

Murdock held up his left hand, his right held low by his pistol. "Hold it right there, Jensen. I'm arrestin' you and Wells for the murder of two men in the saloon. Throw down your guns and come peacefully."

As the sheriff talked, Joey pulled a slab of Bull Durham from his shirt pocket and bit off a corner. He chewed for a moment, then leaned to the side and spit, his eyes never leaving Murdock.

Smoke glanced up and down the street. Though the townspeople had been warned, every window of every shop and storefront was crowded with onlookers. He said, "Murdock, you're a liar. You know that fight was in self-defense, and so do the people of this town."

Murdock shook his head. "Don't matter none what the people of the town think. I'm the sheriff and I say you're under arrest. You gonna throw down your guns, or am I gonna have to kill ya?"

Joey spoke to Smoke, but loud enough for everyone to hear. "If he grabs iron, Smoke, you put one in his heart, and I'll put one 'tween his eyes, then we'll kill everyone with him who tries to draw on us."

The color drained from Murdock's face, and he glanced nervously behind him at the three deputies standing there. "You men don't have a chance." He pointed down the street toward his other seven deputies. "I've got you outnumbered three to one."

Tolson stepped up next to Smoke and Joey. "Two to one, Murdock. I'm standing with them."

Joey spit again. "Two to one makes it about even, I'd say. 'Course, it don't matter what the odds are, 'cause yore gonna git the first two slugs, Murdock. You'll be dead before the smoke clears."

Murdock licked his lips and took a step backward. "Wait a minute . . ."

Joey called out loudly, "Either make yore play, you sniveling coward, or throw down that badge and crawl on home to your big brother."

That was too much for Murdock, coward though he was. He growled and slapped leather.

Before his gun moved an inch, both Joey and Smoke had their Colts out and firing. One slug pierced the sheriff's badge on his left breast and another punched a hole at the top of his nose between his eyes, exploding his head and showering the men behind him with blood and brains.

The three deputies grabbed iron, a lifetime too late. Joey and Smoke both let go with both barrels of their scatterguns, firing left-handed, shooting fire and smoke and buckshot toward the men. Their bodies were shredded by the .38-caliber shot and thrown backward to land all tangled up, pieces of arms and legs and guts intermingled in one pile.

When Smoke and Joey fired on Murdock, the seven men to the right all grabbed for their guns. Tolson leveled his Greener and took out two of them with a double-barreled blast that rocked windows for a city block. Cal's and Pearlie's fists were full of iron in an instant, and the two young men cocked and fired so fast, it sounded to onlookers as if a Gatling gun were exploding in one long staccato blast. Of the five remaining men, three managed to clear leather and get off some shots, their bullets pocking dirt and wooden posts behind Cal and Pearlie.

Pearlie grunted once but kept firing. Cal emptied his right-hand Colt Navy and drew his other left-handed. He and the last standing deputy fired simultaneously. The deputy's head rocked back, the top of his scalp blown off. Cal bent and spun around, a short cry escaping his lips before he hit the dirt.

The street was heavy with the smell of gun smoke and blood and the excrement of dying men. Ears rang and gunshots still echoed between buildings for seconds after the last shot was fired.

Smoke and Joey, untouched, looked to see how their compatriots were doing, Smoke moaning low under his breath when he saw Pearlie's face covered with blood and Cal lying unmoving on the ground. Tolson was standing, eyes wide, breathing hard, not a mark on him.

The entire episode had taken less than two minutes from start to finish, and had cost the lives of seven men and wounded four more, two of whom would later die from their wounds.

Smoke bent over Cal while Joey turned Pearlie around to see where the blood was coming from. He removed Pearlie's hat, and saw a neat groove down the side of his head, just above his ear, where a bullet had gouged his scalp. Joey pursed his lips as he removed his bandanna and placed it against the laceration. "Looks like you stood too close to Cal, Pearlie."

Pearlie grinned. "Yeah, how is . . ." His face dropped and he quickly knelt next to Smoke and grabbed Cal by the cheeks. "Cal, you little shit, don't you die on me!"

Smoke slipped his Bowie knife out and slit Cal's shirt, peeling the blood-soaked fabric away from his chest. Just below his rib cage was a small, neat hole. Smoke rolled him over, and where the slug exited was a wound as big as a fist, oozing blood.

Joey pushed Pearlie out of the way and bent to examine the wound. "I don't see no guts nor smell any shit." He raised his eyes to look at Smoke, who had tears coursing down his cheeks. "If the slug missed his bowels, he's gonna be all right." He looked up at Pearlie. "Git the doc over here pronto, boy, an' maybe yore friend will live."

* * *

While the undertaker was still picking up bodies off the street, Ben Tolson called an emergency meeting of the town council. Pearlie told Smoke and Joey to go on and attend the meeting, he would stay by Cal's side while the doctor stitched up the hole in his back. When the doctor stuck the needle in, and Cal groaned in pain, Pearlie said, "It's your own damn fault, Cal. If you didn't have such an attraction for lead, you wouldn't be lying here, moanin' and groanin'."

Cal looked up through pain-clouded eyes and touched the bandage on Pearlie's head. "You okay, partner?" he croaked through dry lips.

Pearlie grinned. "Yeah, 'ceptin' I wish the doc would hurry up and get you back together. I'm getting hungrier by the minute."

Cal's lips curled in a small smile. "When he's done, I'll buy you some lunch, to make up fer bringing all those bullets our way."

Pearlie nodded. "You're on, partner."

At the council meeting Tolson stood before the mayor and businessmen. "Now that Sam Murdock and his men are dead, I've got evidence they threatened a number of people before the last election." He held up a stack of papers. "I have over a hundred signatures on this affidavit that men were told they'd be killed if they campaigned or voted for me."

The mayor banged his gavel, nodding his head. "I've heard the same thing," he said. "In light of this new evidence, I make a motion that pending a new election next month, we ask Ben Tolson to once again assume the duties of sheriff of Pueblo."

The council members all shouted out aye. The mayor banged his gavel again. "Motion passes unanimously. Mr. Tolson, you are now sheriff of this city."

"Before I take the job," Tolson said, "I want to make sure I have the complete support of the council and can do whatever I deem necessary to make this city safe for all citizens."

The mayor looked around, and the councilmen all nodded their heads. "That will not be a problem, sheriff," he said.

Ben stood and pinned on the star that Murdock had been wearing, the one with a bullet hole through the center, still covered with the dead man's blood. "My first official act will be to appoint Smoke Jensen and Joey Wells as deputy sheriffs."

Smoke and Joey glanced at each other; this was news to them.

"Then I'm going to post the town as a gun-free zone, all weapons to be checked upon entering the city limits. Next, I'm posting the town off limits to any employees of the Lazy M ranch, including Jacob Murdock."

One of the councilmen raised his hand. "Can we do that?"

Tolson shrugged. "I'm the sheriff, I can do whatever I want."

Smoke stood up. "Ben, you're right. You and the town can do whatever you want, but I don't think Murdock is going to take this lying down." He looked around the room, his expression serious. "Murdock has over thirty hard cases working for him. Know this, if you try to shut him out of town, he's liable to fight. If the town isn't ready to back Ben's play, with your guns and perhaps your lives, you better let him know now."

Ben nodded. "Smoke's right. As soon as I post the town, it's gonna be like waving a red flag in front of a bull. We can expect trouble, and probably sooner rather than later."

The mayor stood. "I for one am tired of living under Murdock's thumb. This was a decent, law-abiding town before he moved here and took over the Lazy M. I would like for it to be that way once again, and if it takes the blood of good men for that to happen, then so be it."

All the councilmen stood and clapped and cheered. The mayor said to Ben, "There is your answer, sheriff. Go and do what you think is necessary."

"I'll post the town tonight, and I'd like you to call a town meeting first thing in the morning, Mr. Mayor. We'll need to get the people ready for what is almost sure to happen next."

Chapter 11

That night, over supper in the hotel dining room, Tolson met with Smoke and Joey. Cal and Pearlie were also present. Other than looking pale and drawn, and occasionally taking a nip from the bottle of laudanum the doctor had given him, Cal was doing okay.

Tolson, between bites of steak, said, "All of my previous deputies have agreed to come back to work, and I've hired another five, who I know are handy with long guns. All together, that gives me fifteen men, counting you four."

Smoke nodded. "What are your plans for sealing up the town?"

"I haven't had time to give it much thought."

Smoke looked over at Joey. "Joey, you've had some experience in getting in and out of garrisons in the past. Any suggestions?"

Joey nodded. "We need some warnin' when Murdock's men are comin'. I'd post a couple of sentries three or four miles out of town on the main roads from the Lazy M. I don't think Murdock will be expectin' much resistance, so

I doubt if he'll go to the trouble of circling around and comin' in on our back side.''

Tolson nodded, and began to make some notes on a scratch pad with a pencil.

"Second, I'd post a man at every entrance to the city, with a big fire bell, in case Murdock's men git by the sentries for one reason or another.''

"What about placement of men in the town?''

"No question about it, the best place for your men with long guns and scatterguns is on the roofs. I'd have most of your men on both sides of the street, about every two or three buildings. They'd have a clear field of fire and they'd be hard to hit from horseback with pistols.''

Tolson looked up from his pad. "Anything else?''

"Yeah, at the meeting in the mornin' I'd tell all the womenfolk and kids to stay off the streets for the next couple of days. The way you're puttin' the pressure on and screwin' it down tight, I don't 'spect it'll take Murdock long to make his play.''

Smoke nodded. "That's right. Without being able to buy supplies, he can't afford to wait too long.''

"One other thing. I'd hold off posting the town against firearms until this is over. I'd warn every citizen to carry a shotgun or a pistol, even those that don't know how to use 'em. If there's enough lead flying around, some of it's bound to hit somebody, hopefully Murdock and his men.''

Tolson looked up, his eyes worried. "This could turn out to be a bloodbath, couldn't it?''

Joey shrugged. "It's your town, you got to decide if it's worth fightin' for or not.''

One of Tolson's deputies came running in the hotel dining room. "Hey, boss. Jacob Murdock and some of his men are riding into town.''

Tolson stood, put his hat on, and pulled it down tight. He grinned. "Time to let Murdock know who's running the show now.''

The group went outside to stand in the twilight in front of the hotel. Murdock reined in his horse and sat looking down at Tolson and the men behind him.

"I hear Jensen and Wells gunned down my brother in cold blood." His eyes flicked over Smoke and Joey, who stared back at him. Then he noticed the star on Tolson's chest. "You the sheriff now, Tolson?"

"Yes."

"Well, what are you going to do about it?"

Tolson shrugged. "Nothing. It was a fair fight, and your brother drew first."

"I just saw his body. His pistol was still in leather."

"I said he drew first, I didn't say he drew fastest. He made his play and got killed for it. That's all there is to say on the matter."

"That's not all I got to say on it!"

Joey stepped forward, his hands hanging near his pistols. "I shot your cowardly brother right between the eyes, Murdock. If you"—he cut his eyes to Vasquez and Garcia, whose face was still heavily bandaged, sitting on their horses behind Murdock—"or anyone else has anything to say about it, I'm ready."

Vasquez muttered, "Let me kill this *gabacho*, Mr. Murdock."

Murdock held up his hand. "Not now, Emilio. They got us outnumbered." He tipped his hat at Tolson. "You win for now, Tolson. I'm going to pick up my brother's body and take it out to the ranch, but I'll be back tomorrow with more men."

"You better come prepared to fight, Murdock. I'm posting Pueblo off limits to you and your men. The only way you'll get into town is to blast your way in."

"That the way you want it, Tolson?"

He shrugged. "That's the way it is, Murdock. Now, get your brother and get your trash out of my town."

Before he rode off, Murdock growled, "I'm gonna tree this town, Tolson, and you with it."

The town meeting the next morning went as expected. Smoke stood up to address the citizens. "People of Pueblo, it is time for you to take a stand against the tyranny of Jacob Murdock. He and his men are planning to try and take your town away from you, and force you to live under his thumb. Let me say this, nobody has ever treed a western town, nobody. Nearly every man in this town is a combat veteran of some war, whether it was against Indians, outlaws, the Union Blue or the Rebel Gray. Back in September of seventy-six, Jesse James and his outlaw gang tried to collar Northfield, Minnesota. They were shot to rags by the townspeople." He looked out over the crowd. "Your sheriff and I expect no less of you."

The crowd cheered and waved shotguns and rifles in the air, and showed they were solidly behind Tolson and his plan to rid the area of Murdock and his gang. Sentries were posted on roads leading to town and at each entrance to the city, with fire bells nearby, as Joey had suggested. Men with rifles and shotguns were on roofs, ready for whatever Murdock had planned.

At the same time as the town meeting was going on, Jacob Murdock was standing on his porch, over forty hard-case gunnies on their mounts in front of him.

"Men, I intend to tree Pueblo and kill those bastards Wells, Jensen, and Tolson. If you men do that for me, there'll be an extra month's pay in your packet."

As the men cheered and waved their guns in the air, he held up his hand for silence. "And to the man who puts a bullet in any of the three I mentioned, it's an extra thousand dollars."

The gun hawks cheered and yelled again. Murdock shouted, "Now, are we ready to ride?"

"*Yes,*" they shouted.

"Then shag your mounts, boys, 'cause there's money to be made in Pueblo today!"

The crowd of gunmen whirled their horses and galloped off toward Pueblo in a cloud of dust, not one of them thinking for a minute that most of them wouldn't be coming back.

By noon the city resembled a ghost town, with no one on the streets other than Tolson and his men. Businesses were locked and barricaded, owners sitting vigil with weapons ready.

At each entrance to the city limits, two wagons were lashed together with ropes, ready to be pulled across to block the streets after the outlaws were within the town. The killers would be able to ride in, but getting out alive was going to be next to impossible.

It was one-thirty in the afternoon when a sentry from the north side of town came galloping down the street in a cloud of dust, firing his pistol. He shouted, "They're comin', they're comin'!"

Smoke, Joey, Cal, and Pearlie joined Tolson on the street. "How many?" Tolson yelled.

"Looks like over thirty men, all wearing bandannas over their faces, and they're all carryin' rifles and shotguns, loaded for bear!"

"Get to your places, men," Tolson shouted, earing back the hammers on his Greener and taking his place in a doorway.

Smoke and Joey went to the opposite side of the street and crouched down behind water barrels stacked there for that purpose. Cal and Pearlie jumped into the back of a buckboard and lay flat, peeking over the sides.

Cal said, "You sure you want in this wagon with me?" He fingered the large bandage on his side. "You know how I attract bullets."

Pearlie snorted, "Somebody's got to be here to plug the holes in your hide so you won't bleed to death. Might as well be me." When Cal grinned, Pearlie added, "Besides, if I let you get kilt, Miss Sally'd probably never make me bear sign again."

Within five minutes the bandits arrived, shooting wildly in every direction, yelling and screaming in Spanish and Apache dialects as they rode down the main street, sending dust and gun smoke billowing around them.

As soon as they were inside the city limits, wagons at either end were pulled across streets behind and before them, trapping the killers between them.

Smoke and Joey stood, ignoring the buzzing and whining of slugs passing all around them, and began to fire into the crowd of riders with deadly accuracy. Smoke's first bullet took a man in the face, blowing half his head away, catapulting him beneath the hooves of his fellow riders.

Joey's first shot took a man's hat off; his second punched a hole in his chest and blew out his spine, killing him instantly.

Tolson stepped out of his doorway and let loose with both barrels, knocking two men from their saddles and spewing blood and guts into the air. In the next instant, a slug slapped into his left shoulder, spinning him around and back through the door.

Cal and Pearlie were firing rapidly, gun barrels glowing a dull red, spitting gun smoke and flames. A huge man, his bandanna barley covering the bandages on his face, rode at the wagon containing Cal and Pearlie, screaming and firing his pistol into the wood of the buckboard.

One of his slugs ricocheted off the wood and sliced through Cal's left earlobe, taking it off clean. As Cal ducked and grabbed at his head, Pearlie cursed and rose up, taking careful aim as the *bandido* charged. He squeezed his trigger and put a bullet in the man's throat, snapping his head back and knocking him from his horse to bounce and roll in the dirt.

Men on the rooftops stood and began to pour a withering blanket of fire into the raiders, decimating their ranks.

Michael Thomas, manager of a general store, aimed over the balustrade and fired twice, knocking two outlaws from their saddles before a slug blew his jaw away, killing him instantly.

Jesse Monroe, gun shop owner, stood calmly, firing from his shop's door, his wife and teenage son reloading for him. He took out six men, then a chest wound drove him to the ground. Two bandits jumped from their horses and ran into the door, to be blown to hell by Mrs. Monroe with her husband's Greener. She screamed furiously, stepped outside, and began to fire a pistol, hitting nothing but scaring the hell out of several riders.

Sammy Layton, a pimply-faced sixteen-year-old livery boy, fired a Winchester .22 pop gun from the hayloft of his father's establishment, stinging and wounding several men, until a bullet tore a chunk out of his side. He was thrown back into the hay, where he vomited once, then rolled back over, picked up his rifle, and continued to fire, blood streaming from his wound.

Twin teenagers, Missy and Bobby Johanson, fired pistols from the open window of their mother's dress shop. A Mescalero Apache jumped from his horse and ran screaming into the room. Mrs. Johanson, her own pistol empty, grabbed a nearby parasol and stabbed the Indian in the gut, running the pointed end of the umbrella through the savage to protrude from his back. He stood there, a look of complete surprise on his face, until he died.

Donovan James, a seventy-year-old veteran of the Indian Wars, fired a .50-caliber Civil War musket until he ran out of gunpowder, then pulled ancient matching army cap-and-ball pistols from his double-rigged holsters and stood in an alleyway, firing and cocking, his frail arms bucking with each shot. When a wounded Mexican wearing a Rurale uniform pitched off his horse in front of James, he aimed and pulled triggers, both guns empty.

The Mexican struggled to his feet, a grin on his face. "Now you die, gringo."

"Not yet, slimeball," the old man growled. He pulled a twelve-inch-long Bowie knife from his belt and stuck it in the Mexican's belly, then shoved the dying man off his knife and began to reload his pistols.

A rider came thundering at Smoke and Joey out of the dust, an Apache tomahawk raised high like a sword, ready to swing. Smoke and Joey both pulled triggers, hammers falling on empty chambers. As the Indian neared, Smoke hurriedly punched out his empties, but knew he didn't have time to reload before the man would be upon them.

Joey didn't hesitate. He threw down his pistol and ran toward the rider. He took a giant leap up onto a hitching rail as he ran and catapulted himself forward into the rider's body, knocking him to the ground. As bullets whined around him, he and the rider came to their feet at the same time. Smoke had his pistol reloaded but couldn't get a clear shot. Joey was in the way, so he gave covering fire to protect him from other riders, killing two and wounding one.

The Apache pulled his mask down and grinned as he raised his tomahawk for a fatal blow. He was one of the group that had attacked Joey's ranch. *"Chinga tú, gringo!"* he shouted.

Joey crouched and pulled his Arkansas Toothpick from its scabbard on the back of his belt. As the tomahawk whistled down, he parried the blow with his knife, sending sparks flying. He screamed a rebel yell and stepped into the Indian's body, burying his blade to the hilt in his stomach.

The Apache's eyes widened in pain and shock, and Joey twisted the blade and jerked it upward, ripping his chest open and tearing his heart out. As the man fell before him, Joey leaned over and spit tobacco juice into his staring, dead eyes as he holstered his knife.

Billy Bob Boudreaux, one of the men on the rooftops, was shot in the neck and fell tumbling to crash through a roof over the boardwalk. Another businessman, Darren Jones, shot in the stomach, fell forward through his window, sending glass shards sparkling in the sunlight.

Smoke saw three of the raiders jump from their horses and run bent over, dodging bullets, into an alley on his side of the street. Smoke began reloading his Colts as he jogged back down an alley next to where he was.

Just before he reached the end of the passageway, he put his back against a wall and eased to a corner of the building, peering around it carefully. The three bandits were walking slowly along the back street, pistols in hands as they looked for a way out of the trap they were in.

Smoke pulled his hat down tight, squared his shoulders, and stepped out into the street, Colts hanging in his hands at his sides. "You boys lost?" he called.

The men whirled and pointed pistols his way, shouting in Spanish as they began to fire wildly. Smoke raised both hands and fired from the hip without taking time to aim. His Colts boomed and bucked in his hands, spitting death and destruction into the killers. One of their bullets nicked Smoke's neck, and another took his hat off, but he kept firing.

Two of the men went down, bleeding from chest and stomach, writhing in their blood in the dirt of the street.

The third spun, hit in his arm by Smoke's last shot. He straightened as Smoke's hammers fell on empty chambers. With an evil grin he raised his pistol and took aim at

Smoke's face. *"Adiós, pendejo,"* he spat out as he eared back his hammer.

From behind Smoke came an explosion and the whine of a bullet passing close by his ear. He ducked instinctively as the man facing him doubled over, clutching his stomach before he toppled to the ground, dead.

Smoke said without looking behind him, "Nice shooting, Joey. Thanks."

Joey didn't answer, he was busy ejecting brass casings from his Colt and reloading.

By the time Smoke and Joey ran back down the alley to the main street, the gunfire had begun to die down as most of the raiders were killed or blown wounded out of their saddles. Three men managed to squeeze their mounts around the wagons at the end of town, shooting sentry Jerry Wilson dead as they made their escape, riding low over their saddle horns back toward the north. One had a machete hanging from his belt, bobbing up and down with the motion of his bronc.

Men gathered riderless, milling horses and began to line bodies along the boardwalk, shoveling dirt over blood pools in the street. The raiders were laid in one section, fallen townspeople in another. The doctor was busily attending to wounded citizens, ignoring wounded bandits.

Smoke and Joey walked over to the buckboard where Cal and Pearlie were still lying.

Smoke shook his head at the sight of Cal with blood streaming down his neck from his partially shot-off ear.

Joey laughed out loud. "Damn, Pearlie, you were right. This boy is plumb lead-hungry."

"Come on, Joey, don't you start on me too," Cal complained, one hand to his torn ear.

Smoke saw Pearlie on hands and knees, crawling in the wagon. "Pearlie, what the hell are you doing?"

Pearlie looked up and winked. "I'm lookin' for Cal's ear. Maybe the doc can sew it back on."

Smoke saw two men carrying Tolson out of a building on a makeshift stretcher. He and Joey rushed over to him, calling out, "Hey, Ben, how're you doing?"

He shook his head, grimacing. "Hell, it's the same damn shoulder I been hit in three times already. This makes four bullets in the same place."

Joey smiled. "That much lead in ya, it's a wonder ya don't lean to the side when ya walk."

"Seriously, Ben, you did a good job. Murdock's gang must be pretty well shut down now," Smoke said.

Tolson waved the men carrying his stretcher to stop. He leaned up on one elbow. "I don't know, Smoke. All the men who got away were wearing masks. We all know it was Murdock, but I don't know as I can prove it."

Joey said, "I don't need no proof, sheriff. I saw the machete hangin' on the belt of one that got away, so my business here isn't finished yet."

"Give it a few days, Joey, just till I get on my feet again, and we'll ride out to Murdock's together and see what he has to say for himself . . . all right?"

Joey scratched his chin. "I guess I can wait a couple o' more days." He looked at Smoke. "Maybe we can spend the time lookin' over the ranch you bought."

Smoke slapped his forehead. "Damn, I clean forgot about the Williams place in all the excitement. We'll go out tomorrow and take a look at it, though I doubt we'll be needing it now that Murdock is finished."

Joey shook his head. "Don't go countin' him out just yet, Smoke. Cuttin' the tail off a snake don't always kill it. You got to git the head to make sure."

* * *

A sweating Jacob Murdock twirled the dial of his office safe as fast as he could. Vasquez stood behind him, pulling a cork from Murdock's bourbon.

Murdock took a handful of cash from his safe, counted out twenty-five bills, and put the rest back in the drawer. He slammed the heavy iron door shut and spun the dial again to lock it.

He rose and took a glass full of whiskey from Vasquez, who merely upended the bottle and gulped his straight.

"Here is twenty-five hundred dollars, Emilio. Five hundred is for you, the other two thousand is for the men I want you to hire."

Vasquez spread his hands. "Señor, *es finito,* give it up. Jensen and Wells beat us. Is time to go to greener pastures."

Murdock took a long, slow drink of the bourbon and sleeved sweat off his forehead. "You don't know who we're dealing with here, do you?"

Vasquez shrugged. "A couple of gringo gunfighters. So? In a few weeks they will move on and forget Emilio and Jacob."

Murdock shook his head. "No, I don't think so. That small one, the one with the Southern drawl, that's Joey Wells."

"Again I say, so?"

"During the Civil War a group of over a hundred and fifty men, called Kansas Redlegs, betrayed and killed Joey's friends. It took him two and a half years, but he tracked every Kansas Redleg in that group, all one hundred and fifty of them, and shot them dead . . . sometimes taking on three or four at a time."

Vasquez narrowed his eyes. "Emilio *es no* Redleg."

Murdock refilled his glass and sat behind his desk, taking out a long, thick cigar and lighting it. As smoke curled around his head, he pointed the cigar at Vasquez. "Tolson told me that a group of Mexican and Indian *bandidos* raided Joey's ranch, stole his cattle, and shot his wife and son. You wouldn't know anything about that, would you, Emilio?''

The Mexican's eyes gave him away, first narrowing, then opening wide as he spread his hands. ''Me, señor?''

''Don't bother denying it, Emilio. Why do you think Wells and Jensen showed up here? They certainly weren't after me.''

The Mexican nodded. ''Señor, one question. What makes you trust Emilio with your money? What if I take money and don't come back?''

Murdock smiled. ''Remember the Redlegs, Vasquez? Joey Wells will hunt you down and kill you unless you come back here with the meanest guns you can buy. It's your only chance of living long enough to get gray hair.''

''You are correct, Señor Murdock.'' Vasquez took the stack of one-hundred-dollar bills and stuffed them in his coat. ''Where will I find these men?''

Murdock pursed his lips. ''Colorado Springs, I think, is the best bet. It is right on the edge of a mountain range, where men on the run from the law go to hide out, and it's only about forty miles from here. From there you can wire other nearby towns and have the word put out I'm hiring, and paying top wages, for men not afraid of Smoke Jensen or Joey Wells. With their reputations, there ought to be plenty of men willing to make their name by taking them down. Tell them they have one week to get here, then we'll make our move.''

Vasquez nodded. ''*Sí* señor.''

''And, Emilio, unless you want to spend the rest of your life looking over your shoulder every time you enter a town, you'd better get some good men.''

Chapter 12

It was three days before the doctor gave the okay for Tolson to ride out to the Lazy M and confront Murdock. Smoke, Joey, Cal, and Pearlie rode along in case some of Murdock's regular ranch hands tried to stop the sheriff.

On the way to the ranch house, the group could see several herds of beeves in the distance, being tended to by punchers on horseback.

Smoke pointed out the activity to Tolson. "Doesn't look much like Murdock has packed up and left, does it?"

The sheriff looked over his shoulder at Smoke. "You didn't expect it to be that easy, did you?"

Murdock was waiting for them on his front porch as they approached. "Howdy, gents. What can I do for you?"

Tolson said, "We come to talk to you about the raid on Pueblo a few days ago."

Murdock took the cigar out of his mouth and examined its tip. "Yeah, I heard about that. Seems some of those Mexican workers I hired went crazy and attacked the town." He looked back up at Tolson. "I certainly hope you killed or captured all of them."

Tolson pursed his lips, his eyes narrow. "And you didn't know anything about all this?"

Murdock spread his arms. "Of course not, sheriff. I'm a law-abiding rancher. One day last week the men just up and left the ranch without a word to me about where they were going." He shrugged. "I thought maybe they just quit and were going looking elsewhere for work, you know how Mexes and half-breeds are."

"What about Vasquez? He leave with the others?" Joey asked, staring intently at Murdock.

Murdock shook his head. "No, Mr. Vasquez is on an errand for me." He glared back at Joey, his gaze flicking to Smoke for a moment. "I sent him over to . . . to another town to hire some men to replace the Mexicans that left."

"You know when he'll be back?"

"I think he'll be here within the next couple of days. Why do you ask?"

Joey smiled with his lips but not with his eyes. "Oh, I got a few things I wanna discuss with him."

Now it was Murdock who smiled, just as evilly as Joey. "Well, I'll be sure and tell him to look you up when he gets back, Wells. Now, if there's nothing further, gentlemen?"

Tolson snorted. "We'll be seeing you, Murdock."

Murdock nodded. "Yes, yes, I think you will, sheriff."

As they walked their horses toward town, Joey said, "Sheriff, I know Vasquez was in that raid. I recognized him."

Tolson glanced to the side, then shook his head. "Not good enough, Joey. With those masks on, we'd never prove it was him. Hell, half the Mexes I know carry those machete things when they work."

"So, what next, Ben?" Smoke asked.

"Damned if I know," Tolson answered. "Guess we'll just have to wait and see what Murdock's got up his sleeve."

He glanced at Smoke. "But I can tell you one thing, I'll bet we won't like it one bit."

After a few minutes he asked, "What do you gents plan to do?"

Joey said, "I'm waitin' fer Vasquez ta git back ta town. Once I'm done with him, I guess I'll head back ta Texas."

Smoke spoke up. "Joey, let's cut to the north on the way back to town and take a look at the ranch I bought."

"Okay with me. See ya later, Ben."

The Williams spread was only a matter of an hour's ride north of Murdock's place. As the four men crested a ridge, they could look down over sprawling hills and meadows of lush green mountain grass.

"What do you think?" Smoke asked Joey as they sat looking at fields filled with cattle.

"Right purty, Smoke." He grinned. "Mite greener than my place in Mexico." He pulled a plug of Bull Durham out of his shirt and took a bite. "Hell, those ol' longhorns on my ranch had to walk for miles ta find a clump o' grass worth the effort it took ta eat it."

"Let's go check out the ranch house, Smoke. We can see what supplies we need to buy when we get back to town," said Pearlie.

Cal chimed in. "Always thinkin' 'bout your stomach, Pearlie."

Pearlie looked hurt. "If I don't, who will?"

They rode down the hill toward a log ranch house on the horizon. It was a sprawling place, with two large corrals and an open-sided barn nearby.

They opened the door and entered. "Open some windows, boys. It's a little musty in here," Smoke said.

Joey stared at the floor. It was made of split hardwood beams, and Mrs. Williams had scrubbed and polished it until it shined. "Who-eee, Smoke. This sure beats hell out of my dirt floor back home," said Joey.

Smoke nodded, looking at the window curtains and

many small things the Williamses had done to make this cabin a home. "It's a shame someone killed him. From the looks of this place, they must've been a happy couple."

Joey walked around the room, running his hands over the handmade furniture and tables. "Yeah, it looks real homelike, don't it?"

Pearlie emerged from the kitchen with a wide grin on his face. "Pantry's full. We won't have to buy hardly any foodstuffs nor cookin' supplies. The owner just packed up and left everything like it was, I guess."

Smoke looked at Joey. "Probably couldn't wait to get shut of this place and the memories of her dead husband."

Smoke said, "Come on, boys, let's get back to town. We better get those hands Joey hired out here working the cattle before they all wander off."

"Or before someone takes them off," Joey added, glancing out the window to the south, toward Murdock's spread.

As the four men rode into Pueblo, one of Tolson's deputies stepped off the boardwalk and waved them down. "Smoke, Sheriff Tolson wants to see you at his office as soon as you can get there."

"Something wrong?"

The man shook his head. "I'll let him tell you."

They spurred their mounts into a trot toward Tolson's office. As they dismounted, he stepped through the door to meet them. "More bad news."

Smoke and Joey looked at each other, wondering what was going on. Smoke asked, "What is it, Ben?"

"It seems Vasquez has been successful in his search for more hired hands for Murdock. A few of 'em just rode into town on the way to his place." He inclined his head at the saloon down the street. "Wanna go meet them?"

Smoke shrugged. "Sure."

Tolson stepped back into his office, grabbed his

Greener, and joined them as they walked down the board-walk. "These are some of the worst specimens of humanity I've ever seen. Evidently Vasquez went over to Colorado Springs, 'bout forty miles north of here, and spread the word Murdock was hiring gun hands."

Joey smiled. "Good. That's one more reason to kill him."

They stepped into the saloon and took a table over to one side. Across the room was a table with five men seated at it, still covered with trail dust, passing around a whiskey bottle. The gunnies were too intent on their booze to notice Smoke's group enter the saloon.

Smoke's eyes narrowed, then he grinned. "Well, I'll be damned."

Tolson looked at him. "You know these galoots, Smoke?"

Smoke chuckled. "Yeah, you could say that, Ben."

Joey watched the men for a moment, shaking his head. "Jesus, but they look like they been rode hard and put up wet. That one on the end there has had a horse stomp on his face for sure, an' the one in the middle cain't hardly walk, looks more like a duck waddlin'."

Smoke nodded. "And you notice how that other one kind of sits on the edge of his chair, like his butt's not all there?"

Pearlie said, "I recognize the one dressed all in black with the big silver belt buckle. I knew him a bit back when I was sellin' my guns, that's Ace Reilly." He glanced at Smoke. "You said he went back east with Nap Jacobs."

"He did. Matter of fact, I told him if I ever saw him again, I was going to kill him."

Joey leaned back and waved to the barman for a whiskey. He pulled a cigar out of his pocket and lit it with a lucifer. "That sounds like there's a story behind you knowing these fellahs, Smoke. How 'bout tellin' it?"

Smoke shrugged, his eyes boring holes in Ace's back.

"It all started a while back, after a federal judge named Richards issued a phony warrant on me for killing his brother. I had holed up in the high lonesome and a passel of bounty hunters and outlaws came up after me. Man name of Slater put up thirty thousand dollars for anyone who could drill me. . . ."

Smoke hiked what he figured was about three miles through wild and rugged country, then stopped and built a small, nearly smokeless fire for his coffee and bacon and beans. While his meal was cooking and the coffee boiling, he whittled on some short stakes, sharpening one end to a needle point. After eating, he cleaned the plate and skillet and spoon and packed them away. Then he went to work making the campsite look semipermanent and laying out some rather nasty pitfalls for the bounty hunters and outlaws.

Curly Rogers and his pack of hyenas were first to arrive. Smoke was back in the timber with a .44-.40 long gun, waiting and watching.

The outlaws didn't come busting in. They laid back and looked the situation over for a time. They saw a lean-to Smoke had built, and what appeared to be a man sleeping under a blanket, protected by overlaid boughs.

"It might not be Jensen," Taylor said.

"So what?" Thumbs Morton said. "It wouldn't be the first time someone got shot by accident."

"I don't like it," Curly said. "It just looks too damn pat to suit me."

"Maybe Slim got lead into him?" Bell suggested. "He may be hard hit and holed up."

Curly thought about that for a moment. "Maybe. Yeah. That must be it. Lake, you think you can injun up yonder for a closer look?"

"Shore. But why don't we just shoot him from here?"

"A shot'd bring everybody foggin'. Then we'd probably have to fight some of the others over Jensen's carcass. A knife don't make no noise."

Lake grinned and pulled out a long-bladed knife. "I'll just slip this 'tween his ribs."

As Lake stepped out with the knife in his hand, Smoke tugged on a rope he'd attached to the sticks under the blankets. What the outlaws thought to be a sleeping or wounded Smoke Jensen moved, and Lake froze, then jumped back into the timber.

"This ain't gonna work," Curly said. "We got to shoot him, I reckon. One shot might not attract no attention. Bud, use your rifle and put one shot in him. This close, one round'll kill him sure."

Bud lined up the form in his sights and squeezed the trigger. Smoke tugged on the rope, and the stick man rose off the ground a few inches, then fell back.

"We got him!" Bell yelled, jumping up. "We kilt Smoke Jensen. The money's our'n!"

The men raced toward the small clearing, guns drawn and hollering.

Taylor yelled as the ground seemed to open up under his boots. He fell about eighteen inches into a pit, two sharpened stakes tearing into the calves of his legs. He screamed in pain, unable to free himself from the sharpened stakes.

Bell tripped a piece of rawhide two inches off the ground and a tied-back, fresh, and springy limb sprang forward. The limb whacked the man on the side of his head, tearing off one ear and knocking him unconscious.

"What the hell!" Curly yelled.

Smoke fired from concealment, the .44-.40 slug taking Lake in the right side and exiting out his left side. He was dying as he hit the ground.

"It's a trap!" Curly screamed, and ran for the timber.

He ran right over Bell in his haste to get the hell into cover.

Smoke lined up Bud and fired just as the man turned, the slug hitting the man in the ass, the lead punching into his left buttock and blowing out his right, taking a sizeable chunk of meat with it.

Bud fell screaming and rolled on the ground, throwing himself into cover.

Thumbs Morton jerked up Bell just as the man was crawling to his knees, blood pouring from where his ear had once been, and dragged him into cover just as Smoke fired again, the slug hitting a tree and blowing splinters in Thumbs's face, stinging and bringing blood.

"Let's get gone from here!" Curly yelled.

"What about Taylor?" Thumbs asked, pulling splinters and wiping blood from his face.

"Hell with him."

With Curly supporting the ass-shot Bud, and Thumbs helping Bell, the outlaws made it back to their horses and took off at a gallop, Bud shrieking in pain as the saddle abused his shot-up butt.

Smoke lay in the timber and listened to the outlaws beat their retreat, then stepped out into his camp. He looked at Lake. The outlaw was dead. Smoke took his ammo belt and tossed his guns into the brush. He walked over to Taylor, who had passed out from the pain in his ruined legs. He took his ammunition, tossed his guns into the brush, and then jerked the stakes out of the man's legs. The man moaned in unconsciousness.

Smoke found the men's horses, took the food from the saddlebags, and led one animal back to the campsite. He poured a canteen full of water on Taylor. The man moaned and opened his eyes.

"Ride," Smoke told him. "If I ever see you again, I'll kill you."

"I cain't get up on no horse," Taylor sobbed. "My legs is ruint."

Smoke jacked back the hammer on his .44. "Then I guess I'd better put you out of your misery."

Taylor screamed in fear and crawled to his horse, pulling himself up by clinging to the stirrup and the fender of the saddle. He managed to get in the saddle after several tries. His face was white with pain. He looked down at Smoke.

"You ain't no decent human bein'. What you're doin' to me ain't right. I need a doctor. You a devil, Jensen!"

"Then you pass that word, pusbag. You make damn sure all your scummy buddies know I don't play by the rules. Now, ride, you bastard, before I change my mind and kill you!"

Taylor was gone in a gallop.

Later, another bunch tried to sneak up on Smoke. Smoke released his hold, and the thick springy branch struck its target with several hundred pounds of driving force. The outlaw was knocked from the saddle, his nose flattened, and his jaw busted. He hit the ground and did not move. Smoke led the horse into the timber, took the food packets from the saddlebags, and then stripped saddle and bridle from the animal and turned it loose.

Smoke faded back into the heavy timber at the sounds of approaching horses.

"Good God!" a man's voice drifted through the brush and timber. "Look at Dewey, would you."

"What the hell hit him?" another asked. "His entire face is smashed in."

"Where's his horse?" another asked. "We got to get him to a doctor."

"Doctor?" yet another questioned. "Hell, there ain't a doctor within fifty miles of here. See if you can get him awake and find out what happened. Damn, his face is ruint!"

"I bet it was that damn Jensen," an unshaven and smelly

outlaw said. "We get our hands on him, let's see how long we can keep him alive."

"Yeah," another agreed. "We'll skin him alive."

Smoke shot the one who favored skinning slap out of his saddle, putting a .44-.40 slug into his chest, and twisting him around. The man fell and the frightened horse took off, dragging the dying outlaw along the rocks in the game trail.

"Get into cover!" Horton yelled just as Smoke fired again.

Horton was turning in the saddle, and the bullet missed him, striking a horse in the head and killing it instantly. The animal dropped, pinning its rider.

"My leg!" the rider screamed. "It's busted. Oh, God, somebody help me."

Gooden ran to help his buddy, and Smoke drilled him, the slug smashing into the man's side and turning him around like a spinning top. Gooden fell on top of the dead horse, and Cates screamed as the added weight shot pain through his shattered leg.

Horton and Max put the spurs to their horses and got the hell out of there, leaving their dead and wounded behind. Smoke slipped back into the timber.

"He's up there," Ace Reilly said, his eyes looking at the timber line in the morning light. The air was almost cold this high up.

Big Bob Masters shifted his chew from one side of his mouth to the other and spit. "Solid rock to his back," he observed. "And two hundred yards of open country ever'where else. It'd be suicide gettin' up there."

Ace lifted his canteen to take a drink, and the canteen exploded in his hand, showering him with water, bits of metal, and numbing his hand. The second shot nicked Big Bob's horse on the rump, and the animal went pitching and snorting and screaming down the slope, Big Bob yelling and hanging on and flopping in the saddle. The third shot took off part of Causey's ear, and he left the saddle, crawling behind some rocks.

"Jesus Christ!" Ace hollered, leaving the saddle and finding cover. "Where the hell is that comin' from?"

Big Bob's horse had come to a very sudden and unexpected halt, and Big Bob went flying out of the saddle to land against a tree. He staggered to his feet, looking wildly around him, and took a .44 slug in the belly. He sank to his knees, both hands holding his punctured belly, bellowing in pain.

"He's right on top of us," Ace called to Nap. "Over there at the base of that rock face."

Smoke was hundreds of yards up the mountain, just at the timber line, looking and wondering who his new ally might be. He got his field glasses and began sweeping the area. A slow smile curved his lips.

"I married a Valkyrie, for sure," he muttered as the long lenses made out Sally's face.

He saw riders coming hard, a lot of riders. Smoke grabbed up his .44-.40 and began running down the mountain, keeping to the timber. The firing had increased as the riders dismounted and sought cover. Smoke stayed a good hundred yards above them, and so far he had not been spotted.

"Causey!" Woody yelled. "Over yonder!" He pointed. "Get on his right flank—that's exposed."

Causey jumped up and Smoke drilled him through and through. Causey died sprawled on the still-damp rocks from the misty morning in the high lonesome.

"He's up above us!" Ray yelled.

"Who the hell is that over yonder?" Noah hollered just as Sally fired. The slug sent bits and pieces of rock into Noah's face, and he screamed as he was momentarily blinded. He stood up, and Smoke nailed him through the neck. Smoke had been aiming for his chest, but shooting downhill is tricky, even for a marksman.

Big Bob Masters was hollering and screaming, afraid to move, afraid his guts would fall out.

Smoke plugged Yancey in the shoulder, knocking the man down and putting him out of the fight. Yancey began crawling downhill toward the horses, staying in cover. He had but two thoughts in mind: getting in the saddle and getting the hell gone from this place.

"It's no good!" Ace yelled. "They'll pick us all off if we stay here. We got to get down the slope."

The outlaws crawled back downhill, staying in cover as much as they could. Haynes, Dale, and Yancey were the first to reach their horses, well out of range of Smoke's and Sally's guns.

Haynes looked up, horror in his eyes. A man dressed all in black was standing by a tree, his hands filled with Colts.

"Hello, punk!" Louis Longmont said, and opened fire.

The last memory Haynes had, and it would have to last him an eternity, was the guns of Louis Longmont belching fire and smoke. He died sitting on his butt, his back to a boulder. Yancey tried to lift his rifle, and Louis shot him twice in the belly. Dale turned to run, and Louis offered him no quarter. The first slug cut his spine; the second slug caught him falling and took off part of his head.

"We yield!" Nap Jacobs yelled.

"Not in this game," Louis called.

The pinned-down gunmen looked at each other. There were four of them left. Nap Jacobs, Ace Reilly, and two of Slater's boys, Kenny and Summers.

"I ain't done you no hurt, Longmont!" Ace yelled. "You got no call to horn in on this play."

"But here I am," Louis said. "Make your peace with God."

The silent dead littered the mountain battlefield. Below them, an outlaw's horse pawed the ground, the steel hoof striking rock.

"And I don't know who you is over yonder in the rock," Nap yelled. "But I wish you'd bow out."

"I'm Mrs. Smoke Jensen!" Sally called.

"Dear God in heaven," Ace said. "We been took down by a damn skirt!"

"Disgustin'!" Nap said.

Kenny looked wild-eyed. "I'm gone," he said, and jumped up.

Three rifles barked at once, all the slugs striking true. Kenny was slammed backward, two holes in his chest and one hole in the center of his forehead.

Nap looked over at Ace. "This ain't no cakewalk, Ace. We forgot about Smoke's reputation once the battle starts."

"Yeah," Ace said, his voice low. "Once folks come after him, he don't leave nobody standin'."

"I got an idea. Listen." Nap tied a dirty bandanna around the barrel of his rifle and waved it. "I'm standin' up, people!" he shouted, taking his guns from leather and dropping them on the ground. "I walk out of here, and I'm gone from this country, and I don't come back." He looked at Ace. "You with me?"

"All the way—if they'll let us leave."

"I ain't playin', Ace. If they let us go, I'm gone far and long."

"My word on it."

"How about it, Jensen?" Nap shouted.

"It's all right with me," Smoke returned the shout. "But if I see you again, anyplace, anytime, and you're wearing a gun, I'll kill the both of you. That's a promise."

"Let's go," Nap said. "I always did want to see what's east of the Mississippi."*

Joey nodded at the end of Smoke's tale. "And which of them do we have here?"

"Curly Rogers is the one in the brown vest, Taylor's the one with the gimpy legs who can't walk right, Bud's the

* Code of the Mountain Man

one sitting on the side of his chair 'cause I shot his butt off, and Dewey's the one with the ruined face.''

"And that leaves the one in black, Ace Reilly," added Pearlie.

Smoke got up out of his chair, saying, "Excuse me, men, I got some business to attend to."

Tolson put his hand on Smoke's arm. "Smoke, what are you gonna do?"

Smoke inclined his head toward the table across the room. "I told Taylor and Reilly if I ever saw them again, I was going to kill them. That's what I intend to do."

Tolson frowned. "You can't just walk over there and shoot down two men like they was animals."

Smoke grinned. "I gave my word, Ben. Besides, those two *are* animals, and they're wanted in more states than you can count."

Joey cleared his throat. "Ben, stay out of it. Smoke is right, he warned 'em and they decided to try his hand, or they wouldn't be here."

Ben reluctantly let go of Smoke's arm, and the mountain man walked across the room toward the table, hands hanging loose.

Chapter 13

Curly Rogers looked up and saw Smoke Jensen walking toward their table. He nudged Taylor with his elbow, interrupting some story he was telling Bud about the good old days before law came to the West.

"What?" Taylor said irritably, turning to Rogers. He saw him staring and followed his gaze, blanching and turning pale when he saw Smoke standing in front of him, feet apart, hands hanging next to his Colts.

As the men at the table became aware of Smoke, all talking and joking stopped and they turned in their chairs to face the mountain man.

"Afternoon, gents," Smoke said, his voice low and without welcome.

Curly Rogers half stood in his chair. "You got no call to roust us, Jensen. We ain't breakin' no laws or nothin'."

Smoke's eyes flicked around the table, pausing at each man for just a moment, causing each to lower their eyes. "Oh, I'm not rousting you, Rogers." His eyes lit on Reilly and Taylor and his hand came up to point at them. "But I do have some unfinished business with these two."

"Whatta ya mean?" asked Taylor, sweat beginning to form on his forehead.

"Remember the last time we met?" Smoke asked.

"Yeah," answered Taylor, trying to put some bluster in his voice. "You put some wooden stakes through my legs and ruint 'em. I cain't hardly even walk on 'em now," he said, his voice turning from bluster to whine.

"That's not what I meant. Do you remember what I told you as I let you ride off that day?"

"Uh . . . no, I don't believe I do."

Smoke glanced to Ace Reilly. "How about you, Ace? You remember?"

The gunman tried a laugh that didn't come off. "Yeah, you said you was gonna kill me if you ever saw me again."

He looked around at his friends. "But you cain't do that. I'm just sittin' here, peaceably drinkin' with my partners, not causing nobody no trouble."

He glared defiantly at Smoke, then glanced over at the table where Tolson sat, his badge on his chest.

"You, mister, are you the sheriff of this town?"

Tolson nodded once, his lips tight.

"Are you gonna sit there and let this . . . this gunfighter threaten honest citizens for no reason?"

Tolson smirked. "I'll tell ya what I'll do, mister. I'll stop this right here and now and we can mosey on over to my office and go through my wanted posters. If I don't find any mention of you or your friend, I'll let you ride on out of town."

Reilly's face slowly turned red. "And if there is somethin' there? You'll put us in jail?"

Tolson shook his head. "No. If you're wanted for anything more than spitting on the street, then I'll just step aside and let my deputy there, Smoke Jensen, do his duty."

Taylor whined. "But, sheriff, that's not fair."

Curly Rogers spoke up. "Don't worry, men, there's five of us and only one of him. He won't dare start anything with those odds."

Chairs scraped back and four men from Smoke's table stood and spread out—Joey, Cal, Pearlie, and Ben. "I'm Joey Wells," Joey said, "and normally I don't interfere in another man's business." He leaned over and aimed a stream of brown tobacco juice at a spittoon. "And if Smoke wants to call them two out, that's his business. However, if any o' the rest o' ya want to enter the dance, I guess I'll just strike up the band and dance along."

The other three with him nodded, grim smiles on their faces.

Curly held up his hands. "Now, wait a minute. I want no part of this. We just answered a call for work out at the Murdock place. There's a whole lot of us goin' out there."

"Oh, and who might they be?" Smoke asked.

"Uh, why, there's Horton, Max, Cates, and Boots, and maybe Gooden."

Smoke shook his head. "Same sorry bunch of no-account losers who are too lazy to work and too cowardly to face a man. Back-shooters every one."

"If you'll back off, we'll just be headin' on out of town, Jensen," Curly said, preparing to stand up.

"Keep your seat until this is over. Then you can leave, but if you head out to Murdock's, I can promise you the same treatment."

He inclined his head toward Taylor and Reilly. "One at a time, or both together. Guns, boots, fists, or knives makes no nevermind to me, boys, but today you die. Pick your poison."

Taylor said, "I cain't fight, I'm a cripple. Look at what you done to my legs."

"Your hand is okay, and you're wearing a pistol. Use it, or die where you sit."

Taylor started to get up, then tried to draw before Smoke

was ready. His gun was half out of his holster when twin explosions shattered the quiet of the room and he was hit twice in the chest, blown backward over his chair to land sprawled on his back with a look of surprise on his face.

Curly's face fell and he murmured, "Jesus, I never even saw him draw, it was like the guns just appeared in his hands."

Reilly held up both hands, a look of terror on his face. He got up and began backing out of the saloon. "I cain't match that, Jensen. I'm gettin' on my hoss and hightailin' it outta here."

Smoke holstered his guns. He reached into the back of his belt and withdrew a pair of black gloves with pads over the knuckles. As he put them on, he grinned savagely. "No need to leave Pueblo so soon, Ace. You knew I was here when you came, so you must have wanted to dance. Well, let's do it."

Smoke's right hand lashed out and caught Ace flush on the nose, splattering it across his face and sending blood spurting. His head snapped back, and he screamed. "No, leave me alone, you devil!" he said, backpedaling as fast as he could.

Smoke kept walking toward him, keeping time with him. With every step, Smoke whipped a short jab to Ace's body. First his chest, then his ribs, then his stomach. After a few steps, Ace tried to block the blows, which then fell on his arms, bruising them and making them knot up.

As Smoke punched, he breathed out through his nose in short, explosive grunts, to be answered by Ace's bellows of pain as the blows landed. Ace finally saw he wasn't going to get away and tried to make a fight of it. He braced his feet and began to windmill his arms, shouting and yelling as if he could scare the mountain man away.

Smoke leaned right and left, letting Ace's wild blows barely miss his face, answering each swing of Ace's with a punch or jab of his own. In a very few minutes Ace's face began to look like ground-up meat. His nose was broken and spread all over his face, his teeth were broken-off stubs protruding through lacerated, bleeding lips, and his eyebrows were split, pouring blood down his cheeks to drip onto his shirt.

Finally, Smoke, tired of torturing the man, set his feet and swung a right cross with all his might. The blow lifted Ace off his feet and dislocated his jaw with a loud crack. He fell backward to lie unmoving, moaning in the dirt.

Smoke turned his back and began walking to the saloon, when suddenly a warning shout rang out from Cal. "Smoke, watch out!"

Smoke crouched and whirled, drawing his Bowie knife in one smooth motion. Ace was rushing toward him, blood streaming from his ruined face, hand holding a knife above him, ready to strike at Smoke's back.

With a motion quick as a striking rattler, Smoke flicked his Bowie knife underhanded. It spun the regulation three times and impaled itself to the hilt in Ace's chest, stopping his rush instantly.

Ace stood there for a moment, looking at the knife handle protruding from his chest as if he couldn't believe it, then he groaned and fell dead to the ground.

Smoke stepped to him, put his boot on his chest, and yanked his knife out. He paused to wipe the blade on Ace's fancy black silk shirt, then put it in its scabbard.

Rogers, Bud, and Dewey were watching silently from the boardwalk. Smoke glared at them through narrowed eyes. "You men are free to leave, but remember what I said. If you go to work for Murdock, spend your money fast. You won't live to enjoy it."

Curly said, "You cain't tell us who to work for, Jensen. It's a free country."

"You're right, Curly. It is a free country, and you're free to choose to live or to die. I say this to each of you. If I ever see you again and you're wearing guns, I will shoot you down on sight. Do I make myself clear?''

The men nodded and climbed on their mounts. After a brief consultation, Bud rode south out of town, and Curly and Dewey rode north, toward Murdock's ranch.

Joey spit brown juice into the dirt next to Ace's body. "I guess we'll be seein' them again."

Smoke nodded, eyes squinted against the sun as he watched Curly and Dewey ride toward the Lazy M. "I wonder how many of my old enemies Murdock's hired."

Joey chuckled. "If he's managed to find some o' mine too, there ought ta be a passel of folks out there plannin' how ta take us down." He spit again. "That's the price o' leadin' an interestin' life, pardner."

Tolson stepped up and stood over Ace's corpse with his hands on his hips. He said, "If Murdock's put the word out that he'll pay whoever puts lead in you two, we may be seein' a lot of this sort of varmint comin' to town." He removed his hat and scratched his head. "Wonder if I might not oughta start watching the train and stage arrivals?"

"Wouldn't hurt to put a couple of men on that, Ben. At least then we'd have some idea of what we're going to be up against in the next few weeks," Smoke said. He shook his head. "I sure wish he would have given up his idea of treeing this town and starting his own empire here in Colorado. This area's getting too civilized for that sort of thinking nowadays."

"Not all that civilized when you stop to think I'm the only law up against him now. The U.S. marshals won't come unless I ask for 'em, and if I do, why then he'd just lay low and wait for 'em to leave again. This country is just to blamed big to police on a day-to-day basis from the territorial capital."

Joey put his hand on Ben's shoulder. "You haven't done so bad, Ben. I think the people o' Pueblo oughta be proud of how you've stood up to that snake. That took a lotta courage.''

Tolson snorted. ''I got no shortage of courage, but we may have a shortage of gun hands if Murdock lures a bunch of hard cases up here to do his dirty work for him.'' He looked at Cal and Pearlie, then back to Smoke and Joey. ''You men are 'bout the best with short guns I ever seen, but all told, we're only ten to fifteen men. I don't relish goin' up against thirty or forty gun hawks by ourselves.''

Smoke said, ''Can't be helped, Ben. We can't ask the townspeople to take a hand in this, unless they ride on the town itself again, and I don't think Murdock is dumb enough to try that again.''

Joey looked north toward the Lazy M. ''No, I figger he and his men'll try ta hit us out at the ranch, where we won't have no backup. He'll either try an' pick us off one by one, or he'll just come at us one night with lots of guns blazing, hoping to get us pinned down in the ranch house.''

Tolson nodded. ''Joey's right, Smoke. You ain't got a lot of cover out there, you're gonna be sitting ducks for Murdock's men.''

Smoke scratched his chin. ''Well, I have a few ideas about how to fix that.'' He turned to the others. ''Come on, boys, let's go out to our spread and see what we can do to even up the odds a little bit.''

Chapter 14

Low, dark snow clouds covered the sun, accentuating the chill in the north wind blowing down from mountain peaks surrounding Pueblo. Smoke, Joey, Cal, and Pearlie were riding the pastures and fields of the Williams ranch, now known in town as the Jensen spread.

Joey shook his head, a wry smile on his face. "Smoke, even though this is mighty purty land, lots of graze, and a good-lookin' herd o' beeves, I think you paid a mite too much fer it."

Smoke nodded, looking at rolling hills and cattle milling in fields, munching thick, green mountain grass. "Yeah, I guess you're right. But over the years since I've settled down with Sally, a lot of gun hawks have tried my hand looking to make a quick reputation. It turns out a goodly number of those were wanted men with prices on their heads. Every time we planted one of those pistoleers, Monte Carson would wire the governor's office and the money just sorta poured in." He stopped his horse and bent his head, using his hat to shield the wind while he lit a cigar. Exhaling a cloud of smoke into the rushing north wind, he said, "Though I never killed a man for the reward, it seems kind of fitting to use that money for something worthwhile, and right now I can't think of anything more worthwhile than to put a crimp in Murdock's plan of building an empire in Colorado."

"I cain't hardly argue with that." Joey gazed at the surrounding mountains, already topped with snow. "I like it up here, Smoke. The view sometimes gits kinda boring in Texas, an' those longhorns will surely try a man's soul."

Smoke glanced at Joey, knowing what he was feeling. Smoke fell in love with the high country the first time he saw it too. "Thinking about maybe staying up here when this is all over?"

Joey shrugged. "This is a good and decent country, an' most o' the people that come out here are good folks, like you and Sally and Cal and Pearlie." He pulled the brim of his hat down against the wind. "Once we've rid this territory of that skunk Murdock, I may jest bring the wife an' boy up here and see what they think."

Smoke smiled. "Oh, I think they'll feel about like you do. This land needs people like you and your family, Joey, and I hope they get to see it with you."

Their conversation was cut short when Cal and Pearlie, who had ridden on ahead, came galloping back to them. "Smoke," Pearlie yelled, pointing over his shoulder, "I think we found what yore lookin' for!"

Smoke and Joey followed the two younger men as they rode over a nearby hillock into a valley. The river running through the ranch had eroded down into the dirt to create a small canyon carved out of underlying sandstone. The canyon walls were about twenty feet deep and made a sharp bend around a series of boulders left by an ancient glacier.

Smoke rode Horse to a ledge overlooking the course of

the river, noticing how it emerged from a wide, flat valley before it entered the canyon.

"You're right, Pearlie. This is perfect." He pointed at the boulders near the bend in the river. "If we dynamite those rocks there into the canyon, they'll block the water and back it up into the valley over there."

Joey pursed his lips and nodded. "An' from the lay o' the land, by the time the river fills the valley and starts ta overflow, it looks like it'll run on down that slope over yonder and miss Murdock's ranch off to the west." He grinned. "When we cut his water off, his beeves are gonna git mighty thirsty."

Smoke smiled. "If anything will force his hand, that will. I don't want him to be able to sit around and wait for his men to pick us off little by little. Stopping the river means every day he waits, he loses more cattle."

Cal said, "We better make sure we're good and ready for him before we do it, then."

Smoke took Pearlie by the arm. "Pearlie, I want you and Cal to ride over to the west and check out the ranches downstream from us. Talk to the owners and see if they mind if we divert the river to run through their land, but tell them to keep it under their hats. No need giving Murdock any advance warning of what we're up to."

"Yes, sir."

Smoke pulled a burlap sack out of his saddlebags and handed it to Pearlie. He leaned in close and in a low voice said, "There's something else I want you to do for me while you're riding around . . ."

When Smoke finished telling Pearlie what he wanted, Pearlie and Cal wheeled their mounts to leave, and Joey said, "Remember what Vasquez said to me the other day? *Cuidado* partners, *cuidado!*"

As they rode off, Pearlie noticed Cal had a wide grin on his face. "What're you smilin' at, boy?"

"Joey called us *partners!*" He stuck out his chest and sat straighter in his saddle. "Pearlie, we're partners with two of the toughest men on the face of this earth."

Pearlie nodded, replying, "You got that right, Cal."

After they finished inspecting the herd, Joey and Smoke headed for the ranch house. There were twenty cowboys seated on the porch and in the front yard waiting for them.

After Joey fixed several pots of coffee and passed out mugs to the punchers, Smoke stood on the porch in front of the group. "Men, I know some of you owned your own spreads and some of you rode for other brands that were taken over by Jacob Murdock. I suspect that all of you know Murdock and his gunnies aren't happy about me buying the Williams ranch."

One of the cowboys, an older man with salt and pepper hair, called out, "Yore right, Mr. Jensen. You sure put a burr under that bastard's saddle, an' that's fer sure."

As the men laughed, Smoke nodded, his face grim. "Yeah, I did. What that means, though, is that Murdock isn't going to take this lying down. He's hired more hard cases to replace those we killed in town, and I expect him to send his gun hawks around to try and run us off this spread. That means gunplay is more than likely, it's inevitable."

"Let 'em come," a younger puncher called, waving his pistol in the air. "We'll be ready!"

Smoke held up his hands to stop the cheering that followed this remark. "I know you men are game, or you wouldn't be here, but Murdock's *bandidos* and new hires are experienced gunmen and outlaws—murderers all, and most of you have never shot at another man in anger."

The group sobered, some looking at the ground and shuffling their feet as they recognized the truth of Smoke's statement. "Now, here's my plan. My partner, Joey Wells,

is going to work with each and every one of you to determine who is good enough with a gun to stand against
Murdock's killers. Those who are experienced with short
guns and rifles will undergo further training by Joey and
myself and will be used as perimeter guards and sentries."
Smoke smiled. "As most of you know, Joey has had a
little experience fighting against and defeating forces far
superior in numbers and in firepower."

As the men nodded, some winking at Joey, Smoke continued. "The other men will be given shotguns to carry
for protection, but will be used primarily to run the ranch
and take care of the herd." Smoke paused a moment to
light a cigar and finish his cup of coffee. "Make no mistake
about it, boys, this is a dangerous business. Some of us are
going to take lead, and some of us are going to die."

He looked around at the men, liking what he saw. None
appeared daunted by the prospect of giving their lives to
rid Colorado of Jacob Murdock and his henchmen.

"For that reason, I've decided that every man who signs
to ride for my brand will be made a partner, be given an
equal share in the ranch, and will draw double wages until
the operation shows a profit."

As the men cheered at this surprising news, Joey stepped
forward. "You men with wives and young'uns don't need
to worry neither. If worse comes ta worse and ya don't
make it through this dust-up, yore families will be taken
care of an' will git yore share of the ranch."

Smoke held up a paper. "Now, if you men will step up
here and sign or make your mark, you'll all be full partners
in the Rocking C ranch, named in honor of Mr. Colt, who's
going to help us make Murdock wish he'd stayed in Texas
and never set foot in Colorado!"

Two days passed without Smoke and his friends hearing
or seeing anything of Murdock or his new hands. Joey had

been working from dawn to dusk with Smoke's new hired hands to see if any showed an aptitude for using gunplay. Joey shook his head. "Smoke, we may 'o bitten off more'n we kin chew."

Smoke refilled Joey's cup of coffee and sat at the kitchen table with him. As Joey built a cigarette, Smoke lit a stogie. "That bad, huh?"

Joey stuck the cigarette in the corner of his mouth. "Ya know, partner, I been livin' with these Colts strapped on so long, they're like a part o' me. Shootin' an' killin' jest seemed ta come naturally ta me, like it was born in me to be what I am."

Smoke smiled. "I know the feeling, Joey. I started young too." Smoke's eyes glazed as he stared out the window at mountain peaks visible in the distance, thinking back to when he came to the mountains with his dad and met Preacher. . . .

Emmett Jensen returned from the war to Missouri to pick up his son, Kirby. He sold their farm for gold and he took Kirby and headed west on two horses, all they owned trailing behind on two pack mules.

The elder Jensen was heavily armed: a Sharps .52-caliber rifle in a saddle boot, two Remington Army revolvers in holsters around his waist, two more pistols in saddle holsters, left and right of the horn. And he carried a gambler's gun behind his belt buckle, a .44-caliber, two-shot derringer. His knife was a wicked-looking, razor-sharp Arkansas Toothpick in a leather sheath on his left side.

Young Kirby carried a Colt Navy, .36 caliber, with an extra cylinder that a man named Jesse James had given him when Kirby let Bloody Bill Anderson and his men water their horses at his farm in Missouri.

The Jensens were someplace west of Missouri and east of the Pacific Ocean when they met up with the dirtiest, smelliest man young Kirby had ever seen. The man was dressed entirely in buckskin, from the moccasins on his feet to his wide-brimmed leather hat. A white, tobacco-stained beard covered his face. His nose was red and his eyes twinkled with mischief. He reminded Kirby of a skinny, dirty version of Santa Claus. He sat on a funny-spotted pony, two pack animals with him. He said he was called Preacher. It wasn't his real name, but he'd been called Preacher so long, he near about forgot his Christian name.

Shortly after parting ways, Preacher galloped up to the pair, his rifle in his hand. "Don't get nervous," he told them. "It ain't me you got to fear. We fixin' to get ambushed . . . shortly. This here country is famous for that."

"Ambushed by who?" Emmett asked, not trusting the old man.

"Kiowa, I think. But they could be Pawnee. My eyes ain't as sharp as they used to be. I seen one of 'em stick a head up out of a wash over yonder while I was jawin' with you. He's young, or he wouldn't have done that. But that don't mean the others with him is young."

"How many?"

"Don't know. In this country, one's too many. Do know this: We better light a shuck out of here. If memory serves me correct, right over yonder, over that ridge, they's little crick behind a stand of cottonwoods, old buffalo wallow in front of it." He looked up, stood up in his stirrups, and cocked his shaggy head. "Here they come, boys . . . rake them cayuses!"

Before Kirby could ask what a cayuse was, or what good a rake was in an Indian attack, the old man had slapped his bay on the rump and they were galloping off. With the mountain man in the lead, the three of them rode for the crest of the ridge. The packhorses seemed to sense the urgency, for they followed with no pullback on the ropes. Cresting the ridge, the riders slid down the incline and galloped into the timber, down into the wallow, the whoops and cries of the Indians close behind them.

Preacher might well have been past his so-called good years, but the mountain man had leaped off his spotted pony, rifle in hand, and was in position and firing before Emmett or Kirby had dismounted. Preacher, like Emmett, carried a Sharps .52, firing a paper cartridge, deadly up to seven hundred yards or more.

Kirby looked up in time to see a brave fly off his pony, a crimson slash on his naked chest. The Indian hit the ground and did not move.

"Get me that Spencer out of the pack, boy," Kirby's father yelled.

"The what?" Kirby had no idea what a Spencer might be.

"The rifle. It's in the pack. A tin box wrapped up with it. Bring both of 'em. Cut the ropes, boy."

Slashing the ropes with his long-bladed knife, Kirby grabbed the long, canvas-wrapped rifle and the tin box. He ran to his father's side. He stood and watched as his father got a buck in the sights of his Sharps, led him on his fast-running pony, then fired. The buck slammed off his pony, bounced off the ground, then leaped to his feet, one arm hanging bloody and broken. The Indian dodged for cover. He didn't make it. Preacher shot him in the side and lifted him off his feet, dropping him dead.

Emmett laid the Sharps aside and hurriedly unwrapped the canvas, exposing an ugly weapon with a pot-bellied, slab-slided receiver. Emmett glanced up at Preacher, who was grinning at him.

"What the hell you grinnin' about, man?"

"Just wanted to see what you had all wrapped up, partner. Figured I had you beat with what's in my pack."

"We'll see," Emmett muttered. He pulled out a thin tube from the tin box and inserted it in the butt plate, chambering a round. In the tin box were a dozen or more tubes, each containing seven rounds, .52 caliber. Emmett leveled the rifle, sighted it, and fired all seven rounds in a thunderous barrage of black smoke. The Indians whooped and yelled. Emmett's firing had not dropped a single brave, but the Indians scattered for cover, disappearing, horses and all, behind a ridge.

"Scared 'em," Preacher opined. "They ain't used to repeaters; all they know is single shots. Let me get something outta my pack. I'll show you a thing or two."

Preacher went to one of his pack animals, untied one of the side packs, and let it fall to the ground. He pulled out the most beautiful rifle Kirby had ever seen.

"Damn!" Emmett softly swore. "The blue-bellies had some of those toward the end of the war. But I never could get my hands on one."

Preacher smiled and pulled another Henry repeating rifle from his pack. Unpredictable as mountain men were, he tossed the second Henry to Emmett, along with a sack of cartridges.

"Now we be friends," Preacher said. He laughed, exposing tobacco-stained stubs of teeth.

"I'll pay you for this," Emmett said, running his hands over the sleek barrel.

"Ain't necessary," Preacher replied. "I won both of 'em in a contest outside Westport Landing. Kansas City to you. 'Sides, somebody's got to look out for the two of you. Ya'll liable to wander 'round out here and get hurt. 'Pears to me don't neither of you know tit from tat 'bout stayin' alive in injun country."

"You may be right," Emmett admitted. He loaded the Henry. "So thank you kindly."

Preacher looked at Kirby. "Boy, you heeled—so you gonna get in this fight, or not?"

"Sir?"

"Heeled. Means you carryin' a gun, so that makes you a man. Ain't you got no rifle 'cept that muzzle loader?"

"No, sir."

"Take your daddy's Sharps, then. You seen him load it, you know how. Take that tin box of tubes too. You watch out for our backs. Them Pawnees—and they is Pawnees—likely to come 'crost that crick. You in wild country, boy . . . you may as well get bloodied."

"Do it, Kirby," his father said. "And watch yourself. Don't hesitate a second to shoot. Those savages won't show you any mercy, so you do the same to them."

Kirby, a little pale around the mouth, took up the heavy Sharps and the box of tubes, reloaded the rifle, and made himself as comfortable as possible on the rear slope of the slight incline, overlooking the creek.

"Not there, boy." Preacher corrected Kirby's position. "Your back is open to the front line of fire. Get behind that tree 'twixt us and you. That way, you won't catch no lead or arrow in the back."

The boy did as he was told, feeling a bit foolish that he had not thought about his back. Hadn't he read enough dime novels to know that? he chastised himself. Nervous sweat dripped from his forehead as he waited.

He had to go to the bathroom something awful.

A half hour passed, the only action the always-moving Kansas winds chasing tumbleweeds, the southward-moving waters of the creek, and an occasional slap of a fish.

"What are they waiting for?" Emmett asked the question without taking his eyes from the ridge.

"For us to get careless," Preacher said. "Don't you fret none . . . they still out there. I been livin' in and 'round injuns the better part of fifty year. I know 'em better—or at least as good—as any livin' white man. They'll try to wait us out. They got nothing but time, boys."

"No way we can talk to them?" Emmett asked, and immediately regretted saying it as Preacher laughed.

"Why, shore, Emmett," the mountain man said. "You just stand up, put your hands in the air, and tell 'em you want to palaver some. They'll probably let you walk right up to 'em. Odds are, they'll even let you speak your piece; they polite like that. A white man can ride into nearabouts any injun village. They'll feed you, sign-talk to you, and give you a place to sleep. 'Course . . . gettin' *out* is the problem.

"They ain't like us, Emmett. They don't come close to thinkin' like us. What is fun to them is torture to us. They call it testin' a man's bravery. If'n a man dies good—that is, don't holler a lot—they make it last as long as possible. Then they'll sing songs about you, praise you for dyin' good. Lots of white folks condemn 'em for that, but it's just they way of life.

"They got all sorts of ways to test a man's bravery and strength. They might—depending on the tribe—strip you, stake you out over a big anthill, then pour honey over you. Then they'll squat back and watch, see how well you die."

Kirby felt sick to his stomach.

"Or they might bury you up to your neck in the ground, slit your eyelids so you can't close 'em, and let the sun blind you. Then, after your eyes is burnt blind, they'll dig you up and turn you loose naked out in the wild . . . trail you for days, seein' how well you die."

Kirby positioned himself better behind the tree and quietly went to the bathroom. If a bean is a bean, the boy thought, what's a pea? A relief.

Preacher just wouldn't shut up about it. "Out in the deserts, now, them injuns get downright mean with they fun. They'll cut your eyes, cut off your privates, then slit the tendons in your ankles so's you can't do nothin' but flop around on the sand. They get a big laugh out of that. Or they might hang you upside down over a little fire. The 'Paches like to see hair burn. They a little strange 'bout that.

"Or, if they like you, they might put you through what they call the run of the arrow. I lived through that . . .

once. But I was some younger. Damned if'n I want to do it again at my age. Want me to tell you 'bout that little game?''

"No!" Emmett said quickly. "I get your point."

"Figured you would. Point is, don't let 'em ever take you alive. Kirby, now, they'd probably keep for work or trade. But that's chancy, he being nearabout a man growed." The mountain man tensed a bit, then said, "Look alive, boy, and stay that way. Here they come." He winked at Kirby.

"How do you know that, Preacher?" Kirby asked. "I don't see anything."

"Wind just shifted. Smelled 'em. They close, been easin' up through the grass. Get ready."

Kirby wondered how the old man could smell anything over the fumes from his own body.

Emmett, a veteran of four years of continuous war, could not believe an enemy could slip up on him in open daylight. At the sound of Preacher jacking back the hammer of his Henry .44, Emmett shifted his eyes from his perimeter for just a second. When he again looked back at his field of fire, a big, painted-up buck was almost on top of him. Then the open meadow was filled with screaming, charging Indians.

Emmett brought the buck down with a .44 slug through the chest, flinging the Indian backward, the yelling abruptly cut off in his throat.

The air had changed from the peacefulness of summer quiet to a screaming, gun smoke-filled hell. Preacher looked at Kirby, who was looking at him, his mouth hanging open in shock, fear, and confusion. "Don't look at me, boy!" he yelled. "Keep them eyes in front of you."

Kirby jerked his gaze to the small creek and the stand of timber that lay behind it. His eyes were beginning to

smart from the pounding of the Henry .44 and the screaming and yelling. The Spencer that Kirby held at the ready
was a heavy weapon, and his arms were beginning to ache
from the strain.

His head suddenly came up, eyes alert. He had seen
movement on the far side of the creek. Right there! Yes,
someone or something was over there.

I don't want to shoot anyone, the boy thought. *Why can't
we be friends with these people?* And that thought was still
throbbing in his brain when a young Indian suddenly
sprang from the willows by the creek and lunged into the
water, a rifle in his hand.

For what seemed like an eternity, Kirby watched the
young brave, a boy about his own age, leap and thrash
through the water. Kirby jacked back the hammer of the
Spencer, sighted in the brave, and pulled the trigger. The
.52-caliber pounded his shoulder, bruising it, for there
wasn't much spare meat on Kirby. When the smoke blew
away, the young Indian was facedown in the water, his
blood staining the stream.

Kirby stared at what he'd done, then fought back waves
of sickness that threatened to spill from his stomach.

The boy heard a wild screaming and spun around. His
father was locked in hand-to-hand combat with two knife-
wielding braves. Too close for the rifle, Kirby clawed his
Colt Navy from leather, vowing he would cut that stupid
flap from his holster after this was over. He shot one brave
through the head just as his father buried his Arkansas
Toothpick to the hilt in the chest of the other.

And as abruptly as they came, the Indians were gone,
dragging as many of their dead and wounded with them
as they could. Two braves lay dead in front of Preacher;
two braves lay dead in the shallow ravine with the three
men; the boy Kirby had shot lay in the creek, arms out-

stretched, the waters a deep crimson. The body slowly floated downstream.

Preacher looked at the dead buck in the creek, then at the brave in the wallow with them, the one Kirby had shot. He lifted his eyes to the boy.

"Got your baptism this day, boy. Did right well, you did."

"Saved my life, son," Emmett said, dumping the bodies of the Indians out of the wallow. "Can't call you boy no more, I reckon. You be a man now."

A thin finger of smoke lifted from the barrel of the Navy .36 Kirby held in his hand. Preacher smiled and spit tobacco juice.

He looked at Kirby's ash-blond hair. "Yep," he said. "Smoke'll suit you just fine. So Smoke hit'll be."

"Sir?" Kirby finally found his voice.

"Smoke. That's what I'll call you now on. Smoke"*

Smoke forced his mind back to the present as Joey continued talking. "I been workin' with these cowboys fer two days now, an' I'm not too hopeful they'll be of much use to us when the goin' gits rough." He took a drink of coffee and flicked ash off his cigarette with his finger. "Don't git me wrong, they's all game as banty roosters, and they ain't afeared o' nothin', but I'm afraid these boys are gonna git theyselves kilt. They's good punchers an' kin all sit a hoss and wrangle beeves like they was born to it, but cain't but one or two hit a target with a shotgun from more'n twenty feet away. Another two or three are all right with a long gun as long as they got time ta git set an' take aim." He smirked. " 'Course, that's when they ain't got hot lead buzzin' over they heads. In a pitched battle . . ." He shrugged his shoulders and stared down into his cup.

Smoke frowned. "Maybe this wasn't such a good idea I had. I sure don't want the blood of these boys on my hands."

Cal came bursting in the door, pistol in his hand. "Smoke, Joey, we got riders comin'!"

Smoke and Joey grabbed iron and ran out the door.

Chapter 15

In the distance, four riders rode at a leisurely pace toward the ranch house. As they approached, Joey, with both hands full of iron, said, "Murdock must not think too much of us ta send jest four hombres ta call."

Smoke frowned. "That doesn't seem likely." He reached inside the door and grabbed his binoculars and raised them to his eyes. After staring at the riders for a moment, he chuckled. "Well, I'll be damned." He handed the glasses to Joey. "Like the preacher always says, the good Lord will provide." He holstered his Colt and stepped out into the yard to greet their visitors.

When the men rode up, Pearlie slapped Cal on the shoulder. "Ol' Murdock better watch his ass now. We got reinforcements!"

Louis Longmont and his cook, André, were accompanied by Sheriff Monte Carson and the old mountain man, Puma Buck. André was leading a packhorse with two huge boxes strapped to its side.

The men dismounted and shook hands all around. Louis

said, "Puma here came to town for supplies and I told him what you were doing. He said he had too many years invested in teaching you how to be a mountain man to let you come up here and be killed by flatlanders."

Puma leaned to the side and spit brown tobacco juice into the dirt. "That's right, boy," he said to Smoke, his faded blue eyes sparkling. "I promised Preacher I'd watch yer topknot, an' I intend to keep my word."

Louis added, "When he said he planned to come up here and assist you in your endeavor, I decided it was time I took a vacation." He patted the Colt tied down low on his thigh. "Besides, I've been neglecting my firearm practice, and a man in my profession cannot afford to get rusty."

Smoke smiled. "And André?"

The French cook gave a short bow. "Monsieur, food poisoning and malnutrition will kill as surely as a bullet. I am here to make sure that you are fed properly." He pointed at the boxes on the packhorse. "I purchased ample supplies in town so we may eat as God intended man to." Without another word he went into the house to inspect the kitchen facilities. He emerged a moment later, a look of disgust on his face as he emptied a pot of thick black coffee into the dirt. *"Merde,* it is worse than I suspected. You gentlemen will soon have coffee fit to drink." He motioned for Cal and Pearlie to bring in his supplies and turned back into the kitchen, mumbling to himself in French.

Smoke looked at Monte Carson. "What about you, Monte? Who's minding the town?"

Monte shrugged. "I figured it was time for Jim to take on some additional responsibility." He grinned. "When Ben Tolson wired me about your plans and about how you were outnumbered three to one and how Murdock was sending all over the country for hard men to come try your hand, I thought it was time I paid my old ridin' partner a visit. It may have been a few years, but I ain't forgotten how you helped me out when I needed it."

"How'd you all get here so soon?"

Puma Buck glared at Smoke. "We rode on that infernal Iron Horse goin' quicker than God ever intended man to go!" He sniffed and spit again. "I'll tell you what, son, that's the first time this old beaver's been scairt in twenty years."

Joey laughed. "When was the last time ya was scairt, Mr. Puma?"

Puma glanced at Joey and winked. "Back in the winter o' fifty-three, when an injun squaw tole me she was gonna move into my lean-to, permanent!"

André stuck his head out of the door. "Gentlemen, coffee is served."

The group sat around a large dining room table and helped themselves to mugs of André's dark, rich coffee. Puma Buck took a tentative sip and made a face.

André glared at the old mountain man. "You do not approve of my coffee, monsieur?"

Puma took another drink and swished it around in his mouth. "Oh, it tastes jest fine, Mr. André. Right flavorful."

Smoke grinned. "The coffee is excellent, André, it's just that Puma is used to mountain-man coffee. It's a mite . . . thicker."

Puma nodded. "Like my old friend Preacher used to say, the secret to good *cafecito* is it don't take near as much water as you think it do."

As the men laughed, Smoke said, "When a mountain man's through drinking his coffee, he uses what's left over to paint the side of his lean-to. It fills the chinks and keeps wind from whistling through the cracks."

Puma nodded, pursing his lips. "It does git a mite chill up in the high lonesome, boys." His faded blue eyes twinkled and Smoke knew a tall tale was about to follow.

"Why, jest last winter, another ol' mountain man,

Dupree, and I was sittin' 'round the fire after a blizzard blew through, an' it was so cold, we had to thaw our words out in a skillet 'fore we could hear what we was sayin'."

Cal's eyes grew wide, "Jiminy," he said in an awed voice.

Puma glanced at him and smiled. "Yeah, it was so cold that winter, our piss froze 'fore it hit the ground." He took a half-smoked cigar out of his pocket and lit the stub. "We had yeller icicles all 'round camp till the spring thaw."

After a few more stories of mountain lore, the men got serious. Smoke stood and said, "Thanks to our friends from Big Rock, the odds against us are a little better, but we're still sitting ducks out here in the open. Now"—he leaned forward, both hands on the table—"here's what I plan to do to even the odds a little more . . ."

After he finished outlining his plans, Smoke took his visiting friends on a short tour of the ranch. He especially wanted them to become familiar with the terrain surrounding and near the ranch house itself. He led them through a small copse of trees off to the right, a pile of boulders less than a hundred yards from the house, and along a dry creek bed that ran from the left of the house out toward the barns and corrals.

Puma looked around at what Smoke had shown them, then nodded as he recalled Smoke's plan of defense for the ranch. "You got a tricky mind fer a young beaver, Smoke." He lit a cigar and smiled through the smoke. "Ol' Preacher'd be right proud of his young'un if'n he were here."

"Thanks, Puma." Smoke rode back to the ranch house but stayed on his horse as the others dismounted. "Joey, hold on a minute. Let's you and me head on into Pueblo and have a talk with Ben to see what the latest is on Murdock's men coming into town."

Louis said, "You want some company, Smoke?"

"No, Louis. I'd just as soon not have anyone else in town see you. No need for Murdock to know we have help."

"Well, you ride with your guns loose, compadre. Murdock may have some men staked out in town just waiting for a chance at your back."

Smoke inclined his head at the short cowboy riding next to him. "Why do you think I asked Joey to ride along? Because of his good looks?"

Joey grinned, rubbing the deep scar on his face. "Must be that, 'cause I cain't cook worth a damn."

"If you all can get some of those traps and deadfalls and such ready, I'd appreciate it. There's no telling how much time we have before Murdock gets tired of waiting."

Louis tipped his hat. "You got it, boss. We'll stay out here miles from civilization and women and whiskey and cards and do all the dirty work while you go into town and have some fun."

Smoke just shook his head, chuckling as he and Joey rode off toward Pueblo.

When they reached the city limits, Smoke and Joey both reached down and loosed the rawhide thongs on their hammers. They knew they were riding into danger, for there were always cowards and back-shooters who wanted to earn reward money the easy way. Smoke intended to show them it wasn't going to be as easy as they counted on.

As they progressed down Main Street, both pair of eyes were constantly searching for the furtive move, the too-quickly averted face, the downcast eyes. Both also kept their eyes peeled for movement on rooftops and in darkened alleyways, favorite spots for ambushes.

They reached Tolson's office without incident and went inside. He was at his desk, poring over a stack of wanted posters and telegraph wires from other sheriffs in the surrounding states. He looked up quickly when they opened the door, his hand going automatically toward the short-barreled Greener on his desk.

"Whoa there, Ben. It's just us," Smoke said with a smile. "Getting kinda jumpy?"

Tolson grinned, sitting back in his chair and putting his feet up on his desk. "Grab a sit-down, boys. There's coffee in the pot, but it might be a bit thick by now. It's been cookin' since noon."

Smoke said no thanks while Joey poured himself a cup. "Any news from our friend?" Smoke asked, sitting across from Ben in one of two straight-back chairs in front of his desk.

Tolson nodded. "There's been a steady stream of newcomers to town, some of 'em pretty rough-lookin' characters. A couple, with faces I recognized on the posters here, I either sent away or run out of town. But it's gettin' so honest folk won't hardly go into the saloon at all, and I stay away unless I got at least two deputies with me."

Joey frowned. "It gettin' that bad, Ben?"

The sheriff shrugged. "Oh, it's okay, I guess. The obvious gun hawks, the real ones with some experience, know not to make trouble in town. It's the others that are gettin' out of hand."

Smoke smiled, looking at Joey, who nodded. "You mean the young punks with the ivory-handled pistols with notches cut in the handles and an attitude like a dog with a sore paw?" Smoke asked.

"Or the ones who walk around town pickin' fights with store clerks and farmers, acting mean and nasty so everybody will know they're tough?"

Ben grinned. "I can see you have both had some experience with these idiots. Half the time I don't know whether to laugh or to beat the shit out of the little snots."

Joey's face grew serious. "You cain't afford to take them too lightly, Ben. 'Member, a slug from an idiot will make you just as dead as one from an expert." He shook his head. "Over the years, my . . . notoriety has caused me to have to face down dozens of these young punks. I have tried my best not ta kill them, but they are usually too stupid to take a chance ta live if you give it to 'em."

Smoke looked out the window at the setting sun. "Ben, you have been working too hard. How about if Joey and I take you to the saloon for a couple of drinks, then over to the hotel for a steak about two inches thick?"

Tolson arched an eyebrow. "You want to check out the saloon and see what riffraff is there now, don't you?"

"Sure," Smoke answered. "Sometimes a little show of force will save lives in the long run."

Tolson got his hat and Greener and walked with Smoke and Joey down the street to the saloon. As they approached, two men with unshaven faces and wrinkled, dirty clothes threw their cigarettes down and stepped into the saloon ahead of them.

Joey said, "Uh-oh. We may have trouble."

Tolson asked, "Why?"

Smoke answered, having noticed the two men just as Joey had. "Those two men ducked into the saloon when they saw us coming. Now, they may just want a front seat for the action, or they may be getting set to hit us as we come through the front door, 'fore out eyes adjust to the lights inside."

Joey touched Tolson on the shoulder. "Ben, why don't you and your Greener hurry up on ahead of us and slip in the back door to the place. Give a whistle if we need to come in with our hands full of iron."

He nodded and jogged on ahead of the pair of gunfighters, who continued to saunter down the street as if they hadn't a care in the world.

At the batwings they paused, then, hearing no whistle, pushed through and in.

The saloon was crowded, men standing elbow to elbow at the bar, and almost every seat at every table taken. The piano player was plunking his keys, looking nervously over his shoulder, sweat pouring off his forehead and staining his shirt.

Smoke saw Tolson in the rear of the room, next to a post. He spread his arms and shrugged; he hadn't seen anything suspicious.

Smoke glanced at the second-story balcony, but there was no one there and all the doors he could see were shut. They would have ample warning if someone tried to step out of a door and shoot them from above.

Joey looked around the room, his eyes passing over, then stopping and returning to the piano player, whose face looked like that of a man about to faint.

Joey stepped a couple of feet to the side and said quietly, "Smoke," and inclined his head to the piano man.

Smoke nodded. "It doesn't seem that hot in here to me, does it to you, Joey?"

Joey shook his head. He pointed at the piano player and said, "Move aside, please."

The man dove off his bench just as two men rose up from behind the piano with guns in their hands. Before the two could pull triggers, both Joey's and Smoke's hands were full of iron and their Colts were exploding, spitting flame, smoke, and lead.

The two men were both hit in the face and neck and chest, being thrown backward and up against a wall, where they slid to the floor, leaving trails of blood on the wall. Before the echoes of the shots had stopped, Smoke and Joey had holstered their guns and were taking seats at a table in a corner. The two men who were already seated at the table got hastily to their feet and walked to the bar, squeezing in among the men gathered there.

Ben Tolson pushed through the crowd and took one of the empty seats next to Smoke. "How'd you men know they was there?" he asked.

Smoke shrugged. "Instinct, I guess. The place was too

quiet. Other than the piano playing, there wasn't the usual talking and yelling you see when there's a group of men getting seriously drunk.''

Joey nodded. ''They was all standing, staring, as if they was waitin' fer somethin' ta happen. When I saw the piano player was the only man in the place makin' a racket, an' he was sweatin' to beat the band''—Joey shrugged too—''I figgered somethin' behind the piano must be makin' him powerful nervous.''

Tolson shook his head. ''Boys, I spent half my life on the owl hoot trail, and you two make me feel like I didn't learn nothin'.''

Smoke smiled a sad smile. ''Well, it's not exactly the kind of knowledge one is proud to have acquired.''

Joey looked around at the other men in the saloon, then nudged Smoke with his elbow. ''Would ya look at that, Smoke?''

Smoke followed his gaze to a group of men at a table across the room. They were all wearing what they evidently thought rough and tough gunfighters ought to wear: fancy silk shirts in black and red, shiny boots with elaborate engraved designs in the leather, and double-holster rigs with pearl-handled or fancy carved butts on their pistols. A couple even had silver belt buckles and conchos on their hatbands.

Smoke laughed out loud, turning to say to Joey, ''They look more like San Francisco pimps than gunmen.''

Joey cut a plug of Bull Durham and stuck it in his mouth. As he chewed, he smiled back. ''You know, Smoke, over the years I met quite a few o' the best shootists in the country.'' He shook his head. ''An' ain't one of 'em ever dressed like thet.''

One of the men across the way, so young the mustache he was trying to grow looked like it had been chewed on by a rat, called out, ''You gents see somethin' you think is funny?''

The saloon got suddenly quiet as everyone waited to see what would happen.

Smoke said, "And who might you be, young man?"

The skinny youth, acne still on his face, sat up straight and tugged at his vest. "I'm the San Francisco Kid."

This caused both Smoke and Joey to throw back their heads and guffaw uncontrollably.

The San Francisco Kid stood up, hands next to nickel-plated Peacemakers in a double rig. "I don't let nobody laugh at me, mister, especially not some old has-been gun-slingers."

An older man sitting next to him stood up too. "And I think you owe this man an apology."

"And you are?" Joey asked, trying to control his grin.

"Turkey Creek Bob Jackson."

Smoke sobered. He had heard of Jackson. He had a reputation as a man who enjoyed killing, especially when he could do it from behind. He was a bounty hunter, and always brought his men in across their saddles, usually shot in the back.

Smoke and Joey got to their feet while Ben scooted his chair back out of the way. Smoke said, "I hear you should change your name to Back-shooting instead of Turkey Creek."

"Go for your guns, you old farts," the Kid called, hunching his shoulders and spreading his fingers out, getting ready.

Joey asked, "How much money ya got, Kid?"

A puzzled expression came on his face. "Why?"

Joey shrugged. "Just wanted to know if ya got enough on ya to pay the undertaker fer buryin' ya."

The Kid looked around, eyes flicking over the crowd. "I ain't gonna need buryin', you are."

"How about you, Bob?" Smoke asked. "You earned any money by shooting someone in the back this week?"

Bob began to sweat, realizing he had backed himself

into a corner. "Wait . . . wait a minute." He held out his hands, palms out. "This ain't no affair of mine."

Smoke said, "Then you shouldn't have bought chips if you didn't want dealt into this hand. Now, slap leather, or drop your guns and crawl out of here on your yellow belly."

That was too much even for the coward named Bob. Both he and the Kid grabbed iron. Smoke and Joey fired their Colts at almost the same time, Joey's shot hitting the Kid in the stomach and doubling him over, to sprawl facedown on the table. Smoke's bullet hit Bob in the base of his throat, punching through and blowing out his spine, almost decapitating him. Neither of the men had cleared leather. Both their pistols were still in their holsters.

Joey walked over and gently lowered the Kid to the floor. "What's yore real name, Kid?" Joey asked as his eyes fluttered open.

"Jesus, it hurts . . . it hurts so bad."

"Not for long, Kid, it'll be over soon," Joey whispered.

"My name's Sammy, Sammy Beaufort." He reached up and grabbed Joey's shirt. "Will you have someone wire my ma? She lives in Denver. Let her know . . . tell her . . ." The Kid's eyes glazed over, staring at eternity.

"Damn that Murdock," Joey growled. He looked up at Smoke and Ben and his eyes were wet. "I thought when I settled with Vasquez, it'd be enough." He shook his head. "Now he's done made me kill this boy, all 'cause o' that reward he put on our heads."

Joey stood and faced the crowd. "I tell all of ya, git the word ta Murdock. The next time I see him, I'm gonna dust him through and through, whether he's heeled or not. There won't be any talkin' or jawin', but the lead is damn shore gonna fly. Let him know!"

Chapter 16

On the way back to the Rocking C ranch, Joey and Smoke rode with their guns loose. They knew it was even money whether Murdock would have men posted on the trail back to Smoke's ranch. Ben had offered to send some men with them, but they declined.

"No need of putting your men in danger, Ben. We're in this until it's over and we can't hide behind your deputies all the time."

" 'Sides," Joey said, sticking a plug of tobacco in his mouth, "Smoke and me can take care o' ourselves pretty good."

Tolson grinned. "Damned if you can't." He stuck out his hand. "Ride easy, men, and watch your rear."

"Onliest way ta ride nowadays," Joey answered.

They stepped into their saddles and rode out of town at an easy canter, in no great hurry.

As they rode, Smoke cut his eyes over at Red, Joey's big roan stallion. "That Red is some animal, Joey."

Joey reached up and patted his mount's neck. "Yeah,

he is. He ain't never let me down, an' we been in some pretty tough spots together. He's outrun an' outlasted ever kinda animal from Indian ponies to Thoroughbred Morgans from England.'' He grinned at Smoke, his teeth white under a full moon. "Long as he gits his grain, he'll run till I tell 'im ta stop or his heart bursts, whichever comes first.''

Smoke nodded. "Same with Horse here. He's bred out of an old Palouse Preacher gave me name of Seven, but he's got more bottom than most Palouse ponies and an easier gait for long riding.''

Joey glanced at Horse. "Yeah, he looks ta be a mighty fine piece o' horseflesh.''

"When this is over, if we're still upright, how about you letting me breed a couple of Palouse mares I've got back at Sugarloaf to Red? Might make some interesting colts.''

"Only if you let me take one or two back to Texas with me.''

"Deal," Smoke said, "if you go back to Texas.''

Joey's eyes narrowed. "What's that supposed ta mean?''

"Well, I thought when Betty and Tom are healed enough to travel, we might just bring them on up here and let them take a look at Colorado." Smoke shrugged. "After all, I already have one ranch, and someone's going to have to run the Rocking C after I leave." He looked at Joey. "I figure you'd be the logical one for that job, if you're interested.''

Joey stared at Smoke for a moment. "This wouldn't be in the way o' charity, would it?''

"Hell no. Remember, we're all part owners of the ranch, in it together. I'm going to expect a good return on my money, and you'll earn everything you make, believe me.''

Joey nodded. "I'll think on it, Smoke, I surely will." He glanced up at the sky, shining golden in moonlight, snow-covered peaks glistening and sparkling like they were sprinkled with diamond dust. "It is a mighty purty country, one God has smiled on, I think."

They were about halfway to the Rocking C, with heavy timber on either side of the trail, when Joey whistled softly to himself. "Smoke, look up yonder, 'bout a hundred yards or so, on top o' that small hillock. There's some boulders and such, an' I just caught a glimpse of somethin' shiny up there, like moonlight reflectin' off a gun barrel."

Smoke cut his eyes northward but couldn't see anything amiss. "Tell you what, Joey"—he glanced at scudding clouds in the sky—"those clouds are going to cover the moon in a minute. When it gets dark, turn Red into the timber. I'll follow, and then we can injun up on whoever is up there waiting on us."

"You got it, partner."

Five minutes later the moon disappeared behind the clouds and the two men pulled their mounts into the forest on the left side of the trail. They stepped out of their saddles and crouched behind a large stand of pines. Without a word both men knelt in the sandy loam and smeared the dark dirt over their faces and hands to hide their white skin. Then, simultaneously, they pulled their knives from scabbards and took off at a trot through the woods toward a small rise ahead.

At the foot of the hill Smoke waved Joey to the left and he slipped to the right, neither making a sound on the soft carpet of pine needles underfoot.

Slowing to a careful walk, Smoke inched up the rising ground, shuffling his feet so as not to break a branch and give their enemies any warning.

He crouched at the base of a series of boulders and listened. He heard a slight cough and the creaking of leather as someone shifted position above.

Smoke put his back to the rock and eased around it, to find four men kneeling with rifles aimed at the trail below.

One of the men whispered to another, "They oughta

be outta those trees by now. What the hell are they doin' takin' so long?''

"You think they saw us, Jesse?" the man answered.

"Naw, they couldn't see this far at night, even with the moon."

"I don't like this, Dave," another said, his voice hoarse. "I'm shaggin' outta here, boys."

Smoke saw Joey's face appear at the other side of the small clearing, and he nodded at him.

As the man stood and turned to leave, he found himself face-to-face with a huge shape with a blackened face. Smoke growled, "Too late, partner," and stuck his knife to the hilt in the startled man's chest just below the rib cage, angling the blade upward to pierce his heart.

With a short, sobbing gasp, the man looked at the hilt of the blade, then up at Smoke. His eyes clouded and he fell facedown with a soft thump.

Jesse looked back over his shoulder, "Willie, what's . . ."

Smoke stepped toward him, holding his blood-smeared knife in front of him. "Willie's dead, and you're next," he said.

Jesse yelled, "You!"

Smoke said, "Yeah, howdy," and slashed backhanded across Jesse's throat, nearly severing his head from his body. Jesse croaked and gurgled, strangling on his own blood and fell, clutching his bloody neck in both hands.

"Son of a bitch," one of the others yelled, and pointed his rifle at Smoke.

To Smoke, in the moonlight, the hole in the end of the Winchester's barrel looked big enough to fall into.

As the man sighted along the rifle barrel, his eyes suddenly opened wide and he screamed a blood-curdling scream into the night. "Aiyee . . ." and pitched forward onto his rifle with Joey's Arkansas Toothpick protruding from his spine.

The final man aimed his rifle and pulled repeatedly

on the trigger, getting nothing but metallic clicks for his troubles. Joey stepped to him and hit him flush in the mouth with a balled-up fist, flattening his nose and sending blood spraying into the air.

The assassin's eyes crossed, and he fell as if he had been poleaxed, unconscious before he hit the ground.

"Ya gotta cock it first, dummy," Joey said to the fallen man.

Smoke dipped his head. "Thanks, Joey."

Joey shrugged, "Better late than never, I guess."

"I'd say you were right on time, partner."

Smoke bent and effortlessly picked the unconscious man off the ground and slung him over his shoulder. "Let's find their horses and we'll take them and this hombre back with us to the ranch," Smoke said.

"Okay," Joey answered as he bent to pull his knife from the back of the dead bushwhacker.

Joey and Smoke passed two sentries at the edge of his property and waved as they rode on by. "Good to see the boys are taking this seriously," Joey observed.

Smoke nodded. "Yes. Wouldn't do for us to be caught napping when Murdock sends his men to call."

As they approached the ranch house, Smoke and Joey saw a large campfire built about twenty yards from the house.

"What the hell?" Joey said.

Smoke grinned. "That's probably Puma. He never could abide sleeping indoors unless there was a blizzard howlin', and then he'd bitch about feeling closed in."

Sure enough, Puma was sitting cross-legged in front of the fire, Cal and Pearlie sprawled on the ground in front of him, listening raptly to his tall tales of the good old days.

Louis Longmont and Monte Carson had carried chairs

from inside the house and were sitting there, listening and drinking coffee. When Louis saw Smoke and Joey arrive, he inclined his head toward Puma and rolled his eyes, grinning.

Puma was telling the boys about the time Smoke had called twenty old mountain men in from the high lonesome to help him deal with Tilden Franklin and his bunch of hired killers.

"You shoulda seen it, boys, some of those coots were pushin' eighty and more. They was spoilin' fer one more fight, didn't none of 'em wanna die in bed." He lit a stubby cigar off a burning twig from the fire and stared at the two young boys in front of him. The only fittin' way fer a mountain man to die is with his guns blazin' in a hail of lead."

He took a sip of his coffee and made a face. "Anyway, there was at least twenty of the wildest, rootin'est, tootin'est old beavers that ever forded a mountain stream all gathered together to give Preacher's boy a hand. There was Charlie Starr, Luke Nations, Pistol Le Roux, Bill Foley, Dan Greentree, Leo Wood, Cary Webb, Sunset Hatfield, Crooked John Simmons, Bull Flagler, Toot Tooner, Sutter Cordova, Red Shingletown"—he paused—"give me some time and I'll name some more."

Pearlie glanced at Cal. "He's tellin' the truth, Cal. I was there fer that fracas."

Puma continued. "Old Tilden Franklin and his gunnies was holed up in a town he'd founded named Fontana. Well, there wasn't no other way so the mountain men headed on into the jaws of hell. . . ."

Hardrock, Moody, and Sunset were sent around to the far end of town, stationed there with rifles to pick off any TF gun hand who might try to slip out, either to run off or try and angle around behind Smoke and his party for a box-in.

The others split up into groups of twos and threes and rode hunched over, low in the saddle, to present a smaller target for the riflemen they had spotted lying in wait on the rooftops in Fontana. And they rode in a zigzagging fashion, making themselves or their horses even harder to hit. But even with that precaution, two men were hit before they reached the town limits. Beaconfield was knocked from the saddle by rifle fire. The one-time Tilden Franklin supporter wrapped a bandanna around a bloody arm, climbed back in the saddle, and, cursing, continued onward. Hurt, but a hell of a long way from being out.

The old gunfighter, Linch, was hit just as he reached the town. A rifle bullet hit him in the stomach and slapped him out of the saddle. The aging gun hand, pistols in his hands, crawled to the edge of a building and began laying down a withering line of fire, directed at the rooftops. He managed to knock out three snipers before a second bullet ended his life.

Leo Wood, seeing his long-time buddy die, screamed his outrage and stepped into what had once been a dress shop, pulling out both Remington Frontier .44s, and letting 'em bang.

Leo cleared the dress shop and all TF riders before a single shot from a Peacemaker .45 ended his long and violent life.

Pearlie settled down by the corner of a building and with his Winchester .44-.40 began picking his shots. At ranges up to two hundred yards, the .44-.40 could punch right through the walls of the deserted buildings of Fontana. Pearlie killed half a dozen TF gun hawks without even seeing his targets.

A few of Tilden's hired guns, less hardy than they thought, tried to slip out the rear of the town. They went down under the rifle fire of Moody, Hardrock, and Sunset.

Bill Foley, throwing caution to the wind, like most of his friends having absolutely no desire to spend his twilight years in any old folks home, stepped into an alley where he knew half a dozen TF gunnies were waiting and opened fire. Laughing, the old gunfighter took his time and picked his shots while his body was soaking up lead from the badly shaken TF men. Foley's old body had soaked up a lot of lead in its time, and he knew he could take three or four shots and still stay upright in his boots. Foley, who had helped tame more towns than most people had ever been in, died with his boots on, his back to a wall, and his guns spitting out death. He killed all six of the TF gunslicks.

Toot Tooner, his hands full of Colts, calmly walked into what was left of the Blue Dog Saloon, through the back door, and said, "I declare this here game of poker open. Call or fold, boys."

Then he opened fire.

His first shots ended the brief but bloody careers of two cattle rustlers from New Mexico who had signed on with the TF spread in search of what Tilden had promised would be easy money. They died without having the opportunity to fire a shot.

Toot took a .45 slug in the side and it spun him around. Lifting his pistol, he shot the man who had shot him between the eyes just as he felt a hammer blow in his back, left side. The gunshot knocked him to his knees and he tasted blood in his mouth.

Toot dropped his empty Colts and pulled out two Remington .44s from behind his gun belt. Hard hit, dying, Toot laughed at death and began cocking and firing as the light before his eyes began to fade.

"Somebody kill the old son of a bitch!" a TF gunhand shouted.

Toot laughed at the dim figure and swung his guns. A slug took him in the gut and set him back on his butt. But

Toot's last shots cleared the Blue Dog of hired guns. He died with a very faint smile on his face.

Louis Longmont met several TF gun hands in an alley. The gambler never stopped walking as his Colts spat and sang a death song. Reloading, he stepped over the sprawled bloody bodies and walked on up the alley. A bullet tugged at the sleeve of his coat and the gambler dropped to one knee, raised both guns, and shot the rifleman off the roof of the bank building. A bullet knocked Louis to one side and his left arm grew numb. Hooking the thumb of his left hand behind his gun belt, the gambler rose and triggered off a round, sending another one of Tilden Franklin's gun slicks to hell.

Louis then removed a white linen handkerchief from an inside breast pocket of his tailored jacket. He plugged the hole in his shoulder and continued on his hunt.

The Reverend Ralph Morrow stepped into what had been the saloon of Big Mama and the bidding place of her soiled doves and began working the lever on his Henry .44. The boxer-turned-preacher-turned-farmer-turned-gunfighter muttered a short prayer for God to forgive him and began blasting hell out of any TF gun hawks he could find.

His Henry empty, Ralph jerked out a pair of .45s and began smoking. A lousy pistol shot, and that is being kind, Ralph succeeded in filling the beery air with a lot of hot lead. He didn't hit a damn thing with the pistols, but he did manage to scare the hell out of those gun hands left standing after his good shooting with the rifle. They ran out the front of the saloon and directly into the guns of Pistol Le Roux and Dan Greentree.

Ralph reloaded his rifle and stepped to the front of the building. "Exhilarating!" he exclaimed. Then he hit the floor as a hard burst of gunfire from a rooftop across the street tore through the canvas and wood of the deserted whorehouse.

"Shithead!" Ralph muttered, lifting his rifle and sighting the gunman in. Ralph pulled the trigger and knocked the TF gunman off the roof.

Steve Matlock, Ray Johnson, Nolan, Mike Garrett, and Beaconfield were keeping a dozen or more TF gun slicks pinned down in Beeker's general store.

Charlie Starr had cleared a small saloon of half a dozen hired guns and now sat at a table, having a bottle of sweetened soda water. He would have much preferred a glass of beer, but the sweet water beat nothing. Seeing a flash of movement across the street, Charlie put down the bottle and picked up a cocked .45 from the table. He sighted the TF gun hand in and pulled the trigger. The slug struck the man in the shoulder and spun him around. Charlie shot him again in the belly, and that ended it.

"Now leave me alone and let me finish my sodie water," Charlie muttered.

The Silver Dollar Kid came face-to-face with Silver Jim. The old gunfighter grinned at the punk. Both men had their guns in leather.

"All right, Kid," Silver Jim said. "You been lookin' for a rep. Here's your chance."

The Silver Dollar Kid grabbed for his guns.

He never cleared leather. Silver Jim's guns roared and bucked in his callused hands. The Kid felt twin hammer blows in his stomach. He sat down in the alley and began hollering for his mother.

Silver Jim stepped around the punk and continued his prowling. The Kid's hollering faded as life ebbed from him.

Smoke met Luis Chamba behind the stable. The Mexican gunfighter grinned at him. "Now, Smoke, we see just how good you really are."

Smoke lifted his sawed-off shotgun and almost blew the gunfighter in two. "I already know how good I am," Smoke said. "I don't give a damn how good you . . . were."

Smoke reloaded the ten-gauge sawed-off and stepped into a stable. He heard a rustling above him and lifted the twin muzzles. Pulling the triggers, blowing a hole the size of a bucket in the boards, Smoke watched as a man, or what was left of a man, hurled out the loft door to come splatting onto the shit-littered ground.

Smoke let the shotgun fall to the straw as the gunfighter Valentine faced him.

"I'm better," Valentine said, his hands over the butts of his guns.

"I doubt it," Smoke said, then shot the famed gunfighter twice in the belly and chest.

With blood streaking his mouth, Valentine looked up from the floor at Smoke. "I . . . didn't even clear leather."

"You sure didn't," the young man said. "We all got to meet him, Valentine, and you just did."

"I reckon." Then he died.

Listening, Smoke cocked his head. Something was very wrong. Then it came to him. No gunfire. It was over.*

"Jiminy," Cal whispered as Puma finished his story. Then Cal punched Pearlie in the shoulder, giving him a hard look. "Why didn't you tell me about that, you skunk?"

Pearlie blushed. "Shucks, Cal. I didn't do much, Smoke and the mountain men did most of the fightin'."

Louis Longmont stood and stretched. "Puma, you oughta write penny dreadfuls, the way you embellish a story so."

Puma looked up through slitted eyes. "I don't know what that word means, but I hope fer yore sake it don't mean what I think it do!"

Monte laughed. "No, Puma, he just means you tell a hell of a fine tale."

*Trail of the Mountain Man

Smoke stepped out of his saddle and pulled on his dally rope, bringing the horse with the unconscious ambusher forward. They had slung him over the saddle and tied his hands to his feet under the bronc's belly.

When Joey cut him down and rolled him over onto his back in the dirt, Pearlie said, "Jesus, what happened to his face? A mule kick him?"

Smoke grinned. "No, it was just Joey's fist."

Louis called out to the ranch house, "André, some coffee for Smoke and Joey, please." He looked at the blood-splattered shirts and dirt-covered faces of his two friends. "You two look like you've had an eventful ride back from town."

Smoke nodded. "Monte, would you see if you can wake that galoot up while Joey and I wash up? Then we'll see if he can give us any useful information about the size of Murdock's new gang."

Chapter 17

Smoke's friends were arranged around the campfire when he and Joey finished washing the outlaws' blood off their faces and hands and changed clothes.

Smoke walked outside to stand over the man whose face Joey had smashed. He was conscious, tied hand and foot, and squirming on the ground, looking around at the unfriendly faces surrounding him.

"What's your name, cowboy?" Smoke asked, his tone neutral, neither friendly nor angry.

"Moses, Moses Jackson," the gunny answered, blood still trickling from his bent, shattered nose.

"Want to tell me why you and your friends were out there waiting to bushwhack Joey and me?"

"We weren't gonna kill you, we was just gonna—" He stopped, evidently in too much pain to think up a good lie.

"Uh-huh," Joey growled, "you was jest sittin' there, guns cocked and aimed, waitin' to blow us to hell."

Moses lowered his eyes, moaning softly when movement caused his pain to flare.

"Did Murdock send you out to do us in?"

"I ain't sayin' anything else. Go on and get the sheriff and have him take me to jail."

"So that bastard Sam Murdock can let you escape? I don't think we'll send for him just yet," Smoke said, his tone becoming harder.

Puma Buck, his eyes feral in reflected firelight, stepped up to stand practically on top of the young man. "If he's not gonna talk, Smoke, let me skin 'im." He cast cold, furious eyes down at the gunman. "I ain't skinned nobody fer two, maybe three years now, but I'm damned if'n I've forgotten how to git the job done."

Moses' eyes widened at the sight of the old mountain man holding his sharp blade before him. Moses twisted his head around to look up at Smoke. "You can't let that old coot near me. I know my rights."

Joey squatted on his heels next to Moses' head. "You gotta right ta die, boy, that's all. The manner o' yore death is all we gotta decide now." He raised his eyes to stare at Puma's big buffalo-skinning knife. "Personally, as the galoot ya was fixin' ta back-shoot, I kinda like the idee of lettin' old Puma have his way with ya, 'specially since ya don't seem inclined ta tell us nothin' anyhow."

Monte leaned over the wounded man, eyes squinted and mean. "Skinnin's too good for him. Let's just scalp him, cut off his ears and dick, and send him back to Murdock." He grinned. "I'm sure they'll welcome him back with open arms, since he failed in his mission."

"You can't do that!" Moses hollered, twisting against his ropes. "Vasquez'll chop me to bits if you send me back." He looked from man to man, his eyes hopeful. "Just let me go and I'll ride out of Colorado and you'll never see me again."

Smoke chuckled low in his throat. "Cowboy, you're a confessed killer and back-shooter. Why would we let you ride off to hire out your gun and murder somebody else?"

"I swear, I'll put my guns up and never ever shoot anybody again."

At this, everyone around the fire laughed. The man obviously would say anything to save his worthless hide. They had all seen Sunday-morning drunks hung over after getting alkalied on Saturday night swear off booze. This was no different.

Puma placed his knife against Moses' chest and cut his shirt buttons off with a gentle movement. "Hmmm, looks like my old blade is a mite rusty and dull. That'll make skinnin' him awful tough. I might even have to take a rest in the middle o' the job 'fore I'm done and git back to it later."

"No, no, please . . ."

Smoke leaned over, his hands on his knees, staring down at Moses. "Then tell us what you know about Murdock's plans. How many men he has, when he plans to hit us, and who he's got riding with him."

Moses licked blood-caked lips, his eyes flicking from Puma's knife to Smoke and back again. "If I tell you what I know, will ya let me go?"

Smoke pursed his lips, appearing to consider the offer. "If what you have to say helps us, then I'll promise you we won't kill you. But"—he pointed his finger at the man—"if I let you ride out of here in one piece and I ever see you wearing a gun again, I swear I'll shoot you down without a second thought. Deal?"

Moses nodded vigorously. "Murdock's got at least forty or fifty men out at his ranch now, and more may be on the way." He glanced at Joey and Smoke. "I guess the chance to make a name by killin' you and Mr. Wells has attracted a whole bunch of hard men."

Joey smirked. "Havin' a chance to do it don't always git it done, son. Go on."

"Well, Murdock don't let the hired hands in on his plans, but I figger from the way he's talking, he is going to send his men out here to the ranch if he can't get you any other way. He's mighty pissed about you gunning down his brother."

Smoke nodded. "Any idea of when he plans to call the raid?"

Moses shook his head. "Like I said, I'm way down on the totem pole, and he don't confide in me. But he did mention he was afraid if he waited overly long, the U.S. marshals would be called in, and he sure don't want that to happen."

Louis spoke up from the edge of the firelight. "You know any names of the gents riding with him?"

"Lord, you want me to name 'em all?"

"As many as you can remember," Smoke answered, and nodded at Louis, who took a small tablet from his coat pocket and a silver-encased pencil to write the names down with.

"Well, there's a group of about eight or ten who said they owed you from when they went up in the mountains after you a couple o' years ago. They kinda hang together, always talking about how badly you treated 'em. Couple of 'em have some awful scars on their faces where they said you beat the shit out of 'em."

Smoke nodded. "That'd be the men riding with Curly Rogers. Dewey and Boots are the ones wearing scars on their faces from the last time I . . . had a talk with them. Horton, Max, Cates, Gooden, and Art South are the others I suspect have come to get their revenge after they failed to get the bounty on me during the Lee Slater mixup. Continue, Moses."

"There's a handful of half-breeds, Jake Sixkiller, Sam Silverwolf, and Jed Beartooth. They hang with a couple of Mexes name of Felix Salazar and Juan Jimenez, who said you boys killed some kin of theirs at the hotel in town the other night."

"Uh-huh, go on."

"Then there's some real bad hombres, those with a reputation already who aim to make their place in history, so they say. The Silverado Kid, Black Jack Morton, Bill Denver, One-Eye Jackson, and Slim Watkins." He paused and licked his lips again. "I think even Murdock and Vasquez are afraid of those gunmen."

Monte raised his eyebrows and looked at Joey, who was frowning. They had all heard of these men, murderers, rapists, robbers, and killers every one. Men who enjoyed killing and maiming, whether for profit or just for the fun of it.

Moses inclined his head toward Puma. "There's even one like him, an old . . . an elderly man dressed all in buckskins and fur who looks older than dirt, with long, shaggy gray hair and beard. He says he's a mountain man named Beaverpelt Solomon, and he wants a chance to kill some other man's kid, man name of Preacher."

Smoke glanced at Puma, whose face was red with anger. "That old bastard!" he exclaimed. "He once stole some beaver pelts from Preacher. Preacher beat the shit out of him and hung that moniker on 'im to let everyone know he was a thieving son of a bitch." He smiled savagely. "It worked, too, wouldn't nobody have nothin' to do with him after that." He looked off toward the mountain peaks in the distance. "The high lonesome can git mighty lonesome if'n even yore so-called friends won't palaver with ya once in a while, an' Beaverpelt wasn't welcome at anybody else's camps after Preacher put the word out on 'im."

"Any others?" Smoke asked Moses.

"Just Shotgun Sam Willowby and Gimpy Monroe. They're kinda old too, but they still know how to draw and fire. To hear them tell it, they was killin' people back in the gold rush days of forty-eight. The other day, a couple of the younger ones made the mistake of calling them old farts, and they blowed them to hell without even breaking a sweat." Moses' eyes were wide. "Then they put ropes on the bodies and dragged 'em out in the pasture for coyotes and wolves to eat!"

Smoke shook his head at the number of guns Murdock had been able to hire and the speed with which they'd all come to Colorado. "That about it?"

"Oh, there's a passel more, but not any other big names, just a bunch of men like me, trying to make a living the only way they know, from hiring out their guns. A group of men who fought down in New Mexico and Arizona during the time of the Lincoln County war. Pretty hard old boys, I suspect, but they keep to themselves and aren't much for bragging or fighting with the others." He hesitated, then said, "Oh, there's one other man. Wears an old Union Army uniform coat and carries a sword on his belt. Says his name's Colonel Waters and he has a debt to pay to Joey Wells."

Joey smiled, but there was no warmth in it. "He was with the Redlegs who killed my men. He's the only one I couldn't track down. I was told he changed his name and moved back east to get away from me." His grin faded and his eyes turned snake hard. "Guess he got tired of runnin' and is ready to face his maker, and I intend to oblige him."

Smoke said, "That all you can tell us, Moses?"

"That's all I know, Mr. Jensen, honest."

"Put him on his horse, boys, but keep his guns and ammunition."

As Cal untied Moses, Smoke put his hand on his shoulder and stared into his eyes. "Just making sure I remember your face, son, 'cause if I ever see it again, you're a dead man. Now, get out of my sight.''

"Thank you, Mr. Jensen, thank you," Moses said as he stepped into his saddle.

Puma waved his knife at the man. "Smoke's a generous man, Moses, don't you ever forget how close you came to tastin' my steel.''

After Moses rode off at full gallop in case they changed their minds, Smoke poured himself a cup of coffee from a pot Puma had sitting on the campfire embers. He took a drink and looked around at his men, his expression grim.

"Boys, this doesn't sound at all good.''

Monte nodded. "Murdock's sure got himself some prize shooters, that's for sure.''

Louis said, "I've heard of some of them, of course, the Silverado Kid and Black Jack Morton got run out of Tombstone a year or so ago. Evidently they were too mean for even that hellhole.''

Monte added, "Yeah, it's said they killed women and kids, anybody who angered 'em, and they was easy to anger, so I've heard.''

Smoke lit a cigar and puffed as he talked, the smoke whisked away on a cold wind blowing from the mountains. "The bunch riding with Curly Rogers are mean and won't hesitate to back-shoot a man, but they're not overly endowed with either courage or intelligence. Bill Denver and Slim Watkins made their name in the mining country of northern Colorado and New Mexico. There's paper out on them for robbing stages, trains, and miners. They killed without warning and without provocation, according to the newspaper accounts. They have ropes waiting for them in more than twenty towns I know of.''

Monte said, "I ain't heard of but two of the half-breeds, Sam Silverwolf and Jed Beartooth, and they're both wanted in Arizona. Seems they like to rape women to death, mostly

Indian women, or they wouldn't be alive to give us grief. I never read nor heard anything of Jake Sixkiller."

Cal said, "I have. Ned Buntline wrote a piece about him a few months ago in one of my dime novels. Sixkiller likes to use a shotgun loaded with nails and rocks and stuff, and then, if anybody's still alive, he scalps 'em." He frowned. "Buntline said he stayed mostly in California, but I guess he came east to get away from his reputation out there."

"What about Beaverpelt, Puma? He anything special to worry about?" Smoke asked.

"Not if you're armed and facin' him," the mountain man said with a look of disgust and loathing on his face. "He's a sneak and a coward. But he's supposed to be pretty good with an old Sharps .52 he carries. He's the only one we have to worry about doin' us any damage from a distance." He looked down at his knife and wiped it on his pants. "Let me take care of that ol' buzzard. It'd be my pleasure to finish what Preacher started years ago."

Smoke drained the last of his coffee from his mug. "I got an idea."

Louis smiled. "About time, boss. What is on your mind?"

Smoke glanced at Joey. "Joey, what is the last thing a commander with an overwhelming superiority in numbers and firepower expects the opposing army to do?"

Joey grinned and nodded. "Attack."

"How about we even up our odds a little?"

Monte's brow furrowed. "You can't mean we're gonna ride against Murdock and fifty men? That'd be suicide! They'd cut us down like autumn wheat."

"A frontal assault's not exactly what I had in mind. Sally brought some books back from her last trip out east to visit her parents. They were about some Japanese fighters called ninjas."

"What are ninjas?" Pearlie asked.

Louis answered in a thoughtful tone, his eyes on Smoke. "Individuals who swore allegiance to the warlords of feudal

Japan, the shōgun. Ninja were called 'invisible killers' because they dressed all in black, attacked at night, and killed without being seen or heard, using their hands and short swords called *katana* on their victims.''

Smoke grinned. ''Exactly. We're about to become American ninjas.''

Chapter 18

Smoke said to his friends gathered around the campfire, "Here's what we're going to do. Joey, Puma, and me will infiltrate Murdock's compound. Louis, you and Monte and Cal and Pearlie are going to stay back a couple of miles from Murdock's ranch house to hold our horses and give us cover in case we have to make tracks out of there in a hurry. If they come chasing us, they'll ride right into your bullets without expecting an ambush."

Louis frowned. "How come you and Joey and Puma get to have all the fun while the rest of us stay on the outskirts of the action?"

"Because, you young pup," Puma said, "Joey learned how to sneak around enemy camps in the war, and Smoke and I learned how to injun up on people from the best teachers they is, mountain men."

Smoke put his hand on Louis's shoulder and said, "Puma's right, Louis. I know you're not afraid of the devil himself, and you're a hell of a shootist in a gunfight. In fact, there isn't a man I'd rather have on my right hand in a fracas than you. But this is different. One mistake, one inadvertent noise, one slipup, and you not only get *yourself* killed, but all of us. That's why I'm leaving you the to the job you can do best, protecting our backs with your guns.''

Louis held up his hands, smiling. ''Okay, okay, you don't have to shine me on. I agree I haven't your experience in sneaking around at night and being quiet like a ninja, but at the first sound of gunfire, I'm not waiting to see if you come out of there, I'm coming in after you!''

''Me too,'' chimed in Monte.

Smoke nodded. ''Fair enough. That okay with the rest of you—Cal, Pearlie?''

Pearlie nodded and Cal said, ''Yes, sir, but I feel like Mr. Longmont. I'd rather be with you when you go in.''

Pearlie jabbed him with an elbow, frowning.

''Well, I would,'' Cal said, rubbing his arm.

''I know you would, Cal, but this doesn't mean you're going to miss out on the action. Believe me, after we stir up this hornet's nest, there'll be enough fighting for all of us.''

When he finished talking, Smoke went into the cabin and came out with a can of bootblack. ''Here, all of you smear this over any skin showing. Also, I want you to take off anything that sparkles or makes noise, don't wear any spurs or metal that will clank or make a sound. Joey, I've got an extra pair of moccasins you can wear when we sneak into their camp.''

''What about us?'' Monte asked. ''Why do we have to blacken our faces if we're not gonna be near the ranch house?''

Smoke said, ''All of us need to do this. When there's a potential for a night fight, it never hurts to be prepared. Remember, they can't hit what they can't see, and remember how sound carries over open ground.''

He looked at Pearlie. "You have that burlap sack I asked you to get for me?"

The young man nodded.

"Did you do what I asked you to do?"

"Yeah, I did it, but, boss, I gotta tell ya, I thought you was crazy."

Smoke grinned. "You see why, now?"

"I think so, an' I'm sure glad I'm on your side." He went over to the barn and returned a moment later with a large burlap sack with a cord tying off its opening. The bag had a lump in the bottom that writhed and moved on its own.

Joey's eyes lit up. "That what I think it is?"

"Yeah," Smoke answered.

"Whoo-eee, there's gonna be dancin' at Murdock's place tonight."

As they mounted up, Smoke said, "Remember, the object tonight isn't a high body count, the object is to spread fear. A scared man will frighten others, his fear spreading like a plague. A dead man is just dead."

Joey snorted. " 'Course, a dead man cain't shoot ya neither."

On the way to Murdock's, Smoke stopped his group at the edge of his property and alerted the three men serving as sentries that they might be riding hard when they returned and not to fire on them inadvertently.

Smoke signaled his riders to a halt on a crest of a small rise, about two miles from Murdock's ranch house. It was a measure of Murdock's overconfidence in his superior numbers that he hadn't bothered to post guards.

Smoke put his field glasses to his eyes and swept the area for a moment. "I don't see anything between us and the ranch house. There's no sign of dogs or sentries."

Joey shook his head. "The man is dumb beyond belief."

"I guess he figures those desperadoes will protect him from harm," Louis said.

Smoke grinned in the darkness. "Well, we'll see about that shortly."

Smoke, Joey, and Puma dismounted, handing their reins to Louis and Monte, while Cal and Pearlie found some low rocks on the hillock to get behind. Louis made the mistake of asking Puma if he was going to be okay to walk the distance to the house.

Puma glared at him for a moment, then just smiled. "Yeah, an' I kin do it with ya on my back if'n I need to, young'un."

The trio took off toward Murdock's at a fast walk, estimating it would take them about twenty minutes to cover the two miles, being careful not to make any noise. Luckily, the fall skies were full of low-hanging storm clouds and the moon was already set for the night, so there was no light to give them away.

Murdock had two large corrals on the far side of his house, and both were full of mounts. Joey whispered he estimated there to be least fifty horses, maybe more.

The area around the house was quiet, and the bunkhouse was off on the other side of the corrals, almost two hundred yards from the ranch house. Smoke pointed to an area nearer the house, where there were several groups of widely spaced campfires burned down to glowing embers. He cupped his hands around his mouth and whispered, "The regular punchers are probably in the bunkhouse. I think the gun hawks are around the fires, sleeping outside."

The American ninjas noted there were five or six blanket-covered forms around each of the dying fires. Puma whispered, "I count twelve camps. There must be over sixty men down there."

Joey answered in a low voice, "That means either Moses was lyin' or more men have joined up in the last day or so."

Smoke nodded at Joey and motioned to the group of

camps on the left with an outstretched arm. He touched Puma and pointed to the right, then, as they eased off, Smoke took the middle collection of sleepers.

Smoke walked slowly, shuffling his feet in the dirt so he would not step on a twig or stick, and walked crouched over so as not to highlight himself against the horizon.

When he came to the closest of the sleeping outlaws, he put his sack down, placed his hand over the man's mouth, and sliced the blade of his Bowie knife quickly across his throat. The outlaw bucked and struggled for a moment, Smoke holding him down until he quieted, drowned in his own blood.

Smoke then made an incision around his head and pulled the killer's scalp free from his skull. He and Puma and Joey had agreed to kill only one man in each small camp, showing the others it could just have easily been them. He flipped the scalp onto the embers of the fire, where it began to slowly sizzle and burn. He then stepped to the next man and gently wrapped a rawhide thong around his boots, tying them together. A few feet farther on, he slipped a man's gun out of his holster, flipped open the loading gate, and emptied his shells in the dirt next to the fire, close to red-hot coals. Crawling to the next slumbering form, Smoke slit his belt and pants button with his Bowie knife. At the end of this group of men, Smoke opened the end of his sack and shook out one of its inhabitants, then quickly walked to the next camp, fifteen yards away, to repeat his actions.

Puma was overjoyed to find in his second group the mountain man known as Beaverpelt Solomon. He didn't want the thief and killer to die without knowing who did it, so Puma grabbed his mouth and pricked him lightly under the chin with the point of his skinning knife.

Beaverpelt's eyes started to open, then widened in surprise as he recognized Puma's blackened face leaning close to his in the darkness, the old man's eyes glittering white with hate. Puma held his knife where Beaverpelt could see it, whispering low in his ear, "Preacher and Smoke send their regards." As Beaverpelt reached up to grab Puma's hand, Puma sliced quickly across the mountain man's throat. He held on tight, staring into Beaverpelt's face until both light and life died in his eyes.

Not content with merely scalping the traitor to the mountain men, Puma also slit his pants open and cut off his genitals, sticking them in his mouth to protrude obscenely from his beard.

Puma, like Smoke, unloaded many of the sleeping men's weapons and sprinkled bullets near the red-hot embers, knowing it wouldn't be long before they heated up enough to explode, sending slugs of lead flying everywhere.

Joey didn't scalp his last victim. After he was dead, he put his Arkansas Toothpick behind the man's neck and jerked quickly upward. The razor-sharp blade sliced through skin, vertebrae, and windpipe, severing the head from its body. Joey found a long stick next to the fire and impaled the head on it, its lifeless eyes looking nowhere. He stuck the other end in the dirt, to stand like a sentinel next to the man's headless body.

When Joey and Puma were through, Smoke went silently among all the camps, depositing some of his burlap-sack cargo in each one.

He trotted back to them, in a hurry now because the burning scalps were beginning to make a terrible stench. The trio quickly walked for fifty yards, then stopped. They turned their backs to the camps so their lights wouldn't be seen, and Joey and Puma struck lucifers and lit cigars. Holding out the red-hot tips, they all lit fuses to bundles of dynamite and lobbed them into the camps, using the ones with longer fuses first and the shorter fuses last.

After they had thrown all they had, the three men began to jog away at a ground-eating pace toward the rise where their friends waited. About halfway there, they were met by Louis, leading their horses. As they climbed into their saddles, the bundles of dynamite began to explode, and men began to scream and shout. Guns were fired at shadows and at comrades, thought to be enemies in the darkness.

In one of the camps, Charlie Jacobson rolled over and stretched, yawning. His outstretched hand encountered something wet and sticky next to him. He leaned over toward Billy Preston, his riding partner, and gagged at what he saw. He opened his mouth to scream just as all hell broke loose around him.

A packet of two sticks of dynamite tied together exploded fifteen feet away, tearing bark off a nearby pine tree and sending razor-sharp shards of wood spinning through the night to impale Charlie's face and chest. Now he screamed as if his lungs would rupture.

Johnny Blackman jumped to his feet and started to run as dynamite went off behind him. He took one step, and his tied-together feet locked, sending him sprawling facefirst into the campfire embers. As he rolled away, red-hot bullet casings near the fire exploded, sending molten chunks of lead into Johnny's body in three places, killing him where he lay. His clothes, covered with embers, caught fire, and his flesh began to char and roast, adding to the horrible stink of burning scalps.

Willie Clayton rolled over at the first blast of dynamite and covered his head with his hands. As the echoes of the blast died down, he looked up, straight into the dead eyes of a head on a stick, staring sightless down at him. His mind snapped and he jumped to his feet, drew his pistol, and began to fire indiscriminately around at anything he saw moving. After he shot two of his camp mates, the third put a bullet into Willie to save his own life.

Felix Salazar jumped to his feet, his pistol in his hand.

As he tried to run, his pants fell down and tripped him, to land squirming on his friend Juan Jimenez. Jimenez, frightened out of his wits, slashed his long stiletto blade into Salazar, ripping his abdomen open and spilling his guts in the dirt.

Jake Sixkiller's life ended when a packet of dynamite thrown by Joey landed two feet from his sleeping form. He rose when he heard the sputtering fuse and reached to grab it as it went off. It blew his right arm off at the shoulder, and the force of the explosion made pulp of his eyes and mincemeat of his face. The killer of women and children rolled in the dirt in blind agony, screaming for the mercy of a God he had always denied existed, until he bled to death.

Dewey, the man whose face Smoke had caved in and ruined, scrabbled on his hands and knees until he was up against a tree, which he hugged for dear life. As he sat there, something crawled across his leg. Terrified, Dewey brushed it away with his hand. He felt a sharp stinging in his palm, and jerked it back. The rattler whose fangs were embedded in his hand came with it, flying through the air to wrap around Dewey's neck, where it again sank its fangs directly into his jugular vein. When the poison hit Dewey's brain, he began to jerk and dance in a seizure, biting his tongue completely in two, drooling and snapping his jaws until his teeth broke off. He died within three minutes of the first bite.

By now, fire-heated bullets were exploding like strings of firecrackers, drilling men in arms, stomachs, legs, and heads. Over ten men were killed and another fifteen wounded by the dynamite and bullets, either from the fire or from their compatriots, who were shooting in terror at anything that moved.

Smoke and his men sat on the rise, watching the chaos they had caused, laughing at the antics of the screaming, hollering men below when they discovered the Colorado diamondback rattlers Smoke had unleashed in their midst. More than one man shot his foot off that night trying to kill the vicious reptiles, and two actually died from snake-bite and fear.

Finally, as dawn approached, Smoke and his friends rode back to the Rocking C ranch, satisfied with a good night's work.

Vasquez and Murdock finally got their men to calm down and stop shooting each other. Torches and lanterns were lit, and they began to try to make sense of what had happened.

Murdock stood with his hands on his hips, looking around at the mess, and at the dead, dying, and wounded desperadoes he had hired.

"Goddamn that Jensen and Wells!" He grabbed Vasquez by the arm. "Just look at what they've done!"

"Señor, try to calm yourself," Vasquez said, peeling Murdock's grasping fingers from his arm. "It is over for now."

"But, how . . . when . . ."

"I told you we should have guards posted," the Mexican said, shaking his head. "Those hombres are loco, they do not know fear."

"But I've got sixty men here. Who would try and attack when they're so outnumbered?"

"You no have sixty men anymore, señor. Maybe half . . ."

"Fuck the men! There's another fifteen coming in the next few days, we'll just wait for them to get here, then I'm gonna make those bastards pay for this."

"I wonder why they didn't kill more men?"

"What do you call that?" Murdock fairly screamed, pointing at the number of men lying dead or wounded.

Vasquez shook his head. "They were here among us, they could kill many more if they wanted."

Murdock just shook his head. "They killed enough, and

wounded plenty more. Now I'm gonna have to put off killin' 'em until I get some reinforcements, and some of these men need time to heal.''

Only when the sun came up did Murdock realize how badly his men had been demoralized. After the wounded were carried inside and attended to, and the dead stacked in a row behind the house, another seven men packed up their gear and prepared to ride off.

Murdock and Vasquez stood before the men as they sat on their horses. ''Why are you men leaving? We'll have plenty more gun hands in a couple of days and then we'll take out Jensen and Wells and their entire force.''

Black Jack Morton said, ''Mr. Murdock, you don't understand what happened last night. The man lying next to me was gutted and scalped, and my gun was emptied and put back in my holster.'' He shook his head. ''They coulda just slit all our throats and we'd never have known what hit us.''

The man sitting next to him, famous as a fearless fighter in the New Mexico range wars, said, ''They was sendin' us a message. They was tellin' us they're not afraid of us, an' they kin kill us anytime they want to.'' He jerked his horse's reins around. ''An' I fer one believe 'em. Yore money's no good to a dead man, Mr. Murdock. I'll see ya around, maybe.'' With that final word, the seven men galloped off, straight west, to avoid both Pueblo and Smoke Jensen's ranch.

Chapter 19

Murdock paced angrily around his study, scowling and cursing as he sipped his bourbon. "Goddammit, I want to kill that Smoke Jensen and Joey Wells so bad, I can taste it. I knew they were gonna be trouble the minute I laid eyes on them!"

Vasquez was sitting on a couch against a far wall, leaned back with his feet crossed on a small table, smoking a cigar and watching smoke curl toward the ceiling. "You know, Señor Murdock, I think you were right what you tole Emilio. That Wells will never rest until he kill me. I think I plenty glad we have more men coming soon."

Murdock shook his head. "I wish they were already here. If they don't get here in the next day or two, I'm afraid more of our men will leave. That raid last night really spooked them."

Murdock stopped pacing long enough to bend over his desk and pluck a cigar out of his humidor. He ran it under his nose, inhaling its rich aroma, then lit it with a lucifer, rotating it so it would burn evenly. As smoke billowed around his head, he pointed the stogie at Vasquez like a pistol. "Emilio, I want you to watch the men real close. If any of 'em start talkin' about leaving, you got to stop 'em quick, make an example of 'em." He raised his eyebrows. "You understand what I'm saying?"

"*Sí, señor.* We must make them understand they are to be more afraid of me than of the gringos, Wells, or Jensen."

Murdock, braver now that he had some bourbon under his belt, sat one hip on the edge of his desk. "You put a bridle on your men for a week or two, let the dust settle a bit, then we'll deal with Mr. Jensen and Mr. Wells once and for all!"

Over the next few days Joey drilled the punchers they had hired unmercifully, trying to teach them in a short while what it had taken him years to learn about guerrilla warfare. Soon he began to seem less grim and even smiled occasionally. "Smoke, I never woulda believed it, but them boys are makin' real progress." He grinned. "They ain't ever gonna be pistoleers, but at least they ain't gonna shoot themselves in the foot if'n somebody draws down on 'em."

Smoke gripped his shoulder. "That's because they have a good teacher, Joey. You're the best man with a short gun I've ever seen!"

"Well," Joey said, blushing, "I don't know 'bout that, but ever one o' these boys have got some hair. I wished I'd o' had 'em ridin' with me agin those Kansas Redlegs."

Smoke smiled. "Oh? I heard you did all right all by yourself, Joey."

Joey shrugged, smiled, and went out to drill the hands some more. After he left, Smoke and his friends got busy setting up the defenses around the ranch house he had planned against the raid they all knew was coming. Puma Buck, not one to sit around and wait for trouble, took off alone to roam the hills and woods surrounding Murdock's ranch. He would alert Smoke to any movements there signaling preparations for an attack.

When all preparations were made, Smoke dynamited the rocks above the river running through his ranch, blocking its flow down to Murdock's spread. Within two days Murdock and Ben Tolson rode out to the ranch house.

Smoke told Louis and Monte Carson to stay out of sight and walked out to meet the two riders. "Howdy, Ben. What can I do for you?"

Tolson, a half smile on his face, pointed to Murdock. "Mr. Murdock here has lodged a complaint against you, Smoke. He says you've blocked off the water to his ranch."

Smoke frowned. "Oh? And if I have, Ben, is that against the law?"

Murdock's face purpled in rage. He pointed his finger at Smoke. "Jensen, you son of a bitch, I know my rights! That riverbed runs through my place, and I got the right to use any water in it to feed my herd!"

Smoke shrugged. "Why, I reckon you're correct, Mr. Murdock, and you're certainly welcome to use any water that comes onto your property." He smiled. "Trouble is, the river must have eroded the walls of a canyon where it comes through my spread. Seems some boulders fell and dammed up the river." He glanced at Tolson and winked. "I don't see how I can be held accountable for forces of nature."

Murdock looked at Tolson. "Sheriff," he almost shouted, "that ain't all. The other night Jensen and Wells rode onto my place and killed and wounded a bunch of my hands. I want him arrested for murder!"

Tolson glanced at Smoke. "Well, what do you say, Smoke?"

Smoke considered the two men, his face serious. "I sure hate to hear that your cowhands got shot up, Murdock." He raised his eyebrows. "Did anyone see who did it?"

Murdock glared hate at Smoke. "You know we didn't,

Jensen. The murdering bastards attacked us at night, while we were sleeping.''

Smoke spread his hands and shrugged. "If you didn't see the men who attacked you, I don't see how you can blame it on me." He smirked. "Maybe it was some of those Mexican and Indian gunslingers who rode on the town last week coming back to haunt you."

"Bullshit! I know it was you. You've shot up my men and now you're trying to kill my cattle by cutting off my water."

Smoke stared at the rancher, his eyes cold and hard. "Your cattle? Way I hear it, Murdock, there's some doubt about just whose cattle those are on your spread." He smiled, but there was no friendliness in his face. "Maybe we could have the sheriff and some of the other ranchers around here ride on over and take a close look at your brands, just to make sure none of them have been altered. While we're at it, we could also take a look at those cowboys that got killed and see if they're really punchers . . . or gun hawks who got only what they deserved."

"Why, you . . ." Murdock's hand fell toward his pistol, but Tolson laid a hand on his arm.

"I don't think you want to do that, Mr. Murdock." Tolson shook his head. "I don't fancy hauling your body all the way back into Pueblo draped across your horse."

Murdock took a deep breath and settled back in his saddle. Venom dripped from his voice as he said, "You haven't seen the last of me, Jensen."

Smoke's lips curled in a smirk. "No, I reckon not. But I am looking forward to the next time you come calling, Mr. Murdock. And you be sure to bring your friend Vasquez with you. Joey Wells wants to have a little . . . chat with him."

As Murdock jerked his reins and whirled his mount around to leave, Smoke said, "Ben, why don't you come in for a cup of coffee before you head back to town? There's an old friend of yours wants to say hello.''

Tolson watched Murdock ride off in a cloud of dust. He shook his head and climbed out of his saddle. ''I wouldn't underestimate that man, Smoke. He may be full of hot air, but he's had some mean ol' boys come ridin' through Pueblo headin' for his ranch the last couple of days.''

Smoke walked him to the house. ''I've got some hard men with me too, Ben.''

When he entered the room, Ben's eyes lit up and he broke into a wide grin. ''Monte Carson, you ol' son of a gun!''

The two men shook hands, clapping each other on the shoulder. ''What are you doing up here?'' Ben asked.

''Hell, I figured it'd been way too long since I had a palaver with my old sidekick, and when I heard my friend Smoke might be in need of help, I thought I could stand a little time off from sheriffing.''

''It's surely good to see you, partner. Been a long time since I had anybody interesting to swap lies with.''

André appeared in the door to the kitchen. ''Monsieur Tolson, would you care to join the other gentlemen for breakfast?''

Tolson glanced at the Frenchman and raised his eyebrows. ''Why, sure, long as Carson here didn't do none of the cooking. As I recollect, his biscuits an' fatback weren't fit for man nor beast.''

As they walked into the dining room, Monte introduced Louis and André to Tolson. Ben said. ''Longmont? I seem to remember a Longmont ran a saloon in Silver City a while back. That you?''

Louis smiled. ''Yes, sir. I had a small establishment there for a while, until the mines began to play out.''

André spooned heaping helpings of scrambled eggs mixed with chopped onions and hot peppers into their plates, and placed a platter of pancakes and blueberries in the middle of the table.

Tolson speared two flapjacks onto his plate and began to eat. Between bites he said, "Back then I was riding with Curly Bill Bodacious, and he told me you pulled up stakes after . . . a fracas involving one of the city officials."

Longmont nodded. "The mayor's son, actually. He was a headstrong, spoiled young man with an excess of money and a paucity of brains. He fancied the favors of a young . . . lady named Lilly Montez." Louis smiled in remembrance. "She was a beauty. Long, shiny black hair, pretty face and complexion, and legs that went from here to there. Evidently, she and young Boyd had a lovers' quarrel and she decided to make him jealous. She began to hang around my place, trying to interest me in her more obvious charms. About the only ladies I was interested in then were the four that reside in a deck of cards, so I declined her offer of companionship."

Smoke snorted. "That's the first time I've ever heard of you turning a lady down."

Louis shrugged. "I was younger then and intent on making my fortune. Anyway, Lilly complained to Boyd I had 'insulted her honor' and he felt compelled to call me out. . . ."

Louis picked up two gold double-eagles and flipped them nonchalantly into a pile of money in the middle of the poker table. "I'll see your bet, Clyde, and raise you a couple of eagles."

The batwings flew open and Boyd McAlister stormed into the saloon. He stood just inside the door for a moment, breathing hard. His wild eyes searched the room, lighting on Louis at his usual corner table. Hitching up his gun belt, he stomped over to stand across from Louis. "Longmont, I'm callin' you out!"

Louis glanced over the cards in his hand at the young firebrand. "I'm in the middle of a game here, Boyd. Why don't you go to the bar and have a beer. I'll be with you in a few minutes, and we can discuss whatever it is you have on your mind."

Boyd's face turned red. "There ain't nothin' to discuss, Longmont. You insulted Lilly, an' I'm gonna make you pay!"

Louis shrugged. "What's your hurry, boy? If you insist on this foolishness, you're going to be a long time dead. Another few minutes of life shouldn't matter one way or another." Louis looked away and said, "Now, Clyde. I've called and raised. You in or out?"

Beads of sweat formed on Clyde's face as he glanced nervously over his shoulder at Boyd. "Jesus, Louis," he whispered hoarsely, "don't you think . . . ?"

Louis removed his cigar from his mouth and studied its glowing tip. "I think, Clyde, that your two pair won't stand up against my hand. The question before us at the moment is, what do you think?"

Clyde carefully peeked at his hole card again. He had a pair of queens, an ace, and a ten showing faceup, and an ace in the hole. Louis had four hearts showing faceup. If he had a heart in the hole, his flush would beat Clyde's two pair and take the pot, over six hundred dollars.

Finally, Clyde flipped his cards over. "No, I think you got that flush, Louis. No need throwing good money after bad."

Louis raked in the pot with both hands, a wide grin on his face. "Good call, Clyde. You know I never bluff." He stacked coins and folded bills and stuffed them all in his pockets.

Across the room Boyd gulped his beer and yelled, "I'll be waitin' outside for you, Longmont."

Louis flipped a rawhide thong off the hammer of his Colt, tied down low on his right leg, saying, "I've never

seen anyone so eager to die." He walked toward the batwings. He glanced over his shoulder in time to see Clyde
turn over Louis's hole card. It was the deuce of clubs.

Clyde snorted. "A busted flush. Your hand was worthless."

"Like I said, Clyde, I *never* bluff . . . well, hardly ever."
Louis straightened his hat and squared his shoulders,
mumbling "No guts, no glory" to himself as he stepped
through the door into bright Colorado sunshine.

Boyd, with two of his friends flanking him, was standing
in the middle of the dirt street.

Louis stepped off the boardwalk and faced the men.
"Three against one. That makes the odds about even,"
he called. He nodded at the two cowboys with Boyd. "You
boys ready to die for your friend?"

Boyd glanced from side to side. "We ain't gonna die,
Longmont. We're gonna dust you through and through."

Louis shrugged and fastened his coat into the back of
his belt, out of the way of his draw. "You called this dance,
Boyd. Time someone has to pay the band. Make your play."

Four hands slapped leather simultaneously, and Colts
exploded, sending clouds of cordite gun smoke to blot
out the sun. Louis's first shot took Boyd in the chest,
punching out his back and throwing him backward. His
gun was still in its leather. Louis crouched a little and spun
to the right, cocking and firing in one lightning-fast move.
His second shot took the man on Boyd's left full in his
face, blowing teeth and blood into the air. He'd gotten
his gun out, but it was still pointed down. As the dying
man's finger twitched, his gun went off, blowing a hole in
his foot. The third cowboy got off a round that tore through
Louis's coat but missed flesh. Louis swung his gun and
cocked and fired a third time in less than three seconds,
hitting the puncher high in his chest, spinning him around
and dropping him facedown in the dirt.

Louis took a deep breath and holstered his Colt. He

walked to his horse, tied to a rail post nearby, and stepped into the saddle. Louis rode slowly out of town, never looking back.

As Louis finished his tale of the gunfight in Silver City, Cal, with eyes wide, said, "Gosh, Mr. Longmont, that must've been something to see!"

Louis stubbed out his cigar with a wry grin. "Well, Cal, gunfights are always more fun to watch than to participate in."

Joey nodded. "That's for damn sure."

Chapter 20

Puma Buck walked his horse slowly through underbrush and light forest timber in the foothills surrounding Murdock's spread. His mount was one they'd hired in Pueblo on arriving, and it wasn't as surefooted on the steep slopes as his paint pony back home was, so he was taking it easy and getting the feel of his new ride.

He kept a sharp lookout toward Murdock's ranch house almost a quarter of a mile below. He was going to make damned sure none of those *buscaderos* managed to get to drop on Smoke and his other new friends. He rode with his Sharps .52-caliber laid across his saddle horn, loaded and ready for immediate action.

Several times Puma had seen men ride up to the ranch house and enter, only to leave after a while, riding off toward herds of cattle, which could be seen on the horizon. Puma figured they were most likely the legitimate punchers Murdock had working his cattle, and not gun hawks he'd hired to take down Smoke and Joey. A shootist would rather take lead poisoning than lower himself to herd beeves.

Off to the side, Puma could barely make out the riverbed, dry now, that ran through Murdock's place. He could see on the other side of Murdock's ranch house a row of freshly dug graves. He grinned to himself, appreciating the graves, some of them his doing, and the way Smoke had deprived the man of water for his cattle and horses.

Puma knew that alone would prompt Murdock to make his move soon; he couldn't afford to wait and let his stock die of thirst.

As Puma pulled his canteen out and uncorked the top, ready to take a swig, he saw a band of fifteen or more riders burning dust toward the ranch house from the direction of Pueblo. Evidently they were additional men Murdock had hired to replace those he and Smoke and Joey had slain in their midnight raid.

"Uh-huh," he muttered. "I'll bet those *bandidos* are fixin' to put on the war paint and make a run over to Smoke's place."

He swung out of his saddle and crouched down behind a fallen tree, propping the big, heavy Sharps across the rough bark. He licked his finger and wiped the front sight with it, to make it stand out more when he needed it. He got himself into a comfortable position and laid out a box full of extra shells next to the gun on the tree within easy reach. He figured he might need to do some quick reloading when the time came.

After about ten minutes the gang of men Puma was observing arrived at the front of the ranch house, and two figures Puma took to be Murdock and Vasquez came out of the door to address them. He couldn't make out their faces at the distance, but they had an unmistakable air of authority about them.

As the rancher began to talk, waving his hands toward Smoke's ranch, Puma took careful aim, remembering he was shooting downhill and needed to lower his sights a bit, the natural tendency being to overshoot a target lower than you are.

He took a deep breath and held it, slowly increasing pressure on the trigger, so when the explosion came it would be a surprise and he wouldn't have time to flinch and throw his aim off.

The big gun boomed and shot a sheet of fire two feet out of the barrel, slamming back into Puma's shoulder and almost knocking his skinny frame over. Damn, he had almost forgotten how the big Sharps kicked when it delivered its deadly cargo.

The targets were a little over fifteen hundred yards from Puma, a long range even for the remarkable Sharps. It seemed a long time but was only a little over five seconds before one of the men on horseback was thrown from his mount to lie sprawled in the dirt. The sound was several seconds slower reaching the men, and by then Puma had jacked another round in the chamber and fired again. By the time the group knew they were being fired upon, two of their number were dead on the ground. Just as they ducked and whirled, looking for the location of their attacker, another was knocked off his bronc, his arm almost blown off by the big .52-caliber slug traveling at over two thousand feet per second.

The outlaws began to scatter, some jumping from their horses and running into the house, while others just bent over their saddle horns and burned trail dust away from the area. A couple of brave souls aimed rifles up the hill and fired, but the range was so far for ordinary rifles that Puma never even saw where the bullets landed.

Another couple of rounds fired into the house, one of which penetrated wooden walls, striking a man inside in the thigh, and Puma figured he had done enough for the time being. Now he had to get back to Smoke and tell him Murdock was ready to make his play, or would be as soon as he rounded up the men Puma had scattered all over the countryside.

Several of the riders had ridden toward Smoke's ranch and were now between Puma and home. "Well, shit, old beaver. Ya knew it was about time for ya ta taste some lead," he mumbled to himself. He packed his Sharps in his saddle boot and opened his saddlebags. He withdrew two Colt Army .44s to match the one in his holster and made sure they were all loaded up six and six, then stuffed the two extras in his belt. He tugged his hat down tight and eased up into the saddle, grunting with the effort.

Riding slow and careful, he kept to heavy timber until he came to a group of six men standing next to a drying riverbed, watering their horses in one of the small pools remaining.

There was no way to avoid them, so he put his reins in his teeth and filled both hands with iron. It was time to dance with the devil, and Puma was going to strike up the band. He kicked his mount's flanks and bent low over his saddle horn as he galloped out of the forest toward the gunnies below.

One of the men, wearing an eye patch, looked up in astonishment at the apparition wearing buckskins and war paint charging them, yelling and whooping and hollering as he rode like the wind.

"Goddamn, boys, it's that old mountain man!" One-Eye Jackson yelled as he drew his pistol.

All six men crouched and began firing wildly, frightened by the sheer gall of a lone horseman to charge right at them.

Puma's pistols exploded, spitting fire, smoke, and death ahead of him. Two of the gun slicks went down immediately, .44 slugs in their chests.

Another jumped into the saddle, turned tail, and rode like hell to get away from this madman who was bent on killing all of them.

One-Eye took careful aim and fired, his bullet tearing through Puma's left shoulder muscle, twisting his body and almost unseating him.

Puma straightened, gritting his teeth on the leather reins while he continued firing with his right-hand gun, his left arm hanging useless at his side. His next two shots hit their targets, taking one gunny in the face and the other in the stomach, doubling him over to leak guts and shit and blood in the dirt as he fell.

One-Eye's sixth and final bullet in his pistol entered Puma's horse's forehead and exited out the back of its skull to plow into Puma's chest. The horse swallowed its head and somersaulted as it died, throwing Puma spinning to the ground. He rolled three times, tried to push himself to his knees, then fell facedown in the dirt, his blood pooling around him.

One-Eye Jackson looked around at the three dead men lying next to him and muttered a curse under his breath. "Jesus, that old fool had a lotta hair to charge us like that." He shook his head as he walked over to Puma's body and aimed his pistol at the back of the mountain man's head. He eared back the hammer and let it drop. His gun clicked . . . all chambers empty.

One-Eye leaned down and rolled Puma over to make sure he was dead. Puma's left shoulder was canted at an angle where the bullet had broken it, and on the right side of his chest was a spreading scarlet stain.

Puma moaned and rolled to the side. One-Eye Jackson chuckled. "You're a tough old bird, but soon's I reload, I'll put one in your eye."

Puma's eyes flicked open and he grinned, exposing bloodstained teeth. "Not in this lifetime, sonny," and he swung his right arm out from beneath his body. In it was his buffalo-skinning knife.

One-Eye grunted in shock and surprise as he looked

down at the hilt of Puma's long knife sticking out of his chest. "Son of a . . ." he rasped, then he died.

Puma lay there for a moment, then with great effort he pushed himself over so he faced his beloved mountains. "Boys," he whispered to all the mountain men who had gone before him, "git the *cafecito* hot, I'm comin' to meet ya."

Smoke was sitting with his friends around the dining room table as dusk approached.

He looked at Cal and said, "Where's Puma got to? He knows to be back here before dark."

Cal shrugged. "I dunno, Mr. Smoke. He sat up most of last night, starin' at the fire and singing some old Indian song. Then this mornin' he put some red and yeller and blue paint on his face and took off toward the mountains with that big old Sharps of his acrost his saddle."

Smoke jumped to his feet. "Damn, Cal, why didn't you tell me this sooner?"

"Why?" the boy asked, a frightened, puzzled look on his face.

" 'Cause that was his death song he was singing, and that paint on his face meant he was going on the warpath, probably intended to do as much damage to Murdock as he could before they killed him!"

"Jiminy, Smoke, I'm sorry . . . I didn't know."

Smoke grabbed his hat and Henry rifle and ran out the door, everyone in the cabin following him. They all loved the old man and weren't about to let Murdock and his men kill him, that is if they weren't too late.

Smoke and his five friends rode hard toward Murdock's ranch, leaning over their saddle horns, grim, determined looks on their faces.

It was almost an hour before they galloped up to the scene of Puma's charge. Dead bodies lay everywhere, and horses milled, grazing on the green grass near the old riverbed.

Smoke jumped out of his saddle before Horse came to a stop and ran to where Puma lay, still staring at the mountains.

Smoke knelt and cradled the old man's head in his lap. Puma gazed up at him through watery, faded blue eyes. "Hey, pardner, I kicked some ass today," he whispered through dry, cracked lips.

Smoke, tears in his eyes, nodded. "You sure did, Puma."

Puma reached up and put his palm against Smoke's cheek. "Don't fret, young beaver. There's been somethin' goin' wrong inside me the last coupla months, an' I didn't hanker to die in no bed. The only fittin' way fer a mountain man to die is with his hands full of iron, spittin' lead and laughin' at death."

"Puma, I'll make sure the other mountain men know of this day and sing about it around their campfires until there are none of us left."

"Say good-bye to the fellahs fer me, Smoke. An' if Preacher's waitin' fer me on the other side, I'll tell him what a good job we did raisin' our boy."

Smoke started to reply, but then noticed it wasn't necessary. Puma was with his friends, and he had all eternity to hunt, where streams never dried up and the beaver and fox were plentiful, and where there was always someone to listen to his tall tales of the ways of the mountain men.

Smoke stood, cradling Puma in his arms like a baby. He face the others with tears running down his cheeks. "I'm going to take him home, up into the high lonesome, and bury him. I'll be back at the ranch tomorrow."

Louis put his hand on Smoke's shoulder. "Smoke, if it's all right with you, I'd be honored to go with you and see Puma off." The gambler and gunfighter who had killed dozens of men in his life choked back a sob, his eyes filling. "I've ridden with many men in my years out west, but none of them could hold a candle to Puma Buck."

Joey, Cal, Pearlie, Monte, and Ben Tolson all stepped forward, nodding their heads, wanting to go too.

Smoke said, "I think Puma would consider it an honor if all of you came along to wish him well on his last journey."

He climbed up on Horse and began to ride up the hill toward distant mountain peaks, Puma's friends following.

They buried Puma that night next to a high mountain stream, near a beaver dam. As Smoke prepared to place the body in the grave, Cal stepped up and handed Smoke Puma's buffalo-skinning knife. "I took this out of the last man Puma killed."

Smoke glanced down at the long, sharp knife, then back up into Cal's eyes. "I think he would want you to have it, Cal. And, Pearlie, you take his pistols."

Smoke looked down at the small figure in his arms. "He always thought of you boys as his grandkids, and I know he'd be proud if you'd honor his memory by taking the things that he always kept by his side."

After the grave was filled, Smoke built a campfire and the men sat up until dawn listening to Smoke tell them about the life of one of the greatest mountain men who ever lived. "Singing his song," as Smoke called it, paying tribute to a man he held as close in memory as his own father.

The next afternoon Smoke and his friends were gathered around the dining room table. "Joey, when I came up here with you, it was because of a debt I owed you for saving my life." He drained his coffee cup, reddened eyes hard. "Now it's gotten real personal. I don't intend for Murdock or any of his hired thugs to live through the next few days."

Joey spoke up. "Smoke, because of Puma's sacrifice, we've got time ta get ready."

Smoke asked, "When do you think they'll hit, Joey?"

The ex-soldier pursed his lips, humming tunelessly for a moment. He narrowed his eyes. "If'n they're smart, which I'm not sayin' they are, there's only two good times ta attack a fortified position. Once is right at dusk. Man can't hardly see well enough ta shoot anything then, eyes plays tricks on 'im. The other time is round about two, three in the mornin', when a body's deepest asleep."

"You're right," Smoke said. He pulled a cigar out of his pocket and lit it. "However, I'm like you. I don't think Murdock is smart enough to wait for the right time. He's so pissed off now after our two attacks on his home, I think he'll send those hired guns and outlaws of his here as soon as they can get ready."

Joey squinted out the window at shadows along the fence. "Well, it looks ta be 'bout three, three-thirty now, an' it's a good two-hour ride from Murdock's place." He built a cigarette and stuck it in the corner of his mouth, striking a lucifer on his pistol handle. As he puffed, he nodded. "I 'spect they'll be here just 'fore dark, 'bout five or so."

Smoke stepped to the door and surveyed the land between his and Murdock's ranch. "If they come straight here, they'll be coming from the south, and the setting sun will be off to their left, our right. I'll station a group of hands with long guns in that copse of cottonwoods over there, and another with shotguns in that group of boulders about fifty yards south of it. They can dig in and use the trees and rocks for cover, and they'll be firing on Murdock's men from out of the sun as they ride past."

Louis rubbed his cheeks, he hadn't shaved for two days and had an unaccustomed growth of whiskers on his usually clean-shaven face. "What about those other little surprises you have planned for those miscreants? Are they all prepared and ready to go?"

Smoke glanced at Cal and Pearlie, whose job it had been to get the traps and deadfalls ready. "How about it, men?"

Pearlie and Cal both nodded. "We're primed and loaded for bear, Smoke."

Chapter 21

Murdock stood on his porch with his hands on his hips, Vasquez standing next to him, looking at the group of men gathered in front of him.

Curly Rogers had just come back from finding One-Eye Jackson and his men's dead bodies by the riverbed. Sandy Billings, the member of the group who had run away, told him where the fracas took place. Rogers said, "They're all dead, Mr. Murdock. Weren't no other bodies around, though there was some blood might've been from that old mountain man who attacked 'em."

Murdock said to Billings, "You say this old codger rode right down on your group of six men by himself?"

"Yes, sir. His face was all painted with Indian war paint, and he was yellin' and screamin' and firin' them big old Colt Armies like some demon outta hell!"

Vasquez's lip curled in a sneer. "And you, señor, you rode away without fighting?"

Billings dropped his eyes, his face flushing. "Yeah, I did." He looked up defiantly. "And I'd do it again. That old bastard was crazy or something, 'cause he sure wasn't afraid of dyin'."

Vasquez nodded. "But you were, *cabrón*." He stepped down off the porch and walked to stand face-to-face with Billings. "We all ride for Señor Murdock," he said, glancing around at the group of gunfighters gathered there. "He pay us money to fight, not to run away like small children."

He looked back at Billings and slapped him hard across the face, driving the man to his knees. "This is what happens to cowards," Vasquez said, and drew his machete and slashed down at Billings, catching him between his shoulder and neck, almost decapitating him.

Billings flopped to the ground, thrashing and screaming as his blood pumped out to spray several men nearby. After a moment the gunman lay still, his blood soaking into the dry earth around him.

Vasquez held his blood-covered machete above his head. "Remember, vaqueros, is better to stay and die like men than to taste my blade."

Murdock's eyes were squinted, looking hard at his hired guns. "We have Jensen and his men outnumbered three or four to one. Any man who's afraid to ride against those odds, I have no use for." He inclined his head toward Vasquez. "If you want to quit, turn in your resignation to Vasquez right now."

He paused for a moment, but no one moved to take advantage of his offer. "Okay, then. Load up your weapons and feed and water your horses. We ride against Jensen in an hour."

As the men dispersed, the Silverado Kid stepped over to Vasquez. "Emilio, I can see you think you and you're knife are big shit." He took the cigarette out of his mouth and flicked it at the Mexican. "Billings was a friend of mine. When this is over, if you're still alive, I'm gonna dust you for what you just did."

Vasquez smiled, his eyebrow arched. "Why for you defend coward?"

"He was married to my cousin, an' he wasn't no coward. That old man took down five hombres, none of 'em slouches with guns." He pointed his finger at Vasquez. "Sometimes it makes more sense to run than to fight, an' that's somethin' you oughta think about after this little fracas, Mex."

The Kid walked off toward the corral to get his horse without looking back at Vasquez.

Shotgun Sam Willowby leaned across his saddle and spoke in a low voice to Gimpy Monroe. "Gimpy, I don't know about you, but these wages ain't looking as good right now as they did in Pueblo."

Gimpy straightened from adjusting his stirrups. "Yore right, Shotgun." He looked around to make sure no one could hear. "I'm thinkin' o' kinda gittin' lost on the way to this little shindig and makin' my way back to New Mexico."

Shotgun Sam nodded. "Yeah, sounds good to me. We'll just hold back on the reins a mite and ride to the rear till we cross that riverbed, then make a sharp turn and shag our mounts toward home."

Curly Rogers and his group of men stood next to the corral, tightening cinch belts and straightening saddles and blankets on their mounts. "Well, boys, it's about time we paid that bastard Jensen back for what he did to us up on that mountain," Rogers said, looking over his bronc at the others.

Boots fingered his facial scars and bent and misshapen nose. "Yeah, that son of a bitch is goin' to be sorry he marked me up like this. I'm gonna put one 'tween his eyes for leavin' me lookin' like a hoss stomped me."

"You're gonna have to stand in line," Cates said, limping around his horse's rear end to pick up his saddlebags. "I cain't hardly walk on the leg he shattered, an' in the winter it pains me so, I cain't get no sleep at all." He stuck his thumb in his chest. "I'm gonna be the one that curls him up!"

Gooden, another member of the group, shook his head. "You boys don't have nothin' to gripe about. That bullet Jensen put in my side messed up my bowels somethin' fierce. I hadn't had a normal shit in two years, and I can't eat nothin' heavier than oatmeal or I git the runs." He stared at the others. "If anybody has a reason to blow Jensen to hell, it's me."

Twenty feet away, Sam Silverwolf and Jed Beartooth were discussing the upcoming battle. "Jed," Sam said as he flipped open his loading gate and checked the rounds in his pistol. "After we kill the gringos, I want to go back to Pueblo." He raised his eyebrows and grinned. "The women are very pretty there, no?"

Jed Beartooth grinned back and grabbed his crotch with his hand. "*Sí,* I too am ready for another kind of riding, amigo."

Bill Denver said to his partner, Slim Watkins, "Slim, you hear what the Kid said to Vasquez over there?"

Watkins nodded, not being much for talking.

Bill asked, "Who do you think'll win in that little dust-up? The Kid or Vasquez?"

Watkins spit a brown stream over his horse's back, shifted his tobacco wad to his other cheek, and replied, "I'll give you two-to-one odds and bet twenty dollars on the Kid if'n it's with guns. I'll give you even money if'n it's with knives."

Bill said, "You're on, cowboy."

The man named Colonel Waters rode up to where Murdock and Vasquez sat their horses. "Murdock, Vasquez," he said, "I intend to kill Joey Wells personally. He was responsible for the death of over a hundred and fifty of my men after the war."

Vasquez stuck one of Murdock's cigars in his mouth and lit it. "So, *señor,* what you tell us this for?"

Waters shrugged. "Just to let you know what I intend to

do. I don't care overly much about the others you're fighting. My attention is going to be on killing Joey Wells.''

Murdock grinned. "That's fine with me, colonel. But
you're going to have to get through the others to get to
Wells, so take your best shot.''

The man in the Union coat tipped his officer's hat and
rode off to join the rest of the gun hawks as they gathered
in front of the corral.

Vasquez glanced at Murdock and tapped his head. *"Es
muy loco."*

Murdock laughed. "I don't care if he's crazy, long as
he can fire a pistol and don't turn tail and run when the
fighting starts.''

He spurred his horse to the front of his group of men.
"Let's ride, men. *Vamanos!*" he called, and wheeled his
mount and rode off toward the Rocking C, over fifty of the
toughest, meanest gunnies from several states following.

Smoke stepped out the door of the cabin to talk to the
men they had hired in Pueblo, who were waiting outside
for instructions.

"Boys, there's trouble riding our way. Unless I'm mis-
taken, Jacob Murdock has hired a bunch of professional
gunfighters and outlaws to ride for his brand. They're on
their way here to kill us so Murdock can have this land
and set up his empire in Colorado. If that happens, he'll
next take over the town of Pueblo and will again install
his own man as sheriff.''

He pulled a cigar from his pocket and lit it as he talked.
"Do you want that to happen?''

His men all raised their voices to shout *no,* and a few
held up rifles and shotguns and waved them in the air.

"Okay, but are you willing to die to keep Murdock from
having his way?''

The men didn't yell this time, but everyone stared back

at Smoke without flinching, nodding their heads, their eyes filled with determination.

"Thank you, men. Your sheriff, Ben Tolson, along with Joey Wells and Monte Carson and Cal and Pearlie and me are not going to let that happen either. We intend to stand alongside you and fight until Murdock and his men are all dead—or we are."

Louis and the others on the porch with Smoke stepped forward to stand next to him. Smoke said, "I'm going to let Joey Wells, who's been working with you men for the past few days, assign you your places in the upcoming battle. He knows your strengths and your weaknesses, and he's going to put you where you can do the most good."

Joey cut a chunk of tobacco off his plug of Bull Durham, stuck it in his mouth, and chewed as he talked. He pointed to one side of the crowd. "You Sammy, Joel, Tuck, and Benny. You an' your men who have been punchin' the cattle, I want you in the cabin here. Get your shotguns and rifles and get upstairs an' on the roof. I want ev'ry window and door double covered. Ya got a clear field o' fire for a hundred and fifty yards, so open them windows and git yourselves comfy, ya may be there awhile." He leaned over the hitching rail in front of the house and spit a brown stream into the dirt. " 'Member what I tole ya 'bout them guns. Take your time and aim, fire only when ya have a good shot, we don't have a surplus o' ammunition, so use what ya have to good advantage."

He looked to the left side of the crowd. "Mike, Jimmy, Todd, and Josh, I want you to set up in that copse of trees over yonder to the right. We already got you some holes dug there and there's a couple o' fallen logs ta git behind. You are the men who are best with rifles, so you're gonna be a bit farther from the action. I want you all ta wait until Murdock and his gang are even with or maybe a bit past ya 'fore ya start to fire on 'em. Let 'em git good and close, then they'll be trapped 'twixt you and the men in the house.''

Joey waved his arm toward the center group of men. Tyler, you and Billy Joe and Tommy are my shotgun brigade. I want ya each carryin' a sack or two of shells and I want ya to git out there in that mess o' boulders yonder. We done got ya some logs and brush and such around some natural holes and caves in the rocks to git in and git outta the way if'n the lead gits too thick. You men are ta stay hidden until Murdock's riders git by ya. Then we'll have 'em boxed in between the house, the trees, an' the boulders.''

As the men started to disperse, Joey shouted, "Now, remember what I said about our little surprises for the gunnies, and don't none of you fall into any of those traps, ya hear?''

Joey looked at Tolson. "Ben, with yore experience with that Greener, I'd like ya to stay on the first floor of the cabin, ta make sure none of the gunnies git close enough to set fire to it or to git inside. Okay?''

Tolson nodded and grinned. "Sure, Joey. I'll guarantee won't none of those bastards get through the door, unless it's over my dead body.''

"Good. Now, Monte, I need you to get to the upper story of the cabin and keep those punchers calm up there. Ain't none of 'em able to hit nothin' with a gun, so I need someone to show 'em how to do it and to protect them if worse comes to worst.''

Monte nodded, his eyes hard as flint. He glanced at Smoke. "These men are going to do you proud, Smoke, I'll see to it.''

After everyone else had gone to their assigned positions, Joey looked at Cal and Pearlie and Louis and Smoke. "Thet just leaves us, men. What'll it be?''

Smoke said, "I think we get to be the cavalry, boys. If we get on our mounts and wait just over that rise over there until we hear gunfire, then we can swoop down in among the gun hawks and do a powerful lot of damage at close range.''

Louis nodded, as did Cal and Pearlie.

Joey said, ''I been fightin' on hossback fer so many years, I don't rightly know no other way. I'll be ridin' with the Jensen cavalry if'n you boys don't mind a rebel yell now and again.''

Smoke laughed. ''I rode with the Gray during the war too, Joey, and I may just join you in the yelling.''

Joey smiled. ''I knew ya was a man after my own heart, Smoke.'' He looked at Cal and Pearlie. ''If you boys want to help, you can go out there and pour a little kerosene on our piles of wood. If they come at us after dark, we'll light the woodpiles so we can see where our surprises are buried.''

Pearlie chuckled as he grabbed a can of kerosene from the kitchen and stepped off the porch. ''I cain't hardly wait to see them boys' eyes when they come bustin' in here loaded for bear. Yes, sir, that's gonna be a sight to see.''

Joey walked over and put his arm around Pearlie's shoulder, speaking low so only he and Cal could hear. ''Boys,'' he said, ''I've grown right fond o' the two o' you.'' He frowned and stared into Pearlie's eyes. ''If either one o' ya git yoreselves kilt tonight, I'm gonna be right pissed off, ya hear?''

Pearlie grinned. ''Yes, sir. I'll keep that in mind, and I want you to know, I'll watch after Cal and make him keep his fool head down.''

Smoke, who had come up in time to hear what was said, nodded. ''You do that, Pearlie, and don't you forget to keep yours down too.''

Pearlie said, ''Yes, sir, Smoke,'' and left to attend to pouring the kerosene and checking the other deadfalls and traps he and Cal had prepared.

André was in the kitchen, boiling large kettles of water

for treatment of the inevitable wounds that were to occur, and making huge pots of coffee in case the battle lasted well into the night.

Smoke was left alone on the porch with Louis Longmont, Monte Carson, and Joey Wells. He pulled his Colts out and checked his loads as he spoke. "Well, gentlemen . . . friends. I guess it's about time we find out what we're made of."

Joey squinted through narrowed eyes. "Those boys we hired'll stand firm, Smoke, I kin tell ya that."

"I know, Joey. They're a fine bunch of men." He holstered his pistols and looked at his friends.

Louis smiled. "I'm going to enjoy riding with you and Joey. Hell, I may have kids someday and I'll not miss a chance to tell them I once rode and did battle with the famous Smoke Jensen and the infamous Joey Wells."

Smoke and Joey laughed, and Smoke said, "Then let's shag our mounts, boys. I want to get a little ways away from the ranch house so we can ride and attack without getting shot by our own men."

They waited while Cal and Pearlie mounted up and then rode toward Murdock's ranch at an easy trot. Smoke had Colts on both legs, a Henry repeating rifle in one saddle boot, and a Greener ten-gauge scattergun in the other.

Louis rode with one pistol in a holster on his right leg and had two sawed-off American Arms twelve-gauges in saddle boots on either side of his saddle horn. The two-shot derringer behind his belt would be useful only in very close quarters.

Joey had his Colt in his right-hand holster, his 36-caliber in his shoulder holster, and two short-barreled Winchester rifles, one in a saddle boot and one he carried across his saddle horn.

Cal had the twin Colt Navy .36-caliber pistols Smoke had given him that he used while riding with Preacher. He also carried a Henry repeating rifle slung over his shoulder on a rawhide strap.

Pearlie had double-rigged Colt Army .44s and a Greener twelve-gauge shotgun with a cut-down barrel for close-in work.

Joey glanced around at his compatriots and laughed. "Hell, boys, if Lee'd had this much firepower at Appomattox, he wouldn't have had to surrender."

Chapter 22

The riders from the Lazy M came galloping toward Smoke's spread like an invading horde of wild men. They started shouting and hollering and firing their weapons toward the cabin while still well out of range.

Smoke, Joey, Louis, Cal, and Pearlie were bent low over their saddle horns behind a small rise in a group of pine trees, waiting for them to pass.

As they rode by, Joey cut a chunk of Bull Durham and stuck it in his mouth. He chewed a moment, then spit, a disgusted look on his face. "Guess those assholes are tryin' to scare us to death with all that yelping like injuns."

Cal, whose heart had hammered when he saw the number of men who rode by, took a deep breath, praying he wouldn't disgrace himself or Smoke in the upcoming battle.

Pearlie glanced at him and saw the sweat beginning to bead his forehead in spite of the chilliness of the early evening air. He reached over and punched Cal in the shoulder. "Don't worry none, partner, we're gonna teach these galoots a lesson they'll never forget."

Cal nodded, relaxing a little bit, knowing he was among friends who would fight with him, side by side, against the devil himself if necessary.

When Smoke heard gunfire being returned from the area of the cabin, he put his reins in his teeth, took his Greener ten-gauge in his left hand and his Colt .44 in his right, and spurred Horse forward, guiding the big Palouse with his knees.

Joey looped his reins over his neck, took his short-barreled Winchester rifle in his hands, jacked the lever down to feed a shell into the chamber, and rode after Smoke.

Louis filled both his hands with his American Arms express guns, eared back the hammers on all four barrels, and leaned forward, urging his mount over the hill.

Pearlie winked at Cal as he grabbed his Greener cut-down shotgun in his left hand and drew his Colt with his right. Before he put the reins between his teeth, he said, "Come on, cowboy, it's time to make some history of our own!"

Cal drew both his Navy .36s and took off after the others, teeth bared in a grin of both exhilaration and fear.

Murdock's men were in the trap Smoke had devised for them, caught with the shotgun brigade hidden among boulders at their rear, and off to their left, hidden in the setting sun, the men with rifles, and to the front, the cabin with its contingent of men who, though not accurate with their weapons, were pouring lead into the outlaws at a furious rate, hitting some by mere chance.

Cal and Pearlie had scattered a series of twenty small piles of kerosene-soaked wood across the clearing where Murdock's men were trapped, and those were now lighted, making the area look like an army camp with its campfires.

Just before Smoke and his band arrived from the bandits' right side, completing their boxing-in maneuver, Monte

Carson, leaning out of an upstairs window, did as he had been instructed.

He began to fire his Henry repeating rifle, fitted with a four-powder scope, at the base of the small fires. The wood had been piled by Cal and Pearlie over cans of black powder, put in burlap sacks with horseshoe nails packed around them.

When Monte's molten lead entered the cans of powder, they exploded, sending hundreds of projectile-like nails in all directions and spreading smoke and cordite in a dense cloud to blind and confuse the enemy.

Men and horses went down by the dozen. Those not killed outright were severely wounded by both explosions and nails.

Other traps began to become effective. Several trenches had been dug, with sharpened spikes stuck in the bottoms. As first horses, then men on foot, began to step into the trenches, and horrible screams of pain from both men and animals began to ring out in the gathering darkness.

Curly Rogers and his group of bounty hunters were directly behind Vasquez and Murdock as they approached the cabin. Rogers was firing his Colts at the ranch house as he and his men passed the pile of boulders. A sudden explosion came from between two of the rocks, and Rogers felt as if someone had kicked him in the side. He was blown out of his saddle, three buckshot pellets in his side. He bounced and quickly scrambled to his feet, barely managing to avoid being trampled by his fellow outlaws.

Rogers clamped his left arm to his side, pulled out another gun, and ran toward the cabin, hoping to find another horse to get on. His feet went right through one of the deadfalls and his legs fell onto two sharpened spikes, sending agony racing through his body like a fire. He screamed, "Help me . . . oh, dear God, somebody help me!" As he flopped on the ground, wooden stakes impaled in his legs, and a bullet from the cabin aimed at another rider missed its intended target but didn't miss him. It severed his spine, ending his pain and leaving him lying paralyzed on the ground.

Cates, seeing the amount of resistance at the ranch, tried to veer his horse off to the left and escape. As he passed between two pine trees, the baling wire Cal had strung nine feet off the ground caught him just under the chin. Horse and rider rode on, but Cates's head stayed behind to fall bouncing on the ground like overripe fruit.

The half-breeds, Sam Silverwolf and Jed Beartooth, trying to escape the fire from the cabin and the trees, whirled their horses and headed for the boulders, intending to take cover there among the rocks.

Tyler and Billy Joe, leaders of the shotgun brigade, saw them coming and stepped into the open, guns leveled. Silverwolf got off two shots with his pistol, taking Tyler in the chest and gut, doubling him over. Billy Joe, twenty-two years old and never having fired a gun in anger before, stood his ground as slugs from the two half-breed killers and rapists pocked stone and ricocheted around him. He sighted down the barrel, waited until they were in range, and pulled both triggers at the same time. The double blast from the shotgun exploded and kicked back, knocking Billy Joe on his butt.

When he scrambled to his feet, breaking the barrel open to shove two more shells in, he saw the breeds' riderless horses run past. He squinted and looked up ahead of him on the ground. What he saw made him turn his head and puke. Silverwolf and Beartooth had been literally shredded by the twin loads of buckshot. There wasn't much left of the two murderers that would even be identified as human, just piles of blood and guts and limbs and brains lying in the dirt.

Juan Jimenez was jumping his horse over one of the small fires when Monte fired into it. Horse and rider were blown twenty feet into the air. Protected from most of the nails by his mount's body, Jimenez survived the blast, but both his legs were blown off below the knees, the stumps cauterized by the heat of the explosion. He landed hard, breaking his left arm in two places, white bone protruding from flesh.

When Jimenez looked down and saw both his legs gone, he screeched and yelled and began to tear at his hair, his mind gone. His agony ended moments later when Ben Tolson took pity on him and shot him from the doorway to the cabin.

The Silverado Kid, Blackie Bensen, and Jerry Lindy were riding next to each other. When the Kid realized the trap they were in, he yelled at his men to pull their mounts to the left. "Rush the trees over yonder, it's our only chance to get away," he hollered.

The three men rode hard at the trees, guns blazing, lying low over saddle horns. Mike and Jimmy were lying behind a log, their Henrys resting on it as they fired. Jimmy drew a bead on Blackie Bensen and fired. His first shot took Blackie in the left shoulder, spinning him sideways in the saddle. This caused Jimmy's next shot to pierce Blackie's right shoulder blade, entering his back and boring through into his right lung. The ruptured artery there poured blood into Blackie's chest, causing him to drown before he had time to die from loss of blood.

The Silverado Kid fired his Colts over his horse's head, two shots hitting home, one in Mike's chest, killing him instantly, the second careening off a tree to embed itself in Josh's thigh, throwing him to the ground.

Todd raised his Winchester '73 and pumped two slugs into Jerry Lindy, flinging the outlaw's arms wide before the twin hammer-blows catapulted him out of his saddle to fall under the driving hooves of the Kid's mount, shattering his skull and putting out his lights forever.

Jimmy's next shot grooved the Kid's chest on the left, causing him to rethink his objective. The Kid jerked his reins to the side and pulled his horse's head around to head back into the melee around the cabin. He'd had enough of the rifle brigade.

Explosions were coming one on top of another, billowing clouds of gunpowder and cordite hung over the area like ground fog on a winter morning, the screams of men hit hard and dying and those just wounded mingled to create a symphony of agony and despair.

Into this hell rode Smoke and his friends. Joey screamed his rebel yell at the top of his lungs—"Yee-haw"—striking fear into the hearts of men who knew it to be a call for a fight to the death.

Smoke answered with a yell of his own, and soon all five men charging the murderers and bandits were screaming, firing shotguns and pistols and rifles into the crowd as they closed ranks with them.

The mass of men broke and splintered as Smoke and Joey and Louis and Cal and Pearlie cut a swath of death through it with their blazing firepower and raw courage.

Smoke saw Horton and Max shooting at the cabin from horseback, while Gooden, Boots, and Art South were nearby on foot, their broncs lying dead at their feet, pierced by hundreds of horseshoe nails.

Smoke glanced at Louis and yelled, "Remember them?" and pointed at the group of men. Louis nodded, his eyes flashing. "Damn right," he said. Louis had been one of the men who rode up into the mountains to stand with Smoke against the bounty hunters in the Lee Slater fracas.

Louis bared his teeth in a wide grin. "Let's do it!" he yelled, and rode hard and fast at the killers with Smoke at his side.

Horton and Max saw the two men coming, Colts blazing, and screamed in fear. "Oh, Jesus," Horton shouted, "it's Jensen and that devil Longmont." He whirled his horse and tried to run. A slug from Louis's Colt hit him between the shoulder blades, throwing him off his horse. It took him ten minutes to die, ten minutes of blazing pain.

Max, less a coward than Horton, turned his mount toward Smoke and Louis and charged them, firing his pistols with both hands. Smoke fired twice with the Colt in his right hand, missing both times. Then he triggered the ten-gauge Greener he held in his left hand. It slammed back, throwing Smoke's arm in the air, making him wonder momentarily if his wrist was broken.

The load of buckshot and nail heads met Max head-on. The lead exploded his body into dozens of pieces, scattering blood and meat over a ten-square-yard area.

Smoke stuck the Greener in his saddle boot and pulled his left-hand Colt. He began to alternate, firing right, then left, then right again as he continued his charge over Max's body toward Gooden, Boots, and Art South.

Gooden snap-shot at Louis and hit home, the slug tearing into the gambler's left thigh but missing the big artery there.

Louis returned the favor, punching a slug into Gooden's gut, doubling him over and knocking him to the ground. "Oh, no," he screamed, "not the stomach again!" He lay there, trying to keep his intestines in his abdomen, but they kept spilling out. Finally, Gooden gave up and lay back and died.

Art South fired at Louis and missed, but nailed his horse in the right shoulder, knocking Louis to the ground. He rolled and sprang to his feet, left hand pushing his wounded left leg to keep him upright.

Art South stepped closer to Louis and extended his hand, pointing his Colt between Louis's eyes. "Any last words, Longmont?" South asked, grinning.

"No," Louis said, and he pulled his derringer out from behind his belt and shot both .44 barrels into South's chest, blowing him backward to land at Boots's feet.

Boots swung his pistol toward the now-unarmed and

defenseless Louis, who merely stared unflinchingly back at the outlaw.

Boots's lips curled up in a snarl until they disappeared into the hole Smoke blew in his face with his .44s. The bullets entered on either side of Boots's nose, blowing his cheekbones out the back of his head.

Smoke grabbed the reins of a riderless horse while Louis bent and picked up the Colt he had dropped. Smoke reached down and picked Louis up with one arm and swung him into the saddle.

"Thanks, partner," Louis shouted.

Smoke just smiled and rode off, looking for other prey.

Cal and Pearlie had emptied their guns and were reloading, trying to keep their mounts from shying while they punched out empty brass casing and stuffed in new ones.

The Silverado Kid galloped over to where Bill Denver and Slim Watkins were riding, firing up into the cabin. Bill Denver shot into the second-story window, his slug taking Monte Carson in the side of the head and taking out a chunk of his scalp as it knocked him unconscious and blew him back out of sight. Two of the punchers in the room rolled Monte over and began dressing his wound, while a third picked up his rifle and took his place at the window.

The Kid shouted, "Look, Denver, Watkins, over there."

He pointed toward Cal and Pearlie, off to the side of the fracas, surrounded by the gunnies they had killed. "There's only those two young'uns between us and freedom. Let's dust the trail on outta here, boys," he cried.

Denver and Watkins nodded and wheeled their mounts to follow the Kid's lead. The three desperadoes spurred their broncs into a gallop, right at Cal and Pearlie.

Cal shouted, "Look out, Pearlie, here they come!"

With no time to reload his pistols, Cal dropped them and swung the Henry repeating rifle off his back and jerked the lever, firing from the hip without bothering to aim.

Pearlie holstered his still-empty pistols and shucked his Greener twelve-gauge with the cut-down barrel from his saddle boot. He eared back the hammers and let 'em down as Cal began to fire.

The Silverado Kid, scourge and killer of women and children, the man too tough for Tombstone, took three .44-caliber slugs from Cal's rifle, two in the chest and one in the left eye. His entire left side disappeared as he back-flipped over his horse's rump to land spread-eagle and dead in the dust.

Denver and Watkins got off four shots with their pistols. The first shot took Cal in the right hip, above the joint, and punched out his right flank, blowing him out of the saddle.

The next shot missed, but the third and fourth both hit Pearlie, one burning a groove along his neck, and the other skimming his belly, tearing a chuck of fat off but not hitting meat.

Pearlie gave a grunt and doubled over, then straightened up and let both his hammers down, one after the other. Denver took a full load of 00 buckshot in the face, losing his head in the bargain, and Watkins's right arm and chest were disintegrated in a hail of hot lead from Pearlie's express gun.

Both men were dead before they hit the ground.

Pearlie jumped out of his saddle and sat cradling Cal's unconscious body in his arms while he reloaded his pistols. No one else was going to hurt his friend as long as he was alive to prevent it.

Jerry Jackson, train robber from Kansas, screaming curse words at the top of his lungs, rode his horse at the cabin, blazing torch in one hand and Colt in the other.

Ben Tolson stepped out of his doorway and onto the porch, his shotgun blasting back at Jackson.

Jackson was blown off his mount at the same time his .44 slug tore into Tolson's chest on the right side, spinning him around and back through the door he gave his life to defend.

Joey, his pistols and both Winchester rifles empty, stood up in his stirrups, looking for Cal and Pearlie. He wanted to make sure they were all right.

He heard a yell from behind him and looked over his shoulder to see Colonel Waters riding at him, his sword held high above his head, blood streaming from a wound in his left shoulder.

"Wells, prepare to die, you bastard," Waters screamed as he bore down on the ex-rebel.

Joey bared his teeth, let out his rebel yell again, and pulled his Arkansas Toothpick from its scabbard. He wheeled Red around and dug his spurs in, causing the big roan to rear and charge toward the Union man.

They passed, the sword flashing toward Joey's head. He ducked and parried with his long knife, deflecting Waters's blade, sending sparks flying in the darkness. Both horses were turned, and again raced toward each other. At the last minute Joey nudged red with his legs, and the huge animal veered directly into Waters's smaller one, knocking both horse and rider to the ground.

Joey swung his leg over the saddle horn and bounded out of the saddle. He crouched, Arkansas Toothpick held waist-high in front of him, and waited for Waters to get to his feet.

The colonel stood, sleeving blood and sweat off his face. "You killed my men, every one, Wells, and now you are going to die."

Joey spit tobacco juice at Waters's feet. "Yore men, like you, Waters, were cowards who killed defenseless boys who'd given up their guns. They didn't deserve ta live, an' neither do you."

Joey waved the blade back and forth. "Come an' taste my steel, coward!"

Waters lunged, his sword outstretched. Joey leaned to

his right, taking the point of the sword in his left shoulder while striking underhanded at Waters.

Joey's blade drove into Waters's gut just under his ribs and angled upward to pierce the officer's heart. The two men, gladiators from a war long past, stood there, chest to chest for a moment, until light and hatred faded from Waters's eyes, and he fell dead before the last of the Missouri Volunteers.

Murdock saw they were losing the battle and shouted at Vasquez, "Emilio, let's get out of here!"

The two men, who had managed to stay on the periphery of the gunfight, wheeled their horses and galloped back toward the Lazy M. They were able to escape Smoke's trap only because of the heavy layer of smoke and dust in the air. By the time the men in the boulders saw them coming, they were out of range of their shotguns.

The fracas lasted another twenty minutes before all the gunnies were either dead or wounded badly enough to be out of commission.

It was full dark by now, and the punchers in the cabin lighted torches, joined with men from the trees and boulders, and began to gather their wounded and dead. The injured who worked for Smoke were brought into the cabin and were attended to by André and the others. Their gunshot wounds were cleaned and dressed and they were given hot soup and coffee, and for those in pain, whiskey.

Smoke bent over Monte Carson, checking his bandages to make sure they were tight. Carson drifted in and out of consciousness, but Smoke was sure he would survive.

André fussed over Louis's leg wound, cleaning and recleaning it until finally Louis said, "Just put a dressing on it, André, there's others here who need you more than I do."

Smoke glanced at Louis, a worried look on his face. "Have you seen Cal or Pearlie or Joey, Louis?"

Louis looked up quickly. "Aren't they here?"

Smoke shook his head. "No."

Louis struggled to his feet, using a rifle as a cane. "Let's go, they may be lying out there wounded"—he glanced at Smoke, naked fear in his eyes—"or worse."

The two men walked among the dead and dying outlaws, ignoring cries for help and mercy as they looked for their friends. The outlaws deserved no mercy. They had taken money to kill others and would now have to face the consequences of their actions. A harsh judgment, but a just one.

Finally, Smoke spied the horse Pearlie had been riding, standing over near a small creek that ran off to the side of the cabin. "Over here," he called to Louis, and ran toward the animal, praying he would find the young men alive.

He stopped short at what he saw. Joey, his left shoulder wrapped in his bloodstained shirt, was trying to dress Pearlie's neck and stomach wounds, but Pearlie wouldn't let go of Cal to give him access. The young cowboy had one hand holding his wadded-up shirt against a hole in Cal's flank to stop the bleeding, while he held his Colt in the other, hammer back, protecting his young friend from anyone else who might try to harm him.

Smoke heard Joey say, "Come on, Pearlie, the fight's over. Let me take care of where ya got shot, then we kin git Cal over to the cabin fer treatment."

Pearlie shook his head. "I'm not movin' from here till I see Smoke. I promised him I was gonna watch over Cal, and I aim to do just that!"

Smoke chuckled as Louis hobbled up beside him. "Would you look at that, Louis. Like a mother hen with her chick."

Louis grinned. "If I ever find a woman who'll take care of me like that, I'll give up gambling and settle down."

"Pearlie, you've done a good job," Smoke said as he knelt by Cal. "Now let Joey fix you up while I take Cal to the cabin so André can patch his wounds."

Pearlie lifted fatigue-ridden eyes to stare at Smoke. "Smoke, you got him?"

Smoke lifted Cal in his arms. "Yes, Pearlie, I've got him."

Pearlie mumbled, "Good," then let his pistol fall to the dirt and passed out.

The next morning, after the doctor from Pueblo had been summoned and he had come to the cabin to do what he could, Smoke and his friends sat around a campfire outside, the cabin being used to house the wounded.

"Well, we didn't do near as bad as I feared," Joey said. "We lost seven good men, and another eight will be a long time recovering."

He took his fixin's out and built himself a cigarette, sticking it in the side of his mouth and lighting it. He upended his coffee cup and drained it without removing the butt. "I'm damned sorry to lose Ben Tolson." He raised his head and looked at Smoke. "He was a fine man, one any man would be proud to call partner!"

"He'd do to ride the river with," Smoke said. These were two of the best compliments a westerner could give another cowboy.

Joey said, "If'n it's all right with you and the others, I'd like ta give his widow a share of the Rocking C. He earned it."

Smoke nodded. "He damn sure did. From what I'm told, if he hadn't stopped that last rider, he would've burned the entire cabin down and all the men with it."

Cal was lying on a makeshift cot before the fire, spooning down some of André's beef stew as fast as he could. He cut his eyes over to look at the bandage around Pearlie's gut. Though thin as a rail, Pearlie was a famous chowhound, being known to eat everything that wasn't tied down.

"Pearlie," Cal said with an innocent look in his eyes,

"did I hear the doctor correct when he said if you didn't have that layer of fat around yore middle, you would've had a serious wound?"

"Yeah," Pearlie said, a suspicious tone to his voice. "So?"

Cal grinned. "So, I guess you can thank Miss Sally for savin' yore life, what with all the bear sign she makes that you scarf down." He winked at Smoke. "I guess no one will kid you anymore 'bout that gut around yore middle."

Pearlie looked down. "What gut? I don't have no gut!" He glanced back over at Cal, trying to look mean. "And if you didn't have this unnatural affection for lead, neither one of us would've gotten shot!"

After a few minutes Joey said, "Smoke, I've checked all the bodies, an' I don't see no sign of Murdock nor of Vasquez."

"I know. One of the boys you assigned to the boulders, Billy Joe I think it was, said right at the end a couple of riders got past them, headed back toward Murdock's place."

Joey struggled to his feet, unable to use his left arm because of the sling the doctor had put on it. "Well, no need to waste any time. I'm goin' after 'em 'fore they have time to split."

Smoke got up and brushed dirt off the seat of his pants. "I'm coming too. I got a score to settle for Puma Buck."

As the others started to rise, Smoke held out his hand. "No, boys. Joey and I started this alone, and we're going finish it alone." He smiled at his wounded friends. "Thanks for the offer, but this trail is ours and we have to ride it all the way to the end."

Chapter 23

Smoke walked over to talk to Louis while one of the uninjured hands threw a saddle on Red and Horse.

"Louis, there's something I want you to do for me while we're over at Murdock's, settling things."

Louis looked up. "Anything, Smoke, as long as it doesn't include dancing." He tapped the large bandage André had wrapped around his leg. "I'm not too spry on my feet just yet."

"Oh, I think you will enjoy this little errand. You can even take the buckboard, with a pillow for your leg if need be."

"Oh?"

"Yes, I'd like you to ride into Pueblo and pick something up for me. I had Ben send a wire to Big Rock last time we were in town, and the . . . package ought to have arrived on today's train."

A slow smile curled Louis's lips. "I hope this package is what I think it is."

Smoke grinned. "Here's what I want you to do . . ."

Shotgun Sam Willowby and Gimpy Monroe were stuffing their faces and filling their guts at the hotel dining room in Pueblo with their horses packed and loaded outside for the long ride back to New Mexico.

Two pretty, young blond women accompanied by a small boy walked into the hotel. As they sat down at a table across the room and ordered lunch, Shotgun Sam glanced around. They were the only patrons, since the dining hour had passed already.

He nudged Gimpy with his elbow. "Hey, Gimpy. What say we stroll on over there and say howdy?" The killer raised his eyebrows in a lewd grin. "We might git lucky an' knock off a piece or two of that fine-lookin' woman flesh."

Gimpy scowled. "You a randy old coot, Shotgun. Man o' yore age ought not be thinkin' with his dick all the time."

Shotgun spread his arms. "What've we got to lose? The sheriff's out there shootin' it up with Murdock and his gang." His grin turned even more evil. "Who's to stop us from whatever we want to do?"

Gimpy cut his eyes toward the women. He nodded as he chewed his steak. "You're right, an' they is right purty at that."

Shotgun added, "An' we gonna be a long time on the trail 'fore we git another chance like this. Let's do it."

Shotgun Sam picked up the Greener he was never without, hitched his belt over his fat gut, and swaggered over to the table where the ladies sat.

The pair of outlaws stood a few feet in front of their table, hands on hips.

"Howdy, ladies," Shotgun said. "My pardner and me was wonderin' if'n maybe you'd like to come up to our room an' have a little drink of whiskey with us." He tried a smile, revealing dirty yellow teeth.

Sally Jensen glanced up, then smiled, her beauty striking

in the afternoon sunlight from the window. "I don't think so, cowboy. We're married ladies in town to meet our husbands."

Gimpy looked around at the empty room and shrugged. "I don't see no menfolk here. Seems a man shouldn't oughta neglect pretty girls like you two."

Betty Wells, who had grown up around men like these, was less refined and gracious than Sally. She gave the pair a scornful look and said, "Get lost, white trash, 'fore my husband comes in here and makes you wish you'd never been born."

Sally raised her napkin to her face to hide her smile at Betty's earthy way of talking.

Shotgun's face flamed red and he snorted through his nose. "Don't try an' git uppity with me, you bitch!" He eared back the hammers on his Greener with a loud double-click. "I asked ya nice, now I'm tellin' ya, git yore butt up and come with me or I'll have to scatter ya all over the room!"

Sally leaned back in her chair, a small smile curling the corners of her lips. She looked at Betty and winked where the men couldn't see it. "Sure, mister. Is it okay if we powder our noses first?"

Gimpy laughed a nasty laugh. "You can powder anything you want long as you hurry it up."

Sally nodded at Betty and glanced at their purses sitting on the floor. "Why don't you get your powder out, Betty, for these nice gentlemen?"

Betty grinned. "That's a right good idea, Sally."

The ladies picked up their purses and laid them on the table in front of them, snapped open the clasps, and put their hands inside at the same time.

With beautiful, sexy smiles, both Betty and Sally looked up at Shotgun and Gimpy and pulled the triggers on the short-barreled pistols both of them carried.

Their guns exploded, blowing out the bottoms of the

purses, then blowing Shotgun and Gimpy back across the room, smoking holes in the middle of their chests.

The outlaws kicked and thrashed for a moment, then lay still.

The manager of the hotel came running into the room, a Colt in his hand. "You ladies all right?" he yelled.

Sally put her purse back on the floor, wiped her lips daintily with her napkin, and said, "Yes, sir, but could I have another cup of coffee, please?"

Betty looked over at him, smiling. "And could I see the dessert menu? Little Tom has been waiting all day for some cake, if you have any."

Smoke put a hand on Joey's arm and helped him climb up on Red, then he stepped into the saddle on Horse. They rode off toward the Lazy M and Murdock and Vasquez at an easy canter.

After a few miles Smoke noticed fresh blood on Joey's shoulder and a tight grimace of pain on his lips.

"This ride too much for your wound, Joey? If it is, we can go back and wait a few days for the wound the doc stitched to knit together."

Joey shook his head, looking straight ahead. "I want to end this business, Smoke. All my life it seems I've been livin' with hate, first during the war, then after, when I was chasin' Redlegs." He took a deep breath. "The only time I've been at peace was with Betty, and then when little Tom came I thought my life was complete and all that anger was behind me."

He pulled a plug of Bull Durham out and bit off the end. As he chewed, he talked. "Since Vasquez and his men rode into my life, I've found all that hate and more back in my heart." He looked over at Smoke. "At first I thought I'd missed all the excitement of the chase, an' the killin'. But I've found that the hate festers inside of ya, an' I'm afraid if I don't git shut of it soon, I won't be fit ta go back to Betty. She's just too fine a woman ta have ta live with a man all eat up inside with hate an' bitterness.''

Smoke smiled gently. ''I don't think you, or Betty and Tom, have to worry about that, Joey. You've just been doing what any man would do, fighting to protect your family and your home.'' He slowed Horse and bent his head to light a cigar. When he had it going good, he caught up with Joey. ''When you see the end of Vasquez, and Murdock, things'll go back like they were. The only hate I can see inside you is anger at the men who hurt your loved ones, and that's a good thing. A man who won't stand up for his family is no good.''

Joey gave a tight grin. ''You ought to be a preachin' man, Smoke. You sure know the right things ta say.''

Smoke laughed until he choked on his cigar smoke. After he finished coughing, he said, ''Now, that's a picture to think on, Smoke Jensen, holding Sunday revivals.''

They stopped at the riverbed and watered their mounts in one of the small pools. ''What are you going to do about the river once this is over?'' Joey asked.

Smoke gave him a look he didn't quite understand, and said, ''Oh, I think I'll leave that to the new ramrod of the Rocking C. It'll be his decision to make.''

Another hour of easy riding brought them to the out-skirts of the Lazy M. In the distance they could see two horses tied up to a hitching rail near the corral, away from the house. Smoke pulled Puma Buck's Sharps .52 from his saddle boot and began to walk toward a group of trees about a hundred yards from the house, keeping the trees between him and the house so Murdock and Vasquez wouldn't be able to see him coming.

Joey walked alongside, carrying a Henry repeating rifle in his right hand, hammer thong loose on his Colt.

Murdock was in his study, down on hands and knees in front of his safe, shoveling wads of currency into a large leather valise.

He and Vasquez had arrived back at his ranch at three in the morning and had taken a short nap, planning to leave the territory early the next morning. They slept longer than intended and were now hurrying to make up for lost time.

Vasquez was sitting at Murdock's desk, his feet up on the leather surface, a bottle of Murdock's bourbon in one hand and one of his hand-rolled cigars in the other.

"What you do now, Señor Murdock? Where you go?"

Murdock looked back over his shoulder, his hands full of cash. "I plan to head up into Montana. There's still plenty of wild country up there, a place where a man with plenty of money, and the right help, can still carve out a good ranch."

"What about Emilio?" Vasquez asked, his right hand inching toward his machete. He was looking at the amount of cash in the safe, thinking it would last a long time in Mexico. He could change his name, maybe grow a beard, and live like a king for the rest of his life.

Murdock noticed the way Vasquez was eyeing his money, so he pulled a Colt out of the safe and pointed it at the Mexican. "Just keep your hands where I can see 'em, Emilio. I was planning on taking you with me, I can always use a man like you." He raised his eyebrows. "But now I'm not so sure that's a good idea. I don't want to have to sleep with one eye open all the way to Montana to keep you from killing me and taking my money."

Vasquez smiled, showing all his teeth. "But, señor, you have nothing to fear from Emilio. I work for you always."

Murdock opened his mouth to answer, when he heard a booming explosion from in front of his house and a .52-caliber slug plowed through his front wall, tore through a chest of drawers, and continued on to embed itself in a rear wall.

Murdock and Vasquez threw themselves on the floor behind his desk, Vasquez spilling bourbon all over both of them in the process.

"Chinga . . ." Vasquez grunted.

"Jesus!" said Murdock.

Smoke hollered to the house, "Murdock, Vasquez. Come out with your hands up and you can go on living . . . at least until the people of Pueblo hang you."

The two outlaws looked at each other under the desk. "What do you think?" Murdock asked.

Vasquez shrugged. "Not much choice, is it? I think I rather get shot than hang. You?"

Murdock nodded. "Maybe I can buy our way out."

Vasquez gave a short laugh. "Señor, you not know man very well. Jensen and Wells not want money, they want our blood."

Murdock didn't believe him. Everyone wanted money. It was what made the world go round. "Jensen, Wells. I've got twenty thousand in here, in cash. It's yours if you turn your backs and let us ride out of here!" Murdock called.

His answer was another .52-caliber bullet tearing through the walls of his ranch house. It seemed nothing would stop the big Sharps slugs.

Murdock said, "I guess you're right."

Vasquez answered, "Besides, after they kill us, they take money anyway."

Murdock scrabbled on hands and knees to the wall, where he took his Winchester '73 rifle down off a rack. He grabbed a Henry and pitched it across the room to Vasquez. "Here, let's start firing back. Maybe we'll get lucky."

Vasquez chuckled to hide the fear gnawing at his guts like a dog worrying a bone. "And maybe horse learn to talk, but I do not think so."

William W. Johnstone

They crawled across the floor and peeked out the window. They could see nothing, until a sheet of flame shot out of a small group of trees in front of the house and another bullet shattered the door frame, knocking the door half open and leaving it hanging on one hinge.

"Goddamn," Murdock yelped. He rose and began to fire the Winchester as fast as he could work the lever and pull the trigger. He didn't bother to aim, just poured a lot of lead out at the attackers.

"Vasquez," he whispered, "see if you can sneak out the back and circle around 'em. Maybe you can get them from behind."

"Hokay, señor," the Mexican answered. He crawled through the house, praying to a God he had almost forgotten existed that he make it to his horse. He wasn't about to risk trying to sneak up on Jensen and Wells. If he got to his horse, he was going to be long gone before they knew it.

He eased the back door open and stuck his head out. Good, there was no one in sight and no place to hide behind the cabin.

Crouching low, he ran in a wide circle to where he and Murdock had left their horses. He slipped between the rails on the far side of the corral and crawled on his belly across thirty yards of horse shit to get to his mount's reins. He reached up and untied the reins and stood up next to his bronc, his hand on the saddle horn, ready to leap into the saddle and be off.

"Howdy, El Machete," he heard from behind him.

He stiffened, then relaxed. It was time to make his play. Maybe, like Murdock said, he would get lucky.

He grabbed iron and whirled. Before his pistol was out of its holster, Joey had drawn and fired, his bullet taking the Mexican in the right shoulder. The force of the slug spun Vasquez around, threw him back against his horse, then to the ground. He fumbled for his gun with his left hand, but couldn't get it out before Joey was standing over him.

"Okay, Señor Wells. I surrender."

Joey's eyes were terrible for the Mexican to behold. They were black as the pits of hell and cold as those of a rattler ready to strike.

Joey leaned down and pulled Vasquez's machete from its scabbard on his back. "I don't think so, Vasquez."

He held the blade up and twisted it so it gleamed and reflected sunlight on its razor-sharp edge. Joey looked at him and smiled. "Guess what, El Machete?"

Suddenly Vasquez knew what the cowboy had in mind. "No . . . no . . . *por favor,* do not do this, señor!"

Joey pursed his lips. "Try as I might, Vasquez, I cain't think of a single reason I shouldn't."

With a move like a rattler's strike, Joey slashed with the machete, severing Vasquez's right arm at the elbow. The Mexican screamed and grabbed at his stump with his left hand.

"Remember Mr. Williams, El Machete?"

As Vasquez looked up through pain-clouded, terror-filled eyes, the machete flashed again, severing his left arm at the elbow.

Vasquez screamed again and thrashed around on the ground, trying to stanch the blood as it spurted from his ruined arms by sticking the stumps in the dirt. It didn't work.

Joey stood and watched as Vasquez bled to death, remembering his wife and son lying in their own blood because of this man.

Smoke continued peppering the house with the Sharps, until one of the slugs tore open the potbelly stove, setting the house on fire.

As flames consumed the wooden structure, Murdock

began to scream. Just before the roof caved in, he came running out of the door, his clothes smoldering and smoking, holding a leather valise in one hand and a Colt in the other. He was cocking and firing wildly at Smoke, who stood calmly, ignoring the whine of the slugs around his head.

"This is for Puma Buck," he whispered, and put a slug between Murdock's eyes. His head exploded and he dropped where he stood, dead and in hell before he hit the ground.

Smoke walked over and picked up the valise, looked in it, smiled, and hooked the handles on his saddle horn.

He helped Joey up on Red, he climbed on Horse, and they headed home.

Chapter 24

On the way back to the Rocking C, Smoke had to stop and reapply the dressings on Joey's shoulder. All the activity had reopened his wound and started it bleeding again.

"What's in the valise?" he asked.

Smoke smiled. "I'll show you when we get back to the ranch."

They got back up on their broncs and continued to ride, slower this time to make it easier on Joey's shoulder.

As they approached the cabin, Smoke glanced at the corral to see if his package had arrived. It had. There were four Palouse mares prancing in there, running and kicking up their heels, glad to be off that train and out in the open air again. There was also a small paint pony. Ready to be ridden.

Joey, tired and weak from loss of blood, rode with his head down and didn't notice the new arrivals.

Smoke helped Joey off Red and called, "Hello, the cabin. We got two hungry cowpokes here."

A petite blond woman walked out on the porch. She

had her arm around a boy, about three or four years old, who walked next to her, a wooden brace on his right leg.

"Hungry cowpokes, are ye'?" she said, her hands on her hips. "And how about your wives, who are starved for a little affection from their men?"

Joey's head jerked up, and his eyes lit up with happiness. "Betty . . . Tom . . ." He ran up the steps to the porch, all fatigue vanished, grinning like a madman. He threw his right arm around Betty and hugged her until she cried, "Stop that, you big galoot, you're going to break my neck." But her eyes were full of laughter. Joey then knelt and hugged, more gently this time, little Tom. "Yore leg . . . you're walkin'?"

Betty stood next to him, running her hands through her man's hair as he knelt next to their son. "The doctor says the brace can come off in two weeks. He thinks the leg will be good as new by then."

Joey looked up, tears in his eyes. "And you?"

"I'm fine, dear. The wound healed without complications." She frowned, looking at his bloody shoulder. "But I don't know about you. It looks like you've been up to your old tricks again."

He stood and laid his head on her shoulder, breathing deep, smelling her hair. "It's over, Betty. The feud is over and done with."

She said, "And you're home for good," mock anger in her voice. "No more galavantin' around doing your man things?"

Joey, famed killer of over two hundred men, looked sheepish. "No, dear. I'm home for good."

From inside the cabin a voice called, "Hey, cowboy, are you going to tell me hello or just stand there with your mouth open?"

Smoke jumped like he'd been shot. He had been so happy to see the Wellses reunited, he'd plumb forgot that Sally had come to Pueblo with them. He ran up the stairs and swept her up in his arms, whirling her around, kissing her, and whispering in her ear that he loved her.

Later, around the dinner table, Smoke explained to Joey what he had done. "I had Ben Tolson send a wire to Sally to see if she could arrange for Betty and Tom to ride the train up here. I knew you wanted them to see the country and see what they thought of it."

Sally patted Betty on the arm. "You have a wonderful wife and son, Joey. We've become fast friends already."

"I also had Sally bring up those Palouse mares we talked about for Red. It's time you carried on his bloodline, and I think they'd make a good cross."

"But what about that little paint pony out there? Surely you can't want to breed it to Red?"

Smoke shook his head. "No, that's for Tom. Soon's that splint comes off, it'll be time to put him on horseback and teach him to ride. That Indian paint will be perfect to learn on, small and gentle until he's ready for more."

"Smoke," Joey said, "I don't know what to say. You've done so much . . ."

Smoke put his hand on Joey's shoulder. "Don't say anything just yet. Take some time, show your family the country. If they, and you, like it up here like I think you will, then I want you to take over the Rocking C ranch."

"But, I cain't . . ."

"Yes, you can, Joey. Remember, you've got lots of partners and we're all counting on you to make this the best ranch in central Colorado." Smoke snapped his fingers. "Oh, I almost forgot."

He reached behind him and placed the leather valise Murdock had been carrying on the table in front of Joey. "Here's a little something from Murdock, to pay you back for all the pain and trouble he's caused you and your family."

Joey opened the valise, and he and Betty glanced in. She sucked in her breath and covered her mouth. "There must be a million dollars in there," she said.

Smoke smiled. "More like twenty thousand. It should be enough to buy the Lazy M and its stock from the bank and combine the two ranches into one big enough to make some real money for all the men and the families of the men who helped us defeat Murdock."

Louis interrupted. "Unless, of course, you'd rather play a little poker with those greenbacks." He cracked his knuckles and smiled. "I'm a little rusty, but if you'll remind me how to play, we could start a game."

Betty reached over and grabbed the valise. "Oh, no, you don't, Mr. Longmont. This money's going straight to the bank, and then it's going to be put to use to help all our new friends at our Colorado home."

Joey raised his eyebrows and grinned.

Sally put her hand in Smoke's. "Looks like we have some new neighbors, Smoke."